SHE WAS DYING ANYWAY

SHE WAS DYING ANYWAY

ZACHARY GOLDMAN MYSTERIES #3

P.D. WORKMAN

ISBN: 9781989080061 (IS Hardcover)

ISBN: 9781989080047 (IS Paperback)

ISBN: 9781988390994 (KDP Paperback)

ISBN: 9781989080030 (Kindle)

ISBN: 9781989080047 (ePub)

pdworkman

Apple-achian Treasure

Vegan Baked Alaska

Muffins Masks Murder

Tai Chi and Chai Tea

Santa Shortbread

Reg Rawlins, Psychic Detective

What the Cat Knew

A Psychic with Catitude

A Catastrophic Theft

Night of Nine Tails

Telepathy of Gardens

Delusions of the Past

Fairy Blade Unmade

Web of Nightmares

A Whisker's Breadth (Coming soon)

High-Tech Crime Solvers Series

Virtually Harmless

Stand Alone Suspense Novels

Looking Over Your Shoulder

Lion Within

Pursued by the Past

In the Tick of Time

Loose the Dogs

AND MORE AT PDWORKMAN.COM

To those who have been silenced

Zachary Goldman?"

Zachary nodded distractedly at the man with the clipboard. The movers were wrestling his couch through the doorway of the apartment, turning and angling it to get it through. He wasn't sure whether they were inexperienced or whether the door was narrower than a standard door. He hadn't expected them to have any trouble getting his few pieces of new furniture inside.

"Mr. Goldman."

"Yes?" Zachary's eyes were drawn back to the bald, sweating man in a grey jacket, who was thrusting a clipboard toward him.

"I'm here to hook up the TV."

Zachary had guessed as much from the crest on his uniform.

"Yeah, sure."

"You need to sign the work order."

Zachary pulled his eyes away from the movers again to scan the heading and the signature line of the form on the clipboard.

"This says you're done."

"I am."

"But you just got here."

"I don't need to do anything here," the man said impatiently. "All of the wiring is done in the utility closet. I'm all done."

"Oh… then I guess I need to test that it's working."

Their eyes were both drawn back to the movers as there was a crunch of the couch meeting the doorframe yet again and one of the movers swore angrily at the other.

"It is working," the TV man said. "I've tested it all out."

"But in here," Zachary motioned to the apartment. "I should test it in here, make sure it's hooked up to the right apartment."

The bald man rolled his eyes at Zachary's presumption. "Come on, buddy. I've got other jobs to do. This one has already taken longer than it should have."

Since Zachary hadn't even seen him until that moment, he had no way of knowing whether it was true, or whether it had been a two-minute hook-up. He knew he really ought to check to make sure everything was working. If he signed the work order saying that everything was done, and then ended up having to call the company to get it fixed, it would be an extra charge. He looked at the movers in the doorway, wondering how much longer it was going to be before they could get the couch in through the door, so he could get in to test the TV and make sure he was getting all of the channels.

"Uh, if you'll just wait for a few minutes…"

"Do you even have your TV unpacked yet?"

That was going to be another problem, Zachary realized. The TV wasn't even out of the box yet. In fact, it was probably still down on the truck. He couldn't remember it being brought in yet.

"No," he admitted. "Could you maybe come back after your next job? Or take your lunch break now and come back in half an hour? I'll get these guys moving and get it all plugged in…"

The man thrust the clipboard at him again. "Just sign the form, buddy. If there's a problem, you'll have to put in a call."

"But how long would it take to get you back here?" Zachary had dealt with enough utility companies to know that it could be days.

"I've done my job. You're not going to need anyone to come back. Just sign the form."

Zachary sighed and took it from him. The form was dense with fine print, and he knew he should read it all, or at least skim through it before he signed it. There was another volley of swearing from the movers, and a long creak of protest from the couch as they tried to bend it through the doorway. Zachary winced and looked over at them. He scribbled an unreadable signature on the form and handed it back to the TV guy, who took it, ripped off a carbonless copy for Zachary's records, and left without a word of thanks. Zachary went over to talk to the movers about the couch.

"We're going to have to cut it into sections," the older of the movers said, wiping his forehead with the back of his arm. "Otherwise, it's never going through this door."

Zachary looked at the damage they had already done to the doorway and the wall around it. The couch was obviously not going to fit. And he wasn't sure how anyone was going to reassemble it if they cut it up to get it through the door. He imagined the pieces sitting in his new living room forever, unusable.

"It will have to go back to the store. I'll have to get something smaller that will fit through."

The two men looked at each other, rolling their eyes.

"Sorry," Zachary apologized. "I'll call them."

At least his phone was a cell and didn't have to be wired in at the apartment. He was sure that would have gone wrong too.

The movers left the couch in the hallway as they went down to bring the next piece of furniture in off the truck. Hopefully, the bed. He could live without anything else for a few days, but he was really looking forward to sleeping on a bed again, after the months of sleeping on Bowman's couch. Not that the couch wasn't comfortable. But it was a couch. He would have his own space back, out of Bowman's way. A bed of his own. His own TV.

Zachary looked around the small apartment. He had viewed it in the evening a couple of weeks before, when the lighting had been softer, and it hadn't looked quite as dingy as it did in the late morning sun. The landlord had said that he would repaint it, but it was obvious he hadn't.

There was a tentative knock on the open door of the apartment, and Zachary pulled himself from his consideration of the merits and deficits of the apartment to turn around and see who it was. Another utility man, the landlord, the movers...

But it wasn't any of those. It wasn't another form or agreement he was going to have to sign. It was a petite blond woman. Her hair was still much shorter than she preferred it, but at least it was her own hair. It had come back in just the same as before chemo, no change in color or curl, as the doctors had warned it might. Bridget's face was filling back out so that she no longer looked sick or waifish, but like herself.

"Bridget! Come in!"

She lifted the grocery bags by way of explanation. "I brought you some things."

Zachary hurried over to relieve her of her load. He hesitated, always unsure how to greet her appropriately.

"You didn't have to do this." Zachary indicated the bags, settling on just taking them from her without any handshake or friendly kiss on the cheek.

"I figured you would be busy with all of the other arrangements and wouldn't have the time to feed yourself properly."

Zachary put the grocery bags on the counter in the kitchen and started to go through them. The fridge was already plugged in, luckily, so nothing would spoil if he put it all away.

"That was really thoughtful. I hadn't even thought about food," Zachary admitted. He ran a hand over his hair. He kept his dark hair short, so it wasn't messy even if he happened to forget to comb it when he got up, but he couldn't remember if he had bothered to shave when he got up that morning. He hadn't expected to have to be presentable for anyone. He scratched his jaw and found it was covered with stubble. Not just one day's growth but probably a few. Another of the things he didn't put a lot of thought into, especially if he was on surveillance. People didn't pay much attention to a man who was a little unclean or rough-looking. They tended to avoid eye contact, in case he might ask for money or a job.

"No, I didn't think you would," Bridget agreed. She grabbed a carton of milk from one of the bags and put it into the fridge, then proceeded to unpack the other items. Zachary grabbed a few dry goods to put into the cupboard before she could do the whole job herself.

When they were finished, Bridget turned and looked at the rest of the apartment. Most of it was visible from the kitchen.

"This is nice."

Zachary was sure that, to Bridget's critical eye, it didn't qualify as 'nice.' He knew how exacting her standards were. She would never even have considered the place for herself. But Zachary wasn't going to be doing a lot of entertaining. His needs were modest and, despite the little bit of recognition he had garnered on a couple of recent cases, his cash flow was thin and irregular, and he needed to be sure not to get anything that would be too expensive for his usual income.

"Thanks. Um… I'd ask you to sit down, but I don't actually have anywhere yet…"

"It will be nice for you to be back in a place of your own again. I'm sure Mario was a good host, but you both need your own space."

"Mario's been great." Mario Bowman really had been a life-saver, letting Zachary come to stay with him for a 'few days' when Zachary's own apartment had burned down, and allowing him to continue to recover there until he was able to get back on his own feet again. Zachary hadn't been comfortable intruding on Bowman all the time; he couldn't imagine how uncomfortable it must have been for Bowman to have someone else in his territory, always underfoot, for what had ended up being weeks on end. "But no one will be happier than him that I'm out of there now."

The movers arrived, with kitchen furniture this time, so in minutes, Zachary and Bridget were able to sit down to visit.

"You'll have to take care of yourself," Bridget said. "You won't be able to rely on Mario to keep the fridge stocked or make supper."

"Yeah, you're right." He would have to make sure he was eating properly, something that was too easy for him to forget when he was distracted by a case or other things going on in his life. "I'll be fine. I've done it before."

"Yes… but not well."

It was strange that Bridget was there. It was nice of her to bring him food and help him to get settled, but he wasn't quite sure why she would. They weren't together anymore. She didn't have any responsibility to look after him, as she was always quick to point out. Yet, in spite of the rift between them, she kept showing up, acting like she still cared what happened to him. She had gone on and was together with Gordon Drake now. Zachary was seeing Kenzie occasionally, though they hadn't really settled into a dating relationship yet. Bridget should have just moved on and not had anything to do with Zachary.

"I'll be fine," he assured Bridget. Maybe that was all she needed. Just some reassurance that he wasn't going to end up starving or in the hospital, somehow making her feel guilty for having broken up with him.

But Bridget didn't make any move to get up and leave. She tapped a nail on the tabletop, a nervous gesture that was out of character for her. The ticking of her nail against the table ratcheted up his anxiety.

"Is… there something wrong?" Zachary ventured. "Is everything okay with you?" He had a sudden sick feeling. What if she had relapsed? What if the cancer had come back?

Bridget instantly read Zachary's expression. "No, no. I'm fine," she assured him. But her eyes filled with tears.

Zachary instantly went into full-blown panic. Her anger and criticism he was used to dealing with. Even her blame. But her tears were something he didn't know how to handle. Bridget never cried. Even when she had told him about her diagnosis, it had been with dry eyes and a flat, stoic voice.

"What is it? What's wrong? What can I do?" He reached out to her, and she actually took his hand, squeezing it for comfort. She blinked rapidly and looked up at the ceiling, trying to avoid shedding the tears that had gathered in her eyes. If it wasn't the cancer, what was it?

Bridget breathed deeply to calm herself. When she spoke, her voice was even, but she talked more slowly than usual, and he knew it was a struggle for her to keep from crying.

"I don't know if I've ever mentioned my friend, Robin Salter, to you."

Zachary flipped through his mental catalog. He was good with names. As a private investigator, he needed to be able to make connections between people quickly, and it was amazing how often a previous name came into play on a new case. Seven degrees of separation became a lot less in a smaller community.

"Not that I remember," he said, feeling bad he couldn't make any connection to the name. Someone she worked with? Was in a club or other organization with? Bridget was very social; she and her family had a lot of friends.

Bridget waved away the apology in his voice. "I didn't know her while we were together. We were in treatment together."

"Oh. She had cancer too?" Was it appropriate for him to ask what kind? Or was that impolite? Invasive?

"Yes. Ovarian, like me. Only…" There was a slight waver in her voice. She was doing her best to hold it together, but she was right on the edge. She cleared her throat and took another deep breath. "Hers didn't go into remission. It metastasized."

Zachary's stomach was a tight knot. That could have been Bridget. The doctor had warned them that treatment might not be successful. Only thirty percent went into remission. Zachary had dealt with the specter of death before, but not like that. Not looking at his beautiful, vibrant wife and knowing that she could die in a matter of months.

"And they... there was nothing they could do?"

"They tried. But she knew she was terminal."

"I'm so sorry, Bridge."

Bridget swallowed. "She died on Friday."

He squeezed her hand, wishing there was more he could do to comfort her. "I'm so, so sorry."

Bridget stared off into space. He wondered whether she was imagining her own life if things had gone differently. Her own death. What if that had been her? What had she accomplished in her life? Who would be mourning for her?

"I need your help."

Zachary blinked, surprised. Even when they were together, Bridget had not asked him for help. She had been happy to be in charge of everything. She took on extra responsibility like it was a new suit to add to her extensive collection. Even now, with the divorce well behind them, she was still bringing Zachary groceries and fussing over his health and his ability to take care of himself.

She never asked for help.

2

I don't think she died of natural causes."

That wasn't what Zachary had been expecting to hear. He furrowed his brow, studying Bridget and trying to divine her meaning.

"You said she had cancer. Terminal cancer. It had metastasized."

"Yes."

Zachary sat back in his chair.

"I want you to look into it. I'll pay your fees."

"You don't need to pay me," Zachary objected. "You're my…" He trailed off. She wasn't his wife. They weren't family, not any longer. Categorizing her as his ex didn't make it sound like a close relationship.

Bridget didn't seem to notice his awkwardness. "Nobody else thinks anything of it. Her family, her boyfriend, not anyone. Or at least, if they do, they aren't saying anything. But I know it wasn't natural. It wasn't her time."

"Sometimes people go before they are expected to," Zachary pointed out. "Pneumonia, or an infection, or just because they gave up."

"She hadn't given up. I had just talked to her. She wasn't ready to go. She was still fighting."

"Chemo can be very hard on the body." He remembered the doctor talking to him and Bridget about how difficult the treatment could be. That for some people with very advanced or aggressive cancers, it was better to have a few months with good quality of life than to eke out a few more in complete misery.

"I know that," Bridget's voice was getting harder the more he protested. Losing that vulnerable, teary edge and growing angry. He could deal with her anger better than her tears. "But I saw her, Zachary. She wasn't ready to go. She wasn't!"

Zachary nodded slowly. "Okay. So, what is it you think happened? You think they made a mistake in her treatment? An accident?"

"Maybe."

Zachary scratched his jaw, thinking it through. He didn't have any big cases on the go. Just the routine insurance claims, cheating spouses, background checks; the kind of cases that were his bread and butter. Routine work he could survive on. As long as Bridget's case didn't take up too much of his time, he could afford to take it on as a favor. If it ended up taking up too much time, she was prepared to pay him. More than likely, it would just be a few inquiries to find out what had happened and then he could put Bridget's mind at ease.

"Are you sure you want to do this, Bridget? It could just end up making you feel worse, keeping it fresh. It might hurt Robin's family and friends and cause resentments."

Bridget nodded. Her jaw muscles were tightly clenched, but otherwise she gave no sign of her deep emotions, smiling pleasantly as if they were discussing the weather. "I realize all that, but... I think it's important."

"Is it what Robin would have wanted? I mean... she was dying anyway, would she really have wanted to make a big deal over it?"

A flush started to creep up Bridget's throat.

"You don't think it's important?" she demanded. "You think

that those few months aren't worth anything? That they can just be written off? Our time here is important, whether it is years, or months, or days. No one has the right to take them away from us."

"Okay. I just want to make sure it's really what you want. When someone starts poking around in a case like this, people can get pretty worked up. You might not think that anyone would care, you think that everyone else would just want to know the truth, but it can cause… really bad feelings… even threats of violence."

"I'm prepared to deal with that." The rosy flush had risen all the way to Bridget's ears. She was steamed, but she was holding back because she wanted Zachary to take the case. She knew that if she exploded, he could simply say he wouldn't take the case. He wasn't obligated.

But he would take it, even if she did blow up at him. He would always do any favor she asked of him.

"So, will you? Will you look into it for me?"

"Yes. Email me all of the information you have on Robin and the hospital or treatment program and I'll see what I can find out. I just wanted to be sure you knew what you were getting into."

Bridget's shoulders dipped and her jaw relaxed. "Thank you, Zachary. You don't know what this means to me."

He allowed himself only a fleeting vision of her expressing her gratitude to him in other ways. Of her softening toward him and realizing how good they were together, how important they were to each other.

But that wasn't why she was there. That wasn't why she had come.

There was a knock on the open door, and Zachary startled, jerking his head around to see who was there. For a split second, he worried that it would be the landlord, upset about the couch sitting in the hallway and the damage to the doorframe and wall. But it was Mario Bowman, smiling at them. He was balding, overweight, and always looked a little seedy when he wasn't wearing his police uniform. But he was a devoted friend who had gone above and beyond the call of duty to help out a man who was hardly more than an acquaintance at the time. Zachary's respect for the cop had only grown as they had gotten to know each other better. Bowman was one of the good guys. One of the best.

"I thought I'd get a start on these boxes." Bowman was leering as if he'd just caught the two of them in a heated embrace. "If you two don't mind being interrupted."

Bridget was on her feet before Zachary, letting go of his hand and stepping over to greet Bowman with a peck on the cheek. "Mario! What a delight to see you again! I'll bet you're happy to be getting rid of this scoundrel."

Zachary made it belatedly to his feet, feeling off-balance for just a split second before he managed to gain his equilibrium. While it appeared to everyone but his physical therapist that he was fully recovered from his last couple of 'accidents,' Zachary was acutely aware of every movement or reaction that took a microsecond longer than it used to. Those instants frustrated him, and all the more when he was the only one who noticed them and everybody else thought he was overreacting or imagining things.

Bowman looked at Zachary with an expression of affection. "Well, to tell the truth…" he trailed off, letting the phrase hang for a moment, "yes, nothing would make me happier than to see the back of him."

He gave Zachary a rough hug around the shoulders to show that he meant no ill will toward Zachary. And Zachary knew it was true, Bowman would be happy to see Zachary out of Bowman's apartment, but even happier to know that Zachary was safely installed in a place of his own.

"So, shall I start bringing things up?"

"Yes, sure," Zachary agreed. "There really isn't much though."

"Not much." Bowman rolled his eyes at Bridget. "It's amazing how much one person can acquire in the space of a few weeks."

He slapped Zachary on the back and headed back out into the hallway to go get the things he'd brought over in the car.

"It isn't that much," Zachary repeated to Bridget, his face warm. When he had moved in to sleep on Bowman's couch, he'd had nothing but the clothes on his back, which weren't even all his own. He hadn't even had a wallet or any means to pay for anything else. But Bowman and others had chipped in to get him clothes, a suitcase, and what other little necessaries Zachary needed until he was able to access his bank account and credit card account, and then to get the settlement money from the insurer so that he'd be able to get established again. He had a new laptop and some photographic equipment, a few files for the cases that he'd worked on since losing everything, his clothing... but it really wasn't more than would fit in a couple of suitcases.

He followed Bowman down to the car and bent over to pick up a suitcase, looking into the car. "What's all this?"

Bowman picked up a couple of boxes, carefully stacked and balanced. "Just a few little things."

Zachary lugged his suitcases, trying to figure out what else Bowman had packed. There couldn't have been that much more than would fit in his suitcases. Bowman had shooed him out of the apartment early that morning, telling him that he'd better be ready well before the first workers were scheduled to get there, and that Bowman would pack everything up and take it over.

Bridget was still there when they got up to Zachary's apartment. He hadn't been sure whether she would stay around or if she would take the first opportunity to disappear. She took the box that Bowman had stacked on top of the one he was carrying and set it down on the kitchen table to look through the contents. Zachary looked down at an assortment of dishes, sheets, and towels. He looked over at Bowman. A bachelor himself, Bowman didn't exactly have a lot to give away.

"Just a few things I wanted to get rid of," Bowman offered with a shrug. "I mean, you're going to need all those sorts of odds and ends, and my place is getting cluttered."

"You didn't need to do that."

Showing no hint of being self-conscious, Bridget started to

remove the dishes and find the appropriate places for them in the kitchen. When Zachary looked at her with his mouth open, looking for a reason to object, she just shook her head.

"Why don't you go unpack your clothes?"

"Uh… okay," Zachary agreed, and took the suitcases into the bedroom to get a start on them.

Zachary was exhausted at the end of the day when everyone was gone, and he was left in his new apartment all alone. He had furniture, other than a couch. The TV and internet were both working, and his various possessions and the donations from Bridget and Bowman were all neatly put away. The apartment felt sparse and empty, but it was a start. After years of being a foster kid barely able to hold on to the one possession that really mattered—the camera given to him by Mr. Peterson—he was used to starting over with nothing. And he knew that he would start to collect new possessions at a rate that would have alarmed Bridget had they still been living together. She never could understand his need to hold on to absolutely everything. Like a grandparent who had lived through the depression, Zachary knew what it was like to want. Parting with anything, no matter how small and insignificant, was difficult.

It was probably a good thing he didn't have a couch, so he couldn't lie down and go to sleep in front of the TV in the living room like he had been doing at Bowman's house. Doctors had always told him that was poor sleep hygiene and that he wouldn't really get the REM sleep he needed to be alert and mentally healthy. It would be his first night sleeping in a bed in months, and he was looking forward to being able to stretch out and not worry about running into the ends of the couch or falling off the side as he had several times.

It was no surprise that when he lay down to go to sleep, he was not the least bit sleepy. His brain whirled around and around, going over everything that had happened during the day, analyzing it, thinking of all of the things he should have said and done instead of what he had. What kept returning to him over and over was the conversation with Bridget about Robin Salter. He probably should have said no. He should have at least been more resistant and given Bridget a day or two to think about it before agreeing to help. The more he looked at the problem, the more obvious it became that it was a minefield, with no safe way across. If he didn't find any evidence that it was not a natural death, Bridget was going to be angry and think that he had not been trying hard enough and had not done a good job. If he did find evidence that the hospital had covered up a mistake or something else, she was going to be angry about Robin's life being cut short before her time was up and she wouldn't have anyone to vent to about it except for Zachary. There was no one else behind her on her mission to find out the truth, so that put Zachary directly in the crosshairs either way.

What if she didn't accept his findings? What if the police or the doctors didn't? What if he had suspicions but couldn't prove anything?

Zachary got out of bed and wandered out to the living room. He turned the TV on and began to pace, trying to silence the arguments going around his head and to get into a rhythm. He checked out the fridge, but he wasn't really hungry, and despite the fact that Bridget had filled it with food, nothing appealed to him. He would have to make a start on it the next day, because otherwise, a few days down the line, things were going to start going bad and he wouldn't be able to keep up with them.

His body was exhausted before he started, so it was no wonder that he quickly tired of the pacing and had to sit down. He had an easy chair, but he wanted to lie on his side rather than recline and was too antsy to stay in the chair.

He ended up lying on the carpet where the couch should be, a throw pillow between his arm and his head, watching inane infomercials on TV until he fell asleep.

3

Bridget had emailed Zachary all of the details she had on Robin Salter and her doctors and treatment. Having been in treatment together, she had some knowledge of when the doctors were likely to be reachable and some other helpful details. She also provided links to Robin's various social media sites, and Zachary spent a few minutes browsing through them to get to know the woman he was trying to get some justice for.

She was a black woman with a narrow face and small features. Attractive in her older pictures, but obviously sick and suffering in the more recent ones. Her hair had been shaved close for a few weeks, and then she only appeared in headscarfs and hats, obviously having lost her hair to her cancer treatments. She had a smile in the older pictures. Grim and determined in the more recent ones.

There was a memorial page set up where her family and friends had posted pictures, memories, and tributes to her. Zachary tried to read them dispassionately, but he couldn't help feeling for the people who had lost her. Her passing had, as Bridget had said, been sudden and unexpected, even though she had been given a terminal diagnosis. Zachary made a list of questions to ask the medical staff, trying to stay focused on the task at hand and not to get distracted by the badges showing that he had announcements to read in his own feed. That would wait; he was working.

Zachary transferred whatever information he would need for the interviews to his phone, grabbed his keys, and headed out. He carefully locked his apartment door behind him and walked to the elevator. The elevator bell dinged, but he didn't get on, instead retreating to his apartment door and double-checking the locks. He looked around for anyone suspicious. He needed to be aware of everyone around him, not allowing himself to be lulled into a sense of false security. There could be no more break-ins, no more fires, no more accidents. He checked the locks one final time and walked down the stairs instead of taking the elevator.

The first person he asked for in the oncology department at the hospital was Dr. Aaron West. The nurse at the nursing station shook her head.

"He's in surgery at the moment. I'm not sure when he'll be available."

"Could I set up an appointment? Or does he do rounds at a certain time? There must be some kind of arrangements I could make."

She looked up at the computer screen, and then down at her paperwork, though she must have had a pretty good idea what Dr. West's regular schedule was if she'd worked there for any length of time. She was an older woman with round glasses and short, limp brown hair. She maintained an air of suspicion listening to him.

"And you want to consult with him on which patient's care?"

Zachary licked his lips. "Robin Salter."

She looked up at him quickly. "Robin Salter? But she died."

"Yes. I still have questions for him with regard to her treatment and prognosis."

"Well, obviously she doesn't have a prognosis at this point."

"No." Zachary's face warmed. "I mean what her prognosis was before she passed. What the expectations were for how she would be treated and… how long she had left."

The nurse still looked at him as if he were crazy. "Why would you want to know that? You're not related to Ms. Salter."

She didn't say it as a question. And he supposed she probably had a pretty good idea that he wasn't blood related to her simply evidenced by his white skin.

"I've been asked to look into any irregularities in Robin's care." He hoped by using her first name, he could humanize Robin Salter and make the nurse more sympathetic to his cause. And to distract her from what he was actually asking.

"Look into…? What are you talking about? Ms. Salter had cancer and she died. There wasn't anything irregular about that."

"There have been some questions…"

She stared at him, not open to the direction of the conversation at all. Zachary tried to give her a warm smile to thaw her cool attitude.

"Were you involved in Robin's treatment? Were you close?"

She scowled. "Patient care is confidential. Do you have some kind of release from the family consenting to this… investigation?"

"No, at the moment I'm just exploring whether there is actually anything to investigate. I take it you don't have any concerns."

"Of course not."

He nodded agreeably. "My wife was treated here. I don't know if you remember… Bridget Downy…?"

Her penciled eyebrows rose. "Your wife is Bridget Downy? I don't remember seeing you before."

"My ex-wife," Zachary amended. He let out a slow breath. "Cancer is very hard on families. She… withdrew from me… our marriage didn't survive."

"But she did. She went into remission, didn't she?"

"Yes." Zachary forced another smile, showing how pleased he was that she had survived her treatment and the horrible disease that had been growing inside her. How pleased he was with the excellent care she had received from the oncology center. People could read things like that in body language and facial expression. Much more clearly than anyone expected. He noticed a slight loosening of the nurse's body muscles. A little more relaxation in her face and shoulders. "Bridget has always been very positive of the care that she received here." That, at least, was true. "Look, I'm sure there is nothing to this business about Robin Salter. But… it is my job to look into it, so that's what I'm doing. Once I've talked to Dr. West and anyone else who might have insight into her care and her death, then I can report to the family that there wasn't anything unusual or unexpected about her death…"

"I suppose."

"Should I make an appointment to see Dr. West? Or do you know when a good time to see him would be?"

The nurse lowered her voice to a more confidential tone. "I don't think it will be too long before he's here for rounds. Unless something goes south with the surgery, it shouldn't take long. He can talk to you then."

"Thank you, that's great. You must have him well-trained."

She gave a little chuckle. "These young doctors. Someone has to take them in hand."

"I can imagine. Were you… closely involved in Robin's care?"

The nurse nodded reluctantly. "Yes, I suppose so. But there wasn't anything unusual about her case. Sometimes… people go before you expect them to. That's just the nature of disease."

"Yes. I'm sure there isn't anything to it." He squinted at her name badge, difficult to make out with black text on a shiny gold background that reflected the light. "Nurse Betty?"

"Betty Hoogner," she agreed, wetting her pink lips and giving a curt nod.

"I think I remember Bridget mentioning you." He paused. "You always remember the good ones. Angels of mercy." He was afraid that might be over the top, but Nurse Betty lapped it up. It didn't matter that Zachary hadn't supplied any details of what she had done to make Bridget so grateful.

"Well, that's so sweet. I remember Bridget being a lot... easier than Robin."

Zachary couldn't imagine Bridget being particularly easy to nurse, given how strong-willed she was. But she was good at managing people and was very gracious when the situation demanded it. In situations that didn't involve Zachary. When they had first met and started to see each other, he had thought she was the sweetest and loveliest women he'd ever met. Everybody had flaws, but finding out Bridget wasn't so perfect after all had been a shock.

"It must be hard being that sick," he said. "I guess you deal with a lot of people who aren't very grateful to be here."

Betty nodded her agreement. "And as nurses, we understand that. We know that nobody chose to get sick and to have to come here. And that we're seeing people at their very worst. Some people... manage it better than others."

"Did you like Robin?"

"Like her?" Betty said blankly. "Well, we do get attached to some of our patients, but mostly we try to maintain a professional distance. Otherwise, it can be very hard working somewhere like this where you lose so many people."

"And Robin wasn't one of the ones you let yourself get attached to."

"No. That isn't because she was a bad person, you know, just..."

"I suppose when you knew she was terminal..."

"It might sound callous," Betty said, "but you have to maintain some emotional distance, or it's just too hard."

"Was there anyone who took care of Robin who was really attached to her? Or who really disliked her?"

"No. I can't think of anyone."

"There isn't anyone who ever said anything about her that worried you?"

Betty shook her head emphatically. "No, certainly not."

Zachary stared off past Betty, committing everything to memory and mentally checking his list of questions to ask. While he would have liked to pull out his phone to write down her answers and consult his notes, he knew if he did, Betty would become self-conscious and stop sharing.

"Can you tell me about the day Robin died?"

Betty patted down her already limp, shapeless hair with one hand. "I don't know what I can tell you."

"You weren't on shift that day?"

"Yes, I was on shift. I'm on every day, really." It was no wonder she seemed so worn. With her obvious years of experience, she should have ranked a little time off. Working every day, especially in an emotionally taxing setting like a cancer treatment center, seemed like a recipe for physical or mental collapse. "I just mean… it wasn't like it was an eventful day. Nothing noteworthy really happened. It was just… the day Robin died."

"Did she have visitors?"

"Yes, a few. She was doing pretty well… up until the end. She had a few people in and out. Her boyfriend, family members…"

"Did she… just die in her sleep? Or did something happen?"

"She was in a lot of pain. We'd increased her painkillers and she slept a lot. Her family was in to see her Thursday evening, and then… Friday morning, she was gone."

"She wasn't on some kind of monitor that would tell you when her heart stopped? Ring an alarm?"

"Despite what you see on TV, very few patients are actually hooked up to a heart monitor at the hospital. Unless they actually have some kind of heart problems that need to be monitored. We aren't notified every time someone's heart stops." Her gaze drifted away from Zachary. "This is a cancer ward. We don't generally take heroic measures. We don't try to bring someone back once their heart stops."

Zachary thought about that. It made sense. And he knew that he himself had rarely been on a heart monitor during his hospitalizations. He *had* been after experiencing a series of electrical shocks, but not during other hospital stays.

"I guess in Robin's case, it was a release? It was good that she didn't suffer longer?" Zachary suggested.

"Yes, that's true… cancer can be a very difficult way to go. We do our very best to fight it back, but often in the end, the monster wins."

"Robin's death was unexpected."

"No."

Zachary focused on Betty's face and raised his brows in query.

"Her death was not unexpected. The timing was," she clarified.

"Ah. Right."

"We knew she was terminal," Betty reiterated. "The cancer had spread through her body. It was only a matter of time."

"But she ended up having less time than you had thought."

"You never really know. Sometimes the doctor gives a person a month, and they live ten years. Sometimes he says they have a few months, and in two or three days, they're gone."

"In cases like that, where they are gone so quickly, is it investigated?"

"No, honey. Why would it be?"

Zachary tried not to bristle at her patronizing manner.

"We know what killed her," Nurse Betty said. "Cancer killed her. We are just grateful she is at rest and no longer suffering. We go on and take care of the living."

Zachary rolled this thought around in his mind for a few moments, examining it. "And you don't think that anyone maybe… decided to help her along? Decided to release her from her pain?"

"Certainly not. You may hear of that kind of thing on TV, but it is very rare. All nurses are not 'angels of death.' Why risk going to prison by interfering with the natural course of things? Patients go when it is their time. Like the coming of the Lord, we don't know the day or the hour. Robin died because she had cancer. That's all. There's nothing else to tell."

The nearby elevator dinged and a group of young doctors and interns got out, chattering away as they entered the unit. Nurse Betty straightened and immediately stared at her screen, typing busily, as if she hadn't been chatting with Zachary.

"There is Dr. West," she said, giving a nod.

Zachary turned and studied the group of young men and women, looking for a gray-haired doctor. But he couldn't sort out which of them was the doctor who had been in charge of Robin's treatment and turned back to Betty for help.

"Dr. West," Betty called out. "There's a gentleman here to see you."

One of the youngsters broke away from the group and approached Zachary. At first glance, he hardly seemed older than twenty, with his geeky glasses and artfully-swept hair. He had to be at least thirty to be in the position he was in, likely much older, but his face was unwrinkled and still boyish. He did hold himself with the upright confidence of an experienced doctor and he didn't have the sleepless eyes of an intern.

"Yes, sir," Dr. West acknowledged. "What can I do for you?"

"I was wondering if I could have a few minutes to talk to you. Privately. I know you have rounds now, and probably a very busy schedule, but if I could get half an hour of your time...?"

Dr. West adjusted his glasses. "I am sure we could find some time, Mr..."

"Goldman. Zachary."

"And what is this about, Zachary?"

"I'm... looking into the death of Robin Salter."

"Looking into... I'm sorry, who are you? Are you with the hospital?"

"No. I'm not—"

"Then I don't understand. There is no reason to 'look into' Ms. Salter's death. Are you a police officer?"

"I'm a private investigator. I've been asked by a friend of Mrs. Salter to look into any... irregularities. Just to put their minds at ease. Her family's and friends'."

"Her family didn't ask me about this. I didn't get the sense anyone had any concerns."

"It will just take a few minutes, and then I can reassure them that everything looks perfectly normal…"

He continued to say 'them' even though there was only Bridget. It sounded better if there were more than just her. Especially since she wasn't even family.

Dr. West didn't look reassured.

"Mr. Goldman's wife was treated here," Nurse Betty told Dr. West. "Bridget Downy. She went into remission."

Dr. West smiled warmly. He was, it seemed, more inclined to humor the spouse of a patient they had managed to save. Maybe he understood that Zachary would be inclined to be positive toward the facility that had helped her.

"Oh, I see. One of our alumni! Then I would guess that you know the quality of the care that our patients get. We are very good at what we do. We have one of the highest-rated cancer treatment programs in the country."

Zachary nodded and continued to look as agreeable as possible as Dr. West extolled the program, the building, the doctors, and even the nurses, finally earning a thin smile and nod from Betty as well. The small herd of young doctors had stopped talking among themselves and were all standing close by, listening in, eyes alight with interest at what was going on.

"I'm sure that's exactly what my report will reflect," Zachary agreed, when Dr. West started to wind down. "We were always very happy with the treatment here. I can see that they continue to hire high-quality staff." He attempted to include both Betty and Dr. West in his smile of approval. There were some people that just couldn't be over-flattered. They would drink up everything he offered and more, without ever suspecting any insincerity. "And I don't want to keep you. You have so much to do here and there are people waiting on you. Are you free after your rounds? Maybe I could buy you lunch?"

"I am engaged for lunch. But maybe this afternoon, three-ish?"

"That would really be great."

"Perfect. You can get the directions to my office from—" Zachary saw Dr. West's eyes slide over to Betty's name badge, but he managed to continue on without a pause, "—Nurse Betty. I won't have a lot of time to meet with you, but we could go over your concerns, provided we are only talking in general terms and not breaking doctor-patient privilege."

Zachary had been worried he was going to run up against claims of confidentiality at some point. He was going to need to get access to confidential patient records, and he wasn't sure how he was going to do that unless he could get the family's consent.

"I'm sure we can work things out," he assured Dr. West. "We could talk about how things were when Bridget was being treated here and discuss hypothetical situations."

Dr. West considered this and then nodded, appearing to accept the suggestion. "Well, I look forward to meeting you, then…"

"Zachary."

"Right. Zachary. I'll see you this afternoon."

He rejoined his group of young cohorts and led them to the first patient room.

Zachary smiled at Betty. "He seems like a very nice fellow."

"He's a good doctor," she agreed. But she looked like she'd eaten something bad. She pulled out a note card and wrote down an address and sketched a small map. She handed it to him slowly. "I didn't say anything to you that was a breach of confidentiality," she asserted.

Zachary shook his head immediately. "Of course not! You're a trained professional. I already knew about Robin's diagnosis and her death. And anything else you said was certainly general knowl-edge. Her family visited her. She was in pain. There's nothing secret about any of that." He intentionally substituted the word secret for confidential. Whether Nurse Betty had actually revealed anything that might be considered confidential or privileged information or not, he wasn't sure. But she hadn't said anything that had surprised him or that Robin or her family would have objected to.

Betty looked reassured. She patted her flat hair down again and nodded. "We do have to be careful of these things."

4

Zachary was left with several hours of dead time. He hadn't really expected to be able to see Dr. West immediately upon just showing up. He would have to be back at the hospital in the afternoon, and in the meantime, he needed to fill the time productively.

Bridget had given him some of the names of Robin's family members and, with a few quick searches, Zachary was able to find phone numbers for them. The first one he managed to reach was Vera Salter, Robin's mother, and she agreed to meet with him if he wanted to drop by and see her. Zachary found her living in a small brick bungalow in a middle-class neighborhood. Despite the fact that she had told him he could stop by, she answered the door in her housecoat and looked surprised to see him.

Zachary introduced himself again, worried that she might not understand why he was there. Grief could do things to a person. Zachary remembered what it had been like to lose his family. And later, to lose Bridget. They weren't even dead, but he still grieved for each one of them, and if he let himself get caught up in it, hours and days could pass while he walked through life in a fog, not really taking in anything that was going on around him.

"I'm Zachary Goldman, Mrs. Salter. My wife is—was—a friend of Robin's."

She nodded slowly, giving Zachary her hand to shake, but she looked right through him as if he weren't even there. Zachary looked into her broad, dark face, searching her eyes for some connection. Her tightly-curled hair was cut close to her head and had more gray in it than black.

"I don't know your wife," Vera said vaguely.

"You've met her. Bridget Downy. She's petite, blond… well, she was blond, is blond now, but when she was in treatment… I don't know if she would have had hair when she met you."

"Bridget," Vera echoed.

Zachary nodded. Vera motioned for him to enter the house, and Zachary looked around, wondering whether anyone else was there to keep an eye on her, or whether she was normally more together. There was a skateboard at the door and a pair of Nike sneakers, which suggested that Vera wasn't the only one living there. Zachary followed her to the living room and looked at the pictures on the mantel and side tables.

"You have a lovely family. Tell me who everyone is."

Vera brightened. Her features livened up a little and she almost smiled. "Here is one of the whole family," she said, choosing one off of the mantel. A posed studio shot, with everyone standing stiffly in front of a fake background. "This is my husband Clarence. He died years ago. And my girls, Robin and Gloria," she indicated the pretty girls standing on either side of their parents. There was a man standing next to Robin. Tall, head shaved bald, a long face that made him look a little sad, in spite of his camera-ready smile. "That was Stanley," Vera said. "He and Robin were engaged. We thought, when we had this picture taken, that he was going to be a member of the family. But… they broke up. Robin always wanted to cut him out of this picture, but I couldn't bear to ruin it that way."

"That's understandable."

"And this…" Vera laid a finger beside a little boy standing in front of Gloria, his dark eyes sparkling with mischief. "This was Rhys."

She pronounced it 'Reese,' like the peanut butter cups. There was something about the way Vera said his name that made Zachary wonder what had happened to her grandson. He took a quick inventory of the other pictures, looking for Rhys in them. There were a few of Rhys, gradually getting older, with his mother or his grandmother, and a couple of school pictures where he was alone. But the sparkling, smiley boy was gone. In his place was a solemn, distant-looking boy. Zachary's mind went back to the children he had met at Summit. Was he autistic? Neurodiverse? What was it that made him look so far away?

"My poor Rhys," Vera said, shaking her head. "He hasn't been the same since Clarence died."

Zachary thought about that. He looked around the room and at the other pictures for more clues as to what had happened to the family. Was the boy still mourning his grandpa so many years later? Had they tried antidepressants? Counseling? Was there something more that Vera wasn't telling him?

"Rhys lives here with you?" he suggested, looking at the skateboard and Nikes.

"Yes. This has always been his home, with Grandma and Grandpa. Sometimes Gloria has lived here with us... and sometimes she's been... other places. But Rhys always stays here with us. And sooner or later, Gloria always comes home again."

Zachary nodded. It was good that Rhys had a stable home. He didn't have to live like Zachary had, passed from one foster family to another, never knowing how long he was going to be there or how bad the next one would be. Or when things got too bad, shunted off to an institution until Zachary could stabilize and they were ready to try something else.

"You must love him very much."

"I do. He's a very special boy."

In the back of his mind, Zachary heard the other boys. The ones who would pick up the word *special* and turn it into something sarcastic and cruel. He wondered again just how Rhys was special. Something set him apart and made him unhappy, and Zachary didn't think it was just losing his beloved grandparent. There was more to it than that.

But that wasn't what he was there to investigate.

Zachary took a surreptitious look at his phone to make sure that time hadn't gotten away from him. He still had plenty of time to visit with Vera before he needed to be back at Dr. West's office. He asked her other questions about the family, trying to get a feel for the dynamics and how Robin had fit into everything. She was the older sister, a bit of a perfectionist, a bit bossy, the sister who always had to be right and needed her parents' praise and attention. Zachary could see parallels between the things Vera said about her daughter and Bridget. The two women had been drawn together by more than the fact that they had both been diagnosed with cancer and were in treatment together. They had an affinity with each other that went much deeper than that.

Zachary sat on the couch beside Vera as she went through the photo albums she had pulled out.

"I know these days everybody has their children's pictures on their phones. But I'm old-school. We used to have them printed and then put them into albums, and I never did get into all of that fancy scrapbooking. Just putting pictures in a book, to look back on later and remember."

"I don't see anything wrong with that." Zachary looked over the pictures of Robin and the others. "I'm an amateur photographer myself, so I understand the magic of developing prints and of being able to hold them in your hands. It's not the same as zipping through pictures on an LCD screen."

"That's right," Vera agreed. She touched the pictures as she turned pages. They were in roughly chronological order, so he could see the girls growing up before his eyes. In the early days, they had always been together. About a year or a year and a half apart in age, Vera had often dressed them up the same way, and the girls had obviously been each other's best playmates in the younger years. But then as they progressed through school, there were pictures of each girl alone, pictures of them with other girls, or with boys, going on to develop separate interests and relationships.

Robin was with boyfriends more often than Gloria, but Gloria was the one who'd had a baby. There was no loving spouse or father in any of the pictures, just Gloria by herself or with Rhys. He'd started out as a small, swaddled baby in arms. There were no pictures where Gloria was looking at her baby with that beatific, Madonna-like expression that photographers were always trying to catch. Instead, she was looking at the photographer or off to the side, the child in her arms barely more than a prop, already forgotten. There were plenty of pictures of Rhys with both his grandma and his grandpa, playing at the park or doing woodwork in Clarence's shop, raking leaves or playing a card game. All of those things that grandparents did with their children, at least in the idealized lives Zachary saw on TV.

And then Clarence was gone. Rhys's smile was gone. In pictures of him with his grandma, he was staring off into the distance, never engaged with her or with the camera man. It was like the whole world was marching by him, and he didn't have a clue.

"He was really affected by the loss of his grandpa," Zachary observed.

Vera nodded. She opened her mouth to explain further, then thought better of it. A secret. Something she wasn't ready to divulge.

"Did Robin and Gloria stay close?" Zachary asked. "Or I should say, did they reconnect again when they got older?"

"Not like when they were children. They were both very strong women. And strong women…"

Zachary thought of Bridget. "They don't always get along with each other. Or with others. My wife always said that if a woman is assertive and says what she wants, she gets called… well…" he didn't want to shock Vera with the language Bridget had actually used. "Some not very complimentary things."

"People say they want men and women to be equal, but the truth is, women are still trained to put others before themselves, to be caregivers first, and to care about outward appearances. You don't get a man by being ugly and pushy. And you need a man."

Zachary sighed. "We still have a ways to go in that department. I know that in the families I lived with, it was always the mother who was in charge of the cooking and cleaning and childcare. She could delegate some of it, but she was the one who was responsible for those areas. It was her job to see that things got done, and to take the blame if they didn't."

"We've come a long way. But we're not there yet."

Zachary nodded his agreement. His eyes were caught by the picture of Robin with someone else on the mantel. It was off in the corner, so he hadn't noticed it right away. It wasn't the same man as had been in the family picture with her. Stanley. It was someone else.

Before Zachary could ask Vera for details, the front door opened and a woman walked in. After looking through pictures for an hour, Zachary knew the oval face and long, carefully-styled wavy hair. She had obviously taken great care to apply her makeup, but it didn't hide the bags under Gloria's eyes or the beginning of crow's feet at the corners of her eyes. Her mouth was turned down even before she realized they had company.

Gloria stopped and looked at Zachary as she kicked off her heels. "Who are you?"

"This is Zachary, Gloria," Vera explained, surprising Zachary by remembering his name after all. "His wife was one of the other ladies in Robin's unit. At the treatment center."

"Was?" Gloria repeated cautiously. "I'm sorry, did she..."

"She went into remission," Zachary was quick to fill her in. "She's starting to get her hair back and feel like herself again."

There was pain in Vera's eyes. Maybe in Gloria's too, but she masked it better.

"I'm sorry. That was insensitive." Zachary's chest hurt when he realized he'd made them feel worse. They had lost their family member, and Zachary blithely told them that his was all better. How could he be so stupid? His brain whirled as he looked for a way to take it back and make them feel better. "I didn't mean it to come out like that. I just didn't want you thinking she was—she had passed—I didn't want you thinking you had to feel sorry for me. You have your own troubles, you don't need to worry about mine."

Both women were silent, apparently uncertain how to deal with his verbal diarrhea. Zachary clamped his mouth shut. Talking wasn't making it any better. If there was a way to make it any worse, that was exactly what he was going to do. So he would shut up.

"Well, anyway…" Vera sighed. "Zachary heard about Robin's passing and he came over for a visit."

Gloria was clearly suspicious. And she had a right to be. Men didn't just go around visiting elderly women who had lost their daughters. Not without some kind of motive. Men were predators and women like Vera were prey. Zachary slid a couple of inches away from Vera as discreetly as he could.

"Bridget was worried about you," he told Gloria, encompassing the whole family with his 'you.' "With Robin passing so unexpectedly…"

Gloria walked the rest of the way into the room and put down a large, heavy-looking handbag. It was brown leather, with lots of shiny clasps and decorations, mirroring the chunky jewelry Gloria wore. She was a forceful woman with a big personality. It was only natural her accouterments would say 'look at me.' The exact opposite to Zachary, who strove to make everything about himself less visible and less memorable. He was always trying to fade into the background where he could just watch and listen and find things out without people even remembering he was there.

"If Bridget was worried, then why isn't Bridget here?"

"She… wasn't up to it. She has to be careful and conserve

her energy for when she needs it." This was far less true than it had been a few months before. He didn't know how much Bridget was able to do, but she seemed to be pretty much back to her old self. The way she had been before the cancer had struck.

Gloria sat down in one of the armchairs. Her gaze was piercing. Zachary had to look away.

"Robin's death was not *unexpected*," Gloria said. "I'm not sure where you got that idea. Surely if your wife had cancer, you know all about it. When the cancer travels to other parts of the body—liver, bones, lungs—then you know they don't have much time left. We knew Robin was living on borrowed time."

"Oh… from what I heard, I was under the impression—Bridget was under the impression—that it happened earlier than the doctor had said. That they thought she still had time left. Months, even."

"What are a few months?" Gloria's voice was thick with grief. "Before the cancer, everyone thought she had a lifetime ahead of her. Time for… all of those things left undone. But a few months? A few months is nothing!"

Zachary looked for a way to formulate an answer. But Vera was sitting beside him shaking her head.

"I would have wanted more time with her. A few months would have been wonderful. I would have taken a few days. A few hours. It was so quick."

"You were surprised, then?" Zachary turned his head back toward her. "You didn't think she was ready to die yet, did you?"

"No," Vera agreed emphatically.

"It doesn't matter if she was ready to die," Gloria said. "That's not the way it works. We don't get to pick our time. It just comes sneaking up behind us, and then… it strikes."

"I didn't think it was Robin's time," Vera said. She looked at Gloria. "Do you?"

Her strength was of a different sort than Gloria's. Gloria was all challenge and hard edges. Vera was strong too, but in a different way. She didn't bend under her daughter's insistence. She just looked at her, waiting for her answer.

Gloria sagged, losing much of her bravado. "No. You're right… she should have had… more time."

That meant there were three people who didn't think it had been Robin's time to go. Maybe Bridget was on to something. Maybe she wasn't just afraid that it could have been her. Frightened that she might be looking in a mirror.

Zachary let them just sit in silence for a few minutes, thinking about Robin and about how she had been taken from them too quickly.

"Do you think…" Zachary wanted to speak as quietly as their own consciences. He wanted them to think it was their own idea. "Is there any possibility that there was a mistake? That the hospital might have done something…? A wrong treatment, maybe? Things do happen…"

Vera and Gloria both stared at him. Neither one jumped in with the exclamation that he could be right. It wasn't something they had already been thinking. It wasn't something that they immediately discounted, though, either. They looked at each other. Gloria shook her head and eventually, Vera followed suit.

"No," she agreed. "The hospital was always very good. The staff was very friendly and respectful and well-trained. I never felt like they didn't know what they were talking about. They were always willing to take the time to explain everything."

"Robin died because she had cancer," Gloria said flatly. "There wasn't anything anyone could have done. She had cancer, and that's what took her. It was her time, even if we didn't like it." Gloria looked at her mother. "God's timing is never the same as ours, is it? The Lord chooses his own time."

"His ways are higher than our ways," Vera agreed. They both seemed to be happy with this answer.

But Zachary had never been a religious person. He had lived in some foster families who had strong Christian beliefs, but he'd never understood their faith in what couldn't be seen or heard or demonstrated in any way. It seemed like people just wanted to delude themselves. Vera and Gloria might believe that Robin had been taken before her time, but they were willing to lay that on God and accept it as His will.

Zachary wasn't willing to do that.

"You wouldn't mind, would you, if I asked around a little bit?" he suggested. "Bridget asked me to look into it, see if anything was suspicious or out of place. I'm sure it's nothing, but you wouldn't mind me asking a few questions, would you?"

Vera shrugged. "We don't know the answers to any of your questions."

"What do you mean?" Gloria raised her voice. "Ask who a few questions? Is that why you're here? To nose around here and see if one of us had anything to do with Robin's death? I can't believe the nerve!"

"No, no, I wasn't accusing you of anything. I just wondered whether... I've been making some inquiries at the hospital, and I wondered if you would mind if I said that you wanted the answers too. That you wanted to make sure it really was Robin's time to go..."

"Who *are* you?"

"He's Bridget's husband," Vera told her daughter, not understanding what Gloria was upset about.

"Something isn't right here," Gloria said. "He's asking questions at the hospital? He comes here asking about Robin? He wants our permission to... what, investigate?"

Zachary shrugged, hoping she would wind down and decide that was okay if he didn't let it become a confrontation.

"I don't remember ever seeing him visiting the cancer unit," Gloria said to Vera. "Do you? Do you remember ever seeing him before?"

"Well, no..."

"Bridget isn't my wife," Zachary explained. "She's my ex-wife. When she found out she had cancer... she didn't want me around. She wanted to face it by herself, without any... distractions. She didn't want to have to worry about anyone else's needs. Just to focus on her own recovery." He swallowed and took a minute to try to slow his breathing and keep himself from getting too emotional. Bridget had been right. She had been able to put all of her energy into healing and had recovered. Robin had not been able to do the same. "We're still on good terms. She asked me if I would look into Robin's death. And just make sure that everything was… usual. Nothing irregular."

Gloria suddenly swore. Zachary could see by her expression that it wasn't that she didn't believe him. She had just put it together. She knew who he was.

"You're that private investigator. You've been on TV and the internet."

"A private investigator?" Vera repeated in a tiny voice.

"He's conducting a murder investigation." Gloria's voice shook. "He thinks someone killed Robin!"

"I'm just looking into it." Zachary tried to calm her. "There isn't any evidence here of murder. I'm just looking at the circumstances. Making sure that there isn't anything that might indicate that it might not have been…" he trailed off, too tangled up in the words and emotions to continue.

"Well, you can leave us out of it. You don't have our permission to do anything on Robin's behalf or my mother's behalf. You can't use our names. We don't want you to pursue this any further!"

Zachary put his hands on his knees and pushed himself up. It was time to be heading back to the hospital again anyway.

"Can I leave you with my card in case you have any questions or you change your minds?"

"No," Gloria snapped.

Zachary took one out anyway and put it beside Vera before leaving.

5

Meeting with Vera had not gone as well as Zachary had hoped, but neither had it gone as badly as he had feared. He had learned a lot about Robin's family and background. They hadn't found the circumstances of Robin's death to be suspicious. He might not have their blessing to continue with the investigation, but he did have more facts and a clearer picture of the person Robin had been.

He was driving back to the hospital when his phone rang. Glancing at the display, Zachary answered it hands-free.

"Bridget? Is everything okay?"

"Why wouldn't everything be okay?"

Zachary didn't respond, momentarily tongue-tied. Was she looking for a status report already? Had she changed her mind and realized looking for an outside cause in Robin's death was a waste of time? She didn't normally call him unless there was something wrong. Usually, because she was upset about something Zachary was doing.

"I just called to see if you were going to look into Robin Salter's death," Bridget said in a more conciliatory tone. "Nothing is wrong."

"Okay. Good. I'm already on it. I've talked to a few people, one of the nurses, her family; I'm just on my way to talk to Dr. West."

"He's probably pretty busy."

"I have an appointment with him."

"Oh. That's great." Bridget took a deep breath. "Thank you so much, Zachary. I really appreciate you taking this on. I know you're probably busy with all kinds of other cases."

"I can make time for it. So far, everything seems to be fine. Nobody seems to be worried or suspicious of anything that happened. Like you say, it was quicker than anyone expected, but that does happen sometimes."

"I know…" Bridget sounded distant. "It's just that… she was still so strong. And then all of a sudden, it was over. She was sick for a few days, and I thought she was just tired and she would get over it with some rest, and then they said she had passed. It doesn't make any sense."

"She was sick before she died?"

"Just a couple of days. It shouldn't have been the end."

Zachary kept his mouth shut and didn't argue with her about it. If Robin had experienced a worsening of symptoms, then that argued for natural causes, not some accident or medical neglect by the hospital.

"I'll do what I can to find out," he promised.

"Thank you, Zachary. I do appreciate it."

Zachary got goosebumps. He remembered the way that she used to talk to him. The way that she used to make him feel. It made him warm and happy to be appreciated by her. Maybe they were getting past the rift that the cancer had caused. Maybe Bridget was getting to the point where she was willing to accept that they had broken up because she had pushed him away, not because he had done anything wrong. Maybe deep down, she still loved him, and this was her way of trying to reconcile with him.

"I lo—you're welcome, Bridget. You know I'm always here to help." He didn't want to be needy. She had asked for his help. That meant she wanted him to be the strong one and to support her.

She had to be the one to set the emotional tone. He'd follow her lead.

"Talk to you later," Bridget's voice was stronger for a moment, and then she was gone, the connection terminated. Zachary's phone decided to start playing his music and he hit the button on the stereo to stop it, not wanting to be distracted by the noise.

For the moment, he just wanted to bask in the knowledge that she needed him. Bridget needed him and appreciated him. Maybe there was a chance for them after all.

***

Dr. West didn't keep Zachary waiting for too long. Zachary sat in the waiting area tapping randomly through his phone, reviewing the notes he had made and questions he should ask. There weren't a lot of coughing children in Dr. West's waiting room, like there were when he went to the walk-in medical clinic for one ailment or another. Instead, it was mostly older women and couples, sitting quietly with magazines or whispering with each other.

He was escorted into Dr. West's office by a receptionist in a flowered nurse's smock. Zachary had been half-expecting to be led to a typical exam room, but of course Dr. West actually had a real office where he got paperwork done and had meetings or made phone calls. It was similar to doctors' offices Zachary had seen on TV; a wall of bookcases filled with thick volumes, a heavy wooden desk, a couple of chairs for visitors to sit in. There was a thin computer monitor on the corner of the desk, and the surface of the desk was covered with various piles and files of paper. There was more to being a doctor like Dr. West than just seeing patients.

"So, Mr. Goldman." Dr. West looked down at a file open on the desk in front of him. Robin's file? Had he been reviewing it before Zachary arrived or was it just an unrelated file and he found it easier to look at something else than to have to look Zachary in the face?

"Zachary."

"Zachary." Dr. West gave a nod. "What can I help you with? Like I said before, there is the matter of privilege to be considered."

"I'm just curious about Robin's last days here. From what Bridget said, Robin seemed to be doing quite well. Bridget is normally a pretty good judge of other people. She was shocked that Robin went so quickly."

"It isn't unusual, after someone finds out they are terminal, for them to… let go. They make peace with their fate, tie up any loose ends, and let themselves go."

"Bridget didn't feel like Robin had done that. She said Robin was still fighting. She wasn't giving in to the cancer."

Dr. West shrugged. "We can't always see what people are really thinking, can we?"

"What was your feeling? How much time did you think she had left?"

"Doctors are notorious for being wrong about these things. You would be amazed at how many doctors get sued for not properly predicting someone's death date. In either direction, early or late."

"Really?" Zachary considered the circumstances under which someone would sue the doctor because they had lived longer than he had predicted. "Wow. But you didn't expect that Robin would die as early as she did?"

Dr. West rubbed his hands together, then folded them on top of his desk. "No. I didn't. But as surprised as I was that she went so quickly… I never suspected any… outside influence. I don't know exactly what you're looking for, but I never saw any problems with Robin's care or sign of outside influences. I think you're just looking at a case where the cancer or a related condition took her sooner than anyone expected."

"That's pretty much what I expected. I know that when Bridget was here, she always said she was treated well and that the staff were very kind. It wasn't like some of the horror stories you hear of people getting sepsis sitting for days in the emergency room. Very clean, very professional." Zachary wasn't worried about laying it on too thick. Doctors had big egos. And the more senior the doctor, the bigger his ego.

Dr. West smiled in appreciation. "We work very hard to provide a clean and homey environment for our patients. We know that no one chose to be there, and that the more comfortable and happier they are, the better they are able to fight cancer and tolerate the treatment protocol."

"You're doing a fine job."

"Thank you. It's really good to hear that."

"You haven't had anyone other than Robin who has died quite a bit earlier than you expected?"

Dr. West frowned and shook his head. "No, there's no pattern that indicates we've got a resistant bacteria on the ward, or some kind of contaminated supplies or medications. Everything has been perfectly normal, no signs of trouble. And Robin's death itself… as I said, it's not abnormal or unexpected. She just went before we predicted. That happens."

"Have you had any staffing changes lately? Anyone new, or anyone you've had to let go?"

"Working in oncology is difficult. People come and go. There's always turnover. It's very taxing to deal every day with people who are dying."

"I would imagine so," Zachary agreed. "You read in the news sometimes about staff in hospital wards or care centers who decide to take matters into their own hands."

"Angels of death," Dr. West said flatly. His smile was gone. He looked toward the door as if he were expecting someone to enter. Or to leave.

"Right. They're not the type of people you expect to be murderers. It's not done out of malice. It's more along the lines of… assisted suicide. Except without consent."

"Just because you've heard it in the news, that doesn't mean it's common. That kind of thing is very rare. Just like nursery nurses stealing infants. It happens a few times, and suddenly it has a name, it's a recognized pattern. People suddenly think it's a common occurrence. But it isn't. There have only been a handful of these 'angels of death' ever identified in the whole country. You're more likely to be hit by lightning than killed by one of these so-called angels."

Zachary nodded. "I've never seen any sign of that kind of thing going on," he agreed. "Certainly, Bridget never had any fear that someone was going to do her in while she was at the treatment center. It's all a little over the top. I'm not even sure what you would look for, if you were administering a department like this. Is there a checklist of things to watch for? Things that should tip you off that you have an 'angel of death' on your staff?" He shook his head in disbelief.

Dr. West fell for it hook, line, and sinker. He leaned forward, dropping his voice like he might be overheard discussing such a thing. "There have actually been studies into this kind of thing. Red flags for medical serial killers. I attended a seminar while on a medical retreat. It's one of those things that comes up during insurance reviews. Are your stats all in line? Are you aware of the red flags for medical serial killers? Do you have a proper vetting program and monitoring in place?"

Zachary nodded, mirroring Dr. West's body language by leaning toward him. "Like what?"

"Carers who have a higher rate of deaths of patients in their care, obviously. Depression, personality disorder, preferring night shifts. People who make their colleagues nervous or have drugs in their possession."

"How would you know that? How would you, as the head of a program like this, be aware of any of that? You'd have access to the death statistics, but do you get a breakdown of what staff members were on duty during each death?"

"It's up to the employees in the department to notice and report any patterns. Obviously, if we had a rash of unexpected deaths or an increase in mortality rate, we would do a deeper review, but these people can be very sneaky. How would you know someone had drugs in their possession without doing a search? You can't just randomly search people's lockers or pockets. How would you know someone had depression or a personality disorder? You're not allowed to ask during an employment interview. We have moms who prefer the night shift because they want to be home with their kids during the day. You can't start accusing them of being serial killers because they've asked for night shift."

Zachary chuckled. "No. Good way to get slapped."

Dr. West laughed, agreeing.

"But you've never had any worries about that?" Zachary asked. "You've never had any scares, or had those doubts cross your mind because a death was unusual or unexpected?"

Dr. West sat back again, hands folded in his lap, staring up at the ceiling. "I'm sure every hospital head of department has at some time or another. Or every head of oncology, anyway. You've been told to be vigilant, so you ask yourself 'could it happen in my unit?' 'Is it happening in my unit?' But no… I've never had any real concerns or suspicions."

"No one you were relieved to let go, because they gave you the creeps? No patients complaining about unscheduled medical treatments or visits…?"

Was there a flicker in Dr. West's eyes before he shook his head? Zachary leaned back as well, thinking it over.

"How does it usually happen? How do these angel-of-death cases go undetected for so long?"

"In a lot of cases, it's insulin overdose. Insulin is naturally found in the body. The person just goes into a coma and dies. When you're dealing with someone who is already on death's door, that's not an unusual event. No one would order an autopsy, and even if one was ordered, the pathologist wouldn't find anything. Insulin breaks down within forty-eight hours, so even if they're looking for it, they're not likely to find it."

And they were already past the forty-eight hour mark since Robin's death.

"You have to get a confession in those cases," Dr. West said. "Or catch them in the act. There's no other way."

"Would you even stock insulin in a cancer ward? Would that be normal?"

"Certainly. Diabetic people get cancer. At a higher rate than non-diabetics, in fact. And anyone with pancreatic cancer is going to get diabetes. Some of the cancer treatments we are using can cause diabetes. It's important to monitor and manage patients' blood glucose levels."

"I didn't know that. I guess that's not something Bridget ever had to deal with, so I wasn't aware of it. What about Robin? Did she have diabetes? Before or after the cancer?"

Dr. West shook his head, but then his eyes drifted down to the file open in front of him. His attention was taken from Zachary as his eyes flicked back and forth over the papers. He turned a couple of sheets over.

"That's confidential information," he said. "I wouldn't be able to tell you if Robin had high blood sugar a day or two before she died that required the administration of insulin."

Zachary stared at him. "She did?" But he understood that Dr. West couldn't confirm or deny the information. He had said only that he couldn't tell Zachary the information. It wasn't something that would ever hold up in court, but it was a direction for him to go.

"I couldn't tell you," Dr. West repeated. "Like I said, a lot of patients get high blood sugar. That's not unusual. It's not cause for concern. It's just something that we keep an eye on."

"Is there any way to tell how much insulin she was given?"

"It's on her chart, if you had permission or a court order. But you don't."

"And can you match your insulin inventory to the charts? Can you tell for sure if she was given the right dose, or do you just assume that she was?"

"My staff know how to administer insulin."

"Yes..." Zachary let Dr. West think about that for a few

minutes. Knowing how to administer insulin made the staff potential suspects, it didn't prove their innocence. Robin could have been given the wrong dosage of insulin either by accident or on purpose. If they had an angel of death on the staff, which Dr. West had pointed out was pretty much impossible to tell, then they could have administered the wrong dosage of insulin and gotten away with it.

Dr. West started to flush. "I don't like your implication, Mr. Goldman."

"Zachary."

"Mr. Goldman. I explained to you why we have insulin stocked. I explained to you that Ms. Salter required insulin because of her cancer or her treatments. You can't then jump to the conclusion that she was overdosed on insulin and that's why she died. I told you there was nothing suspicious about her death and I am sticking to that statement. Ms. Salter died of natural causes. Not insulin overdose.

"Except there's no way to know that."

"I'm telling you."

Dr. West's phone rang. He looked at it for a moment, his brows drawing down in a frown. Then he picked it up. "Dr. Aaron West, oncology."

He listened to the caller, the frown disappearing and his eyes instead going up in surprise. His eyes riveted on Zachary instead of getting that unfocused look people usually got when they talked on the phone, imagining the person on the other end of the call instead of seeing what was in front of them. He nodded and listened to the rapid voice on the other end. Eventually, the caller wound down so that Dr. West was able to speak.

"Yes, Miss Salter," he agreed.

Zachary's heart sank.

"Yes, I understand. Yes. I appreciate your call, thank you for letting me know."

He made a few more calming and affirming noises, and was

eventually able to hang up the phone. He put it down firmly, eyes still boring into Zachary.

"You led me to believe that you had been hired by Robin's family to look into her case."

"No." Zachary kept his voice flat and empty. "I told you that Bridget was concerned. I didn't claim to be hired by the family."

Dr. West scowled. "Whether you said it or not, you clearly wanted me to believe it."

"What you believed isn't my responsibility," Zachary pointed out. "I didn't tell you that Robin's family hired me."

"I think it's time for you to leave."

Zachary nodded, getting to his feet. He kept a purposefully vague and unemotional exterior, but inside, his heart was racing like he was already on the run. He was aware of every twitch Dr. West made, ready for a full-blown confrontation. But luckily, Dr. West kept his own emotions under control and didn't make any threats of violence. He allowed Zachary to simply retreat the way he had come and didn't pursue him or call security.

Zachary walked back past the reception desk and gave the pretty receptionist a smile and a nod, projecting the impression that everything had gone as he had hoped and all was well between him and Dr. West. If he ended up having to call her or ask her for further information, he didn't want to have given away the fact that Dr. West had sent him packing. If she were under the impression that Dr. West had cooperated with him fully, she would be far more accommodating of any further queries.

6

I t was late enough in the afternoon that Zachary decided to simply go home. He could have a bite to eat, check his email and voice messages, and plan out his evening. But when he got home and looked in the fridge at the food Bridget had brought him, nothing appealed to him. His appetite was usually suppressed by his meds, and he and Bridget had never really seen eye-to-eye on dietary choices. Bridget was, of course, big on whole foods, salads, vegetables, and juices, all those things that helped her to keep her figure and to have a strong immune system in order to fight the cancer. While she was not a vegetarian, she eschewed red meat and stuck to occasional skinless chicken and fish. Zachary had no desire to eat either one.

Every foster home had been different, but instead of adjusting to a wide variety of cuisines, Zachary had gotten pickier and pickier. If forced, he would eat whatever was put on the table in front of him. He'd never had a showdown with a foster father over food where he'd been physically force-fed. He'd seen it happen to others. But given the choice, his diet was limited to highly processed foods. Peanut butter sandwiches. Pepperoni and sausage pizzas. Cheese burritos. Greasy fast-food hamburgers. Along with plenty of coffee and cola.

Bridget's "clean" diet of fresh fruits, vegetables, and lean meats just didn't cut it.

Zachary checked his email, made some notes about what he had learned on the Robin Salter case, and pondered over calling Kenzie.

Previously, he wouldn't have hesitated to call her to get her insight and suggest that they go out for dinner. But previously, Bridget had been out of the picture. Not only had she divorced Zachary, but she'd been furious with him. She hadn't wanted to see or hear from him. She didn't want anything to do with him unless it was her own idea.

But that had changed. Suddenly she was in his life again. Asking him for favors. Thanking him. Making him feel like he was worthwhile instead of a piece of dung that had stuck to her shoe after the divorce. He thought he might have a chance with her again.

And that made calling Kenzie a difficult decision. Would it upset Bridget? She'd tried to warn Kenzie away from Zachary before. But she'd also called Kenzie when she thought Zachary needed someone to check in on him. Bridget was too unpredictable for Zachary to be sure how she would react to a potential rival now that she was back in Zachary's life.

Not that he and Kenzie were hot and heavy. They were friends, but Zachary still wasn't sure where he stood with her. Bowman assured him that Kenzie was interested in him and he had a chance of snagging her if he approached it the right way. But Zachary had been too uncertain to pursue her. He'd almost scared her off in the beginning, and he wasn't sure she trusted him yet.

Eventually, Zachary picked up his phone and dialed.

The phone rang a few times before Kenzie picked it up, and Zachary wondered whether she was in the morgue rather than at her desk. She'd been getting a little more time with hands-on work recently, and that meant when the phone rang, she had to decide whether to let it ring, or to stop what she was doing, take off her gloves and whatever other protective gear she was wearing, and then go to the phone.

Eventually, Kenzie answered the phone. "Is this my favorite private eye?"

Zachary snorted. "Do you know any other private eyes?"

"No."

"Then I guess that's a yes. This is your favorite private eye."

"What's up?"

"I have a new case." He wasn't about to tell her that it was an unpaid case, or that it had come to him through Bridget.

"Something of interest to the medical examiner's office?"

"Well… Probably not something that will ever come across your desk, but I am investigating whether it might *not* have been natural causes."

"What makes you think it is not?"

"The client thinks it might not be. I'm not so sure yet."

"What makes him think it wasn't natural causes?"

"It was unexpected. Well, not unexpected… but before it was expected. She had cancer. It had metastasized. But they thought she still had a few months."

Kenzie made an irritated noise. "That doesn't sound like anything to me. Just because someone dies of cancer a few weeks before you expected them to, that doesn't mean anything."

"I know. That's what I keep hearing. But I'm looking into it, asking some questions… just exploring a little."

"And…?"

"I don't really have anything for you. She had high blood sugar, so she was being given insulin. I just wonder…"

"If someone gave her too much?"

Zachary didn't say anything, waiting to see what Kenzie had to say without his input.

"It's a stretch, Zachary. Yes, she could have been given the wrong dosage of insulin, but chances are, they would figure it out right away and would dose her with glucagon. She'd recover just fine."

"What if it wasn't accidental? What if someone gave it to her on purpose?"

"Like who?"

"I don't know. One of the nurses or other staff. An 'angel of death.'"

"Really? You haven't found any evidence that there's an angel of death there. If you had, it would be all over the place. I would have heard."

"No, there's no evidence. It's just… she went before her time. Everybody thought it was too early. I thought… if it wasn't caused by an accident, an accidental overdose, or drug interaction, or allergic reaction… some kind of treatment that was contraindicated… then what? I know it's rare, but you can't deny the fact that it happens."

"There is no angel of death operating in this town. We would have heard something about it if there was."

"These people can operate for years, cause dozens of deaths before they are caught."

"You're going to have to show me some kind of evidence. Show me the numbers. Show me the number of people who died before they should, and that it's different than the averages. Give me bodies, Zachary."

"I can't."

"Of course not," she agreed. "Because there aren't any. No one was murdered. One woman with cancer died before her family thought she would. That's not a crime. That's not a pattern. That's just one person."

"I know."

Kenzie sighed. "I'm about ready to wrap everything up here tonight. Have you eaten?"

Zachary had been debating whether to ask Kenzie or not, puzzling over the complication Bridget posed. He hadn't expected her to ask him.

"Uh… no… not yet."

There were a few seconds of silence as Kenzie analyzed Zachary's clearly hesitant tone.

"Do you not want to eat? Did you have other plans?"

"I could eat." Zachary winced as he heard the pitch of his voice go up. He sounded too cheery. Too bouncy. Like he was trying to cover something up.

"You could eat. But you haven't already. You sound weird. Is everything okay?"

"Yes. Everything is *fine.*"

"Do you want to hit Old Joe's? I'm not really in the mood for buffet tonight."

"Old Joe's is great." Zachary looked at the time on his phone screen. "Is seven too early? Do you need more time than that?"

"Seven would be fine. I'm already famished."

"I'll see you there, then. You don't need to be picked up?"

"I've got my baby."

Kenzie's little red sports car was her pride and joy. Zachary smiled.

"I'll see you at Old Joe's."

Zachary took his time getting to Old Joe's, knowing that Kenzie had to get cleaned up and had farther to travel than he did. He took his time locking the car, checking the door handle to be sure the electric door locks had worked, and scanning the parking lot for anyone behaving suspiciously. He'd never had any trouble with his car in the parking lot of Old Joe's, but he was still wary.

Zachary checked the locks one more time, then went in.

He was surprised to find Kenzie there ahead of him. She already had a drink and had started in on the basket of rolls on the table.

She *had* said that was famished.

Zachary sat down, smiling. Kenzie nodded to the bread basket to encourage him to take a roll for himself, her dark curls bouncing.

"I hope you don't mind, I already ordered."

"You said you were hungry."

"I got you the prime rib and baked potato. That's what you usually go for, isn't it? We can tell them to change it, if you want something else."

"No, that's perfect."

Kenzie nodded. "There's something to be said for having a 'usual.'"

Zachary agreed. The waitress brought over a Coke, also Zachary's usual, and he accepted it with a nod and a smile.

"How long are you going to spend on this case?" Kenzie inquired. Her red-lipsticked lips were marred by a few white crumbs from her roll.

"Did you skip lunch?"

"Uh…" she considered, thinking back over her day. "Yeah, I think I might have. That would explain it, huh?"

"Yeah. You should keep granola bars in your desk or something. So you don't have to starve if you aren't able to get out to eat."

"That would make too much sense. I should do it. Although, maybe substitute 'chocolate bar' for 'granola bar.' Admit it, you would too."

"Uh-huh." Zachary thought about the fridge full of healthy food he had no desire to eat. At least Kenzie had known better than to order him a salad.

"And the case…?"

Zachary tried to circle his thoughts back to Robin Salter. "What about it?"

"How long are you going to dig around looking for something that isn't there? Sometimes people get sick and die. She was under a doctor's care. They certify that she died from the cancer… and unless you've got proof otherwise, you're going to have a helluva time convincing anyone to take another look."

"You're right. But sometimes… I *have* had success in cases that everybody says aren't murder."

"Lucky breaks?" she offered with a teasing smile.

"Hard work," Zachary insisted. And she knew it was true. He had put a lot of time and effort into those cases. It was just when he thought he was at the end of the investigation and there was nothing left to find that everything fell into place. He knew better than to be put off by the appearance of an accidental or natural death. Sometimes, it wasn't an accident.

Zachary took a sip of his cola thinking about this. Could there be an unseen hand tipping the scale in Robin Salter's death? Someone malicious?

"Zachary?"

He blinked and looked at her. "Just thinking about the case."

"Tell me some more. She had cancer. She was terminal. Was she suffering? In a lot of pain?"

"I don't know. I know near the end, she was in more pain, that's what the nurse said. But Bridget saw her and said she still seemed strong. She was still fighting it, and was still in good shape."

"Bridget?"

"Uh…" Zachary looked at Kenzie, realizing he had let her name slip out. He hadn't intended to tell her that. "Bridget knew her. They both had cancer."

"That's quite a coincidence."

"Not really, they met in treatment."

"No, I mean that Bridget happens to know this woman whose death you're looking into. Just coincidentally."

Zachary swallowed. He smiled and nodded. "She said she didn't think it was Robin's time to go. From what she said, Robin still had good quality of life."

Kenzie stared at him and he waited to see whether she was going to challenge him about the origins of the case or whether she would focus on what he was saying.

"That puts a hole in your angel of death theory."

"What? Why?"

"Because medical serial killers are usually one of two types. Either they see themselves as angels of mercy, releasing people from pain and suffering, or they like to be in the middle of the drama, part of reviving or trying to revive the person again."

Zachary concentrated on what she was saying. "Okay. So you think they wouldn't have done it to put her out of her misery if she wasn't really suffering."

"Right."

"And they wouldn't just let her die in her sleep if they wanted to be part of trying to save her."

"Exactly."

Zachary nodded, considering the possibilities. "The nurse that I talked to said they don't take heroic measures to revive patients. Not when they are just going to die anyway. Maybe this angel of death is a new employee. Maybe they didn't know that, and thought there would be a big drama if Robin died, but they were disappointed."

Kenzie shrugged. "That's a lot of speculation."

A cheerful waitress brought them each their dinner orders. Zachary didn't try to talk to Kenzie while she gave her full attention to her dinner. He picked at his prime rib and potato. He had hardly eaten, so he knew he needed to, and it was more appetizing than the rabbit food. Zachary took another bite of the rib as it finally occurred to him that if he wanted something particular to eat, then he'd better stock his kitchen, rather than expecting Bridget or Bowman or somebody else to provide what he wanted. He'd gotten lazy while he'd been living with Bowman, neglecting the things he needed to do for himself. Not that he'd ever been the best at self-care, but he could at least manage to go grocery shopping so he wouldn't need to go out or order pizza every night.

He looked up to find Kenzie studying him.

"Think of something?" she suggested. "About the case?"

"Uh… no. Things I need for the apartment."

"Oh. I should get you a housewarming gift. What do you need?"

Zachary was flummoxed. He couldn't tell Kenzie he needed groceries. The next thing he thought of was the couch, but he couldn't tell her he needed that either. He needed something in between. Something small she could pick up in the housewares department.

"Oh… uh… I could use… a toaster."

"A toaster? I could handle that. Anything particular? Wide slice, retro look, maybe a toaster oven?"

"No. Nothing fancy. Just… a regular toaster."

"Consider it done."

Zachary let out a sigh of relief.

"If you want to pursue this unnatural death angle, you need to have a suspect," Kenzie said, slowing down on her dinner and considering the matter at hand. "Because it doesn't fit an angel-of-death killing."

"It could have been an accident."

"Yes. But you're going to have to get access to her charts and the hospital's other records to prove that. If it was an accidental overdose of something like insulin, you're going to need all of their inventory logs. You'd have to show that it was an accident before being able to get the evidence that it was."

Zachary had a bite of potato and chewed it slowly. In spite of all of the toppings, it was bland and tasteless.

"You're not going to get an autopsy based on baseless speculations, and even if you did, the medical examiner might not be able to find anything. Any insulin in her system would be gone. It could be another cause, but with the extent of her illness and her treatment, all kinds of things are going to be off."

Zachary frowned, a tight band forming across his forehead. "What do you mean?"

"If she was diabetic because of her cancer or because of her treatment, then you can bet that all kinds of other damage had been done to her body as well. Chemotherapy is an attempt to kill cells without killing the person. Sometimes it is successful, but sometimes it causes too much harm for the person to recover from."

"If that was the case... if chemotherapy killed her, that's not considered a medical error?"

"No. The patient signs off on all of the risks. They are told that it could kill them. They're given all of the stats and figures, and have to decide it's worth trying. It's not a medical error or even an error of judgment. You just don't know how a person's body is going to react and what complicating factors might be present."

"Like diabetes."

"Diabetes, anemia, heart problems. A compromised immune system means a simple virus or bacterial infection could kill you. Allergies to one of the medications. The body turning against itself and attacking its own cells."

"That's a lot that can go wrong."

Kenzie picked at her vegetables, cutting a spear of asparagus into short lengths and impaling a few of them on her fork.

"You didn't... go over any of this when Bridget was in treatment?"

"No." Zachary's cheeks heated and he stared down at the puddle of juices on his plate. "I tried to be there for her, but she didn't really want me involved. She didn't want me to come to her doctor's appointments or to her treatments. It wasn't long before she said she wanted me out of there, period. So... I left."

Kenzie shook her head. "I really don't understand her. I would think she would want the support. I can understand breaking up because your partner won't be there for you or thinks you are over-dramatizing your illness... but I don't understand breaking up because you just don't want them around anymore."

"She blamed me for her getting cancer in the first place."

It still hurt to say it. He remembered Bridget's attack, her venom. It was his fault. His fault for being so needy and paranoid and obsessive. The stress of living with him was what had compromised her body's defenses and allowed the cancer to take root.

"You didn't cause Bridget's cancer," Kenzie said firmly.

"But the stress—"

"I've met Bridget, and let me say she has problems that existed long before she met you. I don't know what her childhood or family situation were like, but I have no doubt that this anger she has didn't start when she met you. It goes a lot deeper than that. She's a toxic person. Maybe she's toxic to herself as well as to you."

"No," Zachary protested. "She's very loving. She has a lot of friends and she loves her family. Everyone is drawn to her. When we met, she was so kind and caring. It wasn't until later that she got... angry." He closed his eyes for a minute, trying to focus on the blissful days earlier in their relationship. Before he had screwed everything up. "It was just like my mother... she couldn't deal with my behavior. She tried and tried, but in the end, she couldn't do it anymore. She had to... expunge me from her life."

"What your mother did was incomprehensible. And that's not what Bridget has done. She keeps hanging around, coming back either to rail against you or to take care of you. Or now getting you involved in some nonsense case because she can't stand for you to be out of her life. If you were the problem with the relationship, then why hasn't she gone on?"

"She has." Zachary put a big bite of potato in his mouth to give him a few moments to formulate his objection. "She has a new boyfriend. Gordon. They went home for Christmas, she met his family. They have a normal relationship."

"I highly doubt it."

"They do. She *has* moved on."

Even though he said it, he wanted Kenzie to argue. He wanted her to insist that Bridget wasn't over him and didn't have a good relationship with Gordon.

"Bridget has most definitely not moved on."

Zachary couldn't help the warm, satisfied feeling that flooded through him at Kenzie's words. If Kenzie was right, then Bridget keeping in touch with Zachary even when she insisted she didn't want anything to do with him was a sign that she hadn't let him go. Actions spoke louder than words. She could say all she wanted to that she didn't want Zachary around, didn't want him keeping tabs on her or showing up in any of their old haunts, but her actions said she was still interested in him. Their lives were still intertwined. Even though she was in a relationship with Gordon and claimed she and Zachary were over, there was still a chance at reconciliation.

"You think she still has feelings for me? That she cares about me?"

"I know she does." Kenzie's dark eyes were intense, her gaze so heated that Zachary had to look away from her. "She shows up at your house on Christmas Eve? Asks you to take on an investigation without any merit? I told you before, that level of anger she has against you when you do something she deems to be wrong doesn't mean she hates you. She wouldn't waste time being angry at you if she didn't care for you. She'd just call the police."

Zachary didn't want Kenzie to start thinking about the mistakes he had made in the past. He was doing better at not being so obsessive about his relationships. He was past all of that. He didn't want her starting to worry about it again.

"What about another suspect?" he questioned, changing the topic abruptly back to the investigation. "You think someone other than a doctor or nurse could have been the cause of Robin's death? I met her mother and sister, but I don't see how it could be either of them."

Kenzie's brows squeezed together in a scowl, scrutinizing him and undoubtedly worrying about the reason for his change in direction.

"It could be the same thing as an angel of death. Wanting to end the pain and sickness. Family members can be very sensitive to that kind of thing. Have you considered assisted suicide? Maybe Robin arranged her own death."

"Wouldn't that mean the doctor *was* involved?"

"Maybe, maybe not. Maybe he wouldn't assist her. They might have just looked up methods on the internet."

Zachary sat back, considering it. Neither Vera nor Gloria had given him any reason to suspect them of being involved in Robin's death, but if it was assisted suicide, or euthanasia without her consent, what would he have seen?

"I suppose it's possible. The nurse said that Robin was in more pain before she died. Maybe her sister decided that it was too much…?"

"Only the sister? You've eliminated the mother as a suspect?"

"Well… yes. She didn't strike me as being capable of pulling something like that off. She wouldn't be searching the internet, she's not computer savvy. And she struck me as being… forgetful. Not quite all there."

"Dementia?" Kenzie suggested.

"Not quite… just… old. A little… vague."

"Well, the sister then. Or maybe a boyfriend? Did she have someone?"

Zachary thought back to the pictures at Vera's house. The man Robin had been engaged to, but then broken up with. The other man he had seen a picture of her with that Zachary hadn't had a chance to ask about. He'd been distracted by Gloria's arrival and had forgotten to pursue it.

"Yes… she might have. I'll have to ask the nurse, or maybe Bridget. I did see a picture of her with a man."

"I would suspect him before her sister. I think most women would ask a partner for help before a sibling."

Zachary tried to imagine what Bridget would have done. If she hadn't gone into remission and had been told her case was terminal; if she had been in a lot of pain and knew it wasn't going to get better, would she have asked Zachary for help? Of course, she'd broken up with Zachary, so the situation was different. He couldn't see her ever being desperate enough to ask him for help with something like that. But would she have gone to her family? He couldn't think of a way to ask her.

7

Zachary didn't feel too badly about having to call Bridget up to ask her more questions about Robin and her possible boyfriend. Whether or not there was any chance it had been assisted suicide, he at least had a reason to call Bridget and discuss the case with her more fully. He considered the clock when he got home after dinner and decided she would still be up and it would not be too late for him to call her. They went through the usual 'are you okay?' and reassurances before Zachary was able to introduce his question.

"You didn't say anything in your email about a boyfriend," he said, "but I saw some pictures at her mother's house… it looks like she was in a relationship before she died?"

"Well…" Bridget drew the word out, not committing to an answer immediately, which Zachary thought seemed suspicious. "Yes, she did have a boyfriend. But I didn't want you to jump to conclusions and focus on him, because I'm sure he had nothing at all to do with her death."

But that was what she had asked Zachary to investigate. She should have given him all of the pertinent details if she really wanted him to come to the proper conclusion.

"His name is Lawrence Long," Bridget revealed, uncomfortable with the silence. "He's a really sweet guy. Like I said, I'm sure he had nothing to do with Robin's death, so I don't want you going after him like he's a suspect."

"He has to be a suspect. The boyfriend or partner is always a suspect."

"He didn't have anything to do with it, Zachary. Trust me on this one."

"I still need to talk to him. He might know things that no one else could tell me."

"But he didn't do it," Bridget said firmly. "He didn't have anything to do with Robin's death."

"Do you have any contact information, or do I need to look him up?"

She knew that he could find Lawrence Long and all of his details. Zachary *was* a private investigator. Skip tracing and background searches were his bread and butter. He had access to all of the best tools. If she didn't provide him with the information, it would take him all of ten minutes to search it out himself.

"I don't have his address or his email... but I do have a phone number."

"That will do."

Bridget was still prickly, but she gave it to him with yet another assertion that he hadn't had anything to do with Robin's death.

"Does he know that I'm looking into this? Have you talked to him about your suspicions—your *concerns*," Zachary amended his wording before she could interrupt him to do it herself.

"Yes, on a basic level. He knows that I was surprised by how suddenly she went, and that I have an ex who is a private investigator. I didn't tell him outright that I was going to have you look into it, but he knows enough that he won't be surprised."

"They were just dating?" Zachary asked. "Not married?"

"Uh... yes... just dating."

"Did she give him medical power of attorney?"

"I don't know. Does it matter? He didn't end up having to

make any medical decisions on her behalf. She was gone before then."

"If she gave him medical power of attorney, he might be able to get me access to her hospital records. Her family doesn't want me to have anything to do with it, but if Lawrence was her representative…"

"You'd have to ask him." Zachary was about to speak again when she interrupted him. "But Zachary…"

"What?"

"You may not find him any more accommodating than Robin's family. He believes it was just a natural death."

Zachary wasn't about to give up on Lawrence before he even had a chance to talk to him. There was still a chance the man could get Zachary permission to see Robin's records.

"Bridge…"

"Yes?"

"Out of everybody involved with Robin, you're the only one who thinks that it wasn't a natural death."

"So?"

"Are you sure you're not transferring your own feelings onto Robin?"

"This isn't about me."

"It could be. If you hadn't gone into remission, this is something you could have been facing."

"This is something I *did* have to face," Bridget countered. "I already had to make these decisions. I had to decide how long I was willing to fight the cancer. I had to decide which treatments I would accept, just how far I would go."

There was an unexpected lump in Zachary's throat. He should have poured himself a glass of water before calling her. He cleared his throat and swallowed, trying to continue the conversation without letting his voice break.

"And did you discuss that with Robin?"

"No. No, of course not. It's so personal. The answer is going to be different for everyone. Robin and I were friends, but… not that close."

"She never told you how long she wanted to continue treatment, or whether she would want to end her suffering at some point."

"She wouldn't," Bridget's voice was brittle. "She was still fighting. She hadn't given up. She didn't end her own life."

"Are you prepared for the fact that I might find something different?"

"You won't. I know Robin. This might have been a medical error, but it wasn't suicide."

Lawrence Long was the man Zachary had seen with Robin in the picture on Vera's mantle. He looked younger than Robin, a slight black man with short braids all over his head, a thin mustache and thinner soul patch. Zachary recognized the pain and grief in his eyes, still all too fresh in the wake of Robin's death.

Lawrence had been reluctant to meet with Zachary, but he had agreed. They had arranged to meet at a coffee shop rather than at Lawrence's home. Zachary's brain immediately went into overdrive analyzing this fact. Was there something at Lawrence's home that he didn't want Zachary to see? Was there a secret, or just several days' worth of takeout or dishes that he hadn't been able to deal with during his period of mourning? Did he want to meet at the coffee shop so that he wouldn't be reminded of his grief and would have more incentive not to cry in front of Zachary? Or was it somewhere he had gone with Robin and he wanted to be near her memory?

Lawrence nodded a greeting when Zachary introduced himself, and offered his hand to shake. It was thin and narrow, like a woman's hand, and he offered it like a dead, limp fish, not gripping Zachary's hand when he took it. Zachary let go hastily. Was this spiritless, self-effacing man really the dynamic and strong Robin's partner?

They both sat down, and a waitress came over with two cups of coffee Lawrence had already ordered. Zachary took a sip of his and then set it down.

"I'm so sorry for your loss," he offered. "I can't imagine how difficult this must be for you."

He *could* imagine; he'd been through plenty of loss of his own. But it was a lesson he'd learned from social media articles on dealing with other people's grief. Never presume to know how they are feeling. Let them tell you instead.

Lawrence nodded. "It was such a shock. I know that seems like a ridiculous thing to say, because we all knew she had terminal cancer. But it was still a shock, to leave her seemingly stable and strong one day, and to find out the next day she was dead."

Tears brimmed in his eyes, but he stared off into the distance and didn't shed them.

"That's what Bridget said," Zachary agreed. "It was just such a shock. She didn't feel like it was Robin's time to go yet."

"I guess we were wrong about that." Lawrence took a drink of his coffee.

"I suppose so. Bridget thinks that maybe there was an accident or medical neglect involved. Something the hospital did or didn't do…"

Lawrence tapped his fingers on the table. His eyes were far away. "No. I don't think that. We were all surprised, but the Lord giveth and the Lord taketh away. No one knows the mind of God."

It was similar to what Gloria and Vera had said. Zachary knew better than to let the religiosity bother him. They were just words, platitudes like the prayer Isabella had kept repeating after Declan's death. The words didn't really mean anything, but ritual behavior sometimes helped people deal with their grief. It was better than falling into a bottle.

"You think it was just God's timing?" he asked. "Nothing else?"

"Yes. They were very good at the hospital. I never had any concerns about Robin's care. She never complained about them…" Lawrence trailed off, then made a face, wrinkling his nose and giving a little grimace. "I mean, she didn't complain any more about them than she did about anything else."

"She *did* have complaints, then?"

"Robin had high expectations. She was often disappointed when other people didn't rise to meet them. But there wasn't anything she said that I thought meant anything… it was just normal, everyday stuff."

"Like…?"

"I don't know. Bringing dinner late. Fire alarms going off in the night. Nurses not showing up promptly when she pressed the button." Lawrence shrugged. "I don't want to imply that she was a drama queen, but… the littlest things could set her off."

"Yeah, those don't sound like things that were unusual or indicated a problem with the care."

"Exactly."

"Overall, you think she was satisfied with the care?"

"Overall."

"How was she the last few days? I understand she was in more pain, the staff were trying to control her high blood sugar… was there anything else? How did she seem to you?"

"I really don't see the point of any of this," Lawrence said abruptly. "Nobody has said that there was anything irregular about her death. The doctor already signed a death certificate. Her body was released to the funeral home. Why are you asking questions?"

"I'm sure it's nothing," Zachary assured him. "I'm just asking a few questions, but everything seems to be just fine. Perfectly normal. I just want to be able to reassure Bridget that there was nothing unusual about Robin's death. She just died a little earlier than anyone had expected."

"Bridget," Lawrence repeated.

Zachary wasn't sure where Lawrence was going. They had already mentioned Bridget, that Zachary was her ex, that she had some concerns.

"Yes. You met Bridget…"

"Yes, I know," Lawrence said impatiently. "But what does she have to do with any of this? She's not police or FBI or anything. How can she start an investigation?"

"I'm a private investigator, not a police detective or agent. Anyone can hire me. And Bridget asked me to look into Robin's death."

"But you aren't anyone."

Anyone official, he meant. Anyone with a badge.

"Uh… no. I'm not anyone."

"Don't you need my permission to investigate? Or Robin's family's?"

"No. I don't need anyone's permission." Zachary didn't like the direction the conversation was going. He needed to change something before it all broke down. "Were you Robin's medical attorney?"

"What?"

"Did you have the authorization to make medical decisions on Robin's part if she was unable to? If she had a stroke or went into a coma. Had she appointed you to make decisions for her?"

"No." Lawrence frowned at Zachary like he was saying something crazy. "Robin was able to make her own choices."

"But she knew that at some point, she might not be able to. She didn't make any arrangements?"

"No."

Zachary nodded. So Lawrence would not be of any help with Zachary getting his hands on Robin's medical records. He let his breath out slowly. It didn't matter, then, whether Lawrence approved of the investigation or not. But it was still in Zachary's best interests to distract Lawrence from who had authorized anything.

"That's fine. I just wondered. When was the last time you saw

Robin? Was she in good spirits? Or was she in pain?"

"I saw her on Thursday, but she was pretty tired and I didn't stay for long. Wednesday was the last day I spent any length of time with her."

"How was she Wednesday?"

"She was good."

"One of the nurses said she was in more pain the last few days. But Wednesday was good?"

"She had a lot of pain, down in her bones... I don't know if that meant the cancer had spread to the bones... they weren't monitoring to see how it was progressing... they knew it had spread and they couldn't stop it. We didn't think she'd have any more pain-free days and I guess we were right." Lawrence wrapped his fingers around the mug, trying to draw in the heat. "We had... our last date."

Zachary blinked away the stinging in his own eyes. He gave a nod of encouragement. "What did you do on this last date?"

He expected something brief. Watching a movie together on her in-room TV or having bowls of ice cream. One poignant moment that they never guessed would be their last bit of happiness together.

"Robin had planned the whole day. She had it all laid out. We went to the park for a horse and buggy ride. She'd always wanted to do that. She bought a hat just for that ride. We had a picnic on a blanket in the grass, wicker basket and real china and all. Laid in the sun for a long time. She said the sun felt good on her bones. She was very tired, but she'd planned it all out, so she didn't want to go back to the hospital..." Lawrence paused for a sip of coffee. He cleared his throat and went on. "We went to the carousel. She couldn't sit on one of the horses, but the ones with a sleigh and a bench... I wrapped the blanket around her, and we just went around and around until I was too woozy to handle it anymore. We ordered popcorn and cotton candy, but she couldn't eat more than a bite or two of each." Another pause while Lawrence wiped his eyes and stared out the coffee shop window for a while. "We sat in the car, listening to the radio, and she fell asleep. When the sun went down and the stars came up, I woke her up, and we watched for a falling star to wish on."

He didn't seem inclined to say anything else. Zachary let him sit in silence for a few minutes before speaking up.

"That sounds like a wonderful day."

"It was our last date. She had it all planned out, exactly what she wanted to happen."

"Maybe she did sense that her time was getting short."

Lawrence's mouth twisted. Zachary looked away, giving him his private grief.

Zachary thought for a long time about his meeting with Lawrence. It left him with an unsettled feeling; too many questions had not been answered. It didn't fit together the way he expected it to, even though Lawrence had provided some of the key pieces that should have laid Bridget's worries to rest.

He wasn't sure what path to pursue. He knew how he wanted to proceed, and that was to bring Bridget into the investigation. He always appreciated Kenzie's suggestions and her medical knowledge, and there was always the tantalizing possibility that they might be able to move on to a more intimate relationship; but his relationship with Kenzie wasn't the same as what he had had with Bridget. Bridget had been his one love, the one bright light in his life, and if there was a chance of getting her back…

"Zachary?" He was startled by Bridget's voice in his ear.

"Oh—Bridget!" He blinked at the phone in his hand, not even aware he had dialed it.

"You *did* call me."

"Sorry, I was distracted. I wondered if you wanted to… get together to talk about the investigation. Discuss what I've found so far and where to go next."

"Oh…" Bridget's voice was hesitant. "Have you found

anything?"

"Nothing certain. No real evidence. But some things came up in my discussion with Lawrence…"

"Okay. Well, then, I guess we should get together to talk. Later this afternoon?"

"That would work for me, if you're free." Zachary assumed that Gordon would still be at work, so there would be no chance that Bridget would bring him along or be pressed for time. "Do you want to come here?"

"Better if we meet in a neutral setting, I should think," Bridget decided. Even though she never seemed to have a problem showing up at Zachary's apartment on her own whim.

Zachary accepted her suggestion, and a couple of hours later, they were wandering through the very park Robin and Lawrence had spent their last date in. Bridget selected a bench for them to sit on for their chat. Zachary sat close to her, but his mind was drawn to the romantic ride, picnic, and other special experiences Robin planned before her death.

"So…?" Bridget prompted, attempting to bring Zachary back down to earth. "What did you find out?"

"Do you mind waiting for a minute?" Zachary didn't wait for her to answer. He stood up and fished a tiny digital camera from his pocket. He took a panorama of shots, turning in a circle to get the full 360 degrees. "Could we walk over to the carousel?"

"Zachary…"

"I'm not just being impulsive. Come with me and I'll tell you what happened."

She conceded and walked by his side over to the carousel, while he told her about the last date. Bridget's eyes darted around the park as she envisioned everything that had happened. She was quiet while Zachary took pictures of the carousel and other sights.

"What do you think it means?" she asked finally. "You think she knew she was dying, and it was her final good-bye? A bucket list of all of the things she wanted to do on a date?"

Zachary shrugged. He had been telling himself that all of the pieces fit together, but he knew that they didn't.

"Vermont has legal euthanasia."

She frowned at him, tiny creases appearing between her eyebrows. "End of life choice," she corrected. "Not euthanasia."

"If Robin had wanted to end her life after finding out that her cancer was metastasized and she only had months to live, she could have asked her doctor for assisted suicide."

"Yes."

"But she didn't do that. No one has said that she wanted to choose to end her life on her own terms."

"No. They're all pretty religious. They probably thought it would be a sin."

"If she were going to end her own life, then that last date with Lawrence made sense, right?"

She nodded.

"But Lawrence never said that's why she did it. He said she had the day all planned out, but he didn't say she had planned her death. He was surprised she died when she did, just like everyone else."

"So...?"

"So, if she hadn't planned her death, why have one last date? Why not... a number of special little events that would be easier for her to tolerate? Lawrence said how tired she was. She couldn't manage to get through the day on her own and was wiped out the day after. If she hadn't planned to die, she could have sprinkled each of those date ideas over the next two or three months, or however long she had."

Bridget considered. "I don't know."

"She never told you she'd planned her death. Her doctor didn't say he'd helped her. Her family didn't say she did, and Lawrence didn't say she did. So it wasn't suicide, right?"

"Right."

"Then it doesn't fit."

"Okay..." Bridget's voice was cautious. "Then it doesn't fit. So... what, then?"

"Then is Lawrence lying?"

"Why would he?"

"Nobody else was with them. He took her out for the day… brought her back exhausted… she slept all the next day, and then she died."

"You think he did something to make her sick?" Bridget shook her head adamantly. "No. I don't believe it."

"Something didn't feel right. When he was telling me all of this, I knew something was off. His eyes, his body language, he was trying to hide something."

Bridget watched the carousel. It was a cooler day, so there weren't a lot of families out in the park or a lot of children on the carousel. The cheerful music played and the horses circled endlessly. Zachary pictured Robin and Lawrence there.

"Zachary, Lawrence didn't kill her. He didn't do anything to make her sick. He didn't help her commit suicide. I saw him with her. He worshiped her."

"Maybe he wanted to put her out of her misery. The nurse said that her pain was getting worse, more difficult to manage. Lawrence said the pain was deep down in her bones. He was afraid the cancer had gotten into them. Bone cancer is one of the most painful things a person can go through. Maybe he didn't want her to have to deal with it."

"I don't believe it. No. I was there when he found out that Robin had passed. I was at the hospital. He was devastated by the news."

"Someone can still be devastated when they are the cause of a tragedy." This Zachary knew without a doubt. He had plenty of personal experience in that area.

"No. He was shocked. He couldn't believe it. No one is that good of an actor."

Zachary scowled to himself. Bridget had a knack for reading a situation so that she could respond in just the right way; the perfect hostess, friend, and lover. Could she be that wrong?

"Something is off," Zachary repeated. "It doesn't fit."

8

Zachary went back to the treatment center the next day, hoping to find Nurse Betty on duty again on the same shift. She was, but she was busy away from the reception desk taking care of patient needs and minor emergencies, so it was some time before he could talk to her again.

"You're back again," Betty observed. "Didn't you get everything you needed from Dr. West?"

"Dr. West was very helpful." Zachary searched Betty's face for any sign that Dr. West had told her not to talk to Zachary or informed her that he didn't have the permission of the family to conduct his investigation. Apparently, he had either not gotten around to it, or hadn't thought it necessary to let his staff know. "I just had a few more questions. I'm sorry, I know I'm being a pain."

"You've been very patient. We like patience around here." She laughed at her word play.

Zachary smiled along with her. "You know Robin's fiancé, Lawrence," he said, deciding to promote Lawrence from boyfriend to fiancé for increased sympathy.

Betty nodded immediately. "Yes, of course. Poor fellow. We were the ones who had to inform him that Robin had passed."

"That must have been hard on you too. He took it pretty hard?"

"Of course. Anyone would. It was a shock; we hadn't anticipated her dying that soon."

"But at least he'd had a chance to say goodbye."

Betty's penciled brows drew down. "What?"

"Their last date. On Wednesday. Wasn't that their goodbye date?"

Betty pursed her lips. She started to shake her head, but then stopped, uncertain.

"I just thought..." Zachary let his voice trail off, giving her time to think about it before going on. "They went out and did everything Robin was never going to be able to do again, and then on Friday, she..."

"She didn't commit suicide," Betty said, providing Zachary with the nugget of information he was fishing for. "There was no end of life prescription. We would know. Everyone on the nursing staff knows if there is an end of life prescription."

"Oh." Zachary let his puzzlement show. "Then what happened on Wednesday?"

"She went out on a day pass. They went out together, she and Lawrence. I don't know if it was a date. I thought... maybe they had people to see or arrangements to make..." Betty shifted uncomfortably. She let her gaze wander to her computer while she reviewed the past week's events. "She was very tired when they came back. It was obvious she had done too much. She was in a lot of pain. She said, 'I'm just glad I got that out of the way.'"

"Not exactly something you would say about a big romantic date."

Betty rubbed the space between her eyebrows as if trying to remove the frown lines there. "No."

"They didn't show you pictures of everything they had done? The carriage ride, the picnic, the carousel...?"

"No."

"How did Lawrence seem? He must have been happy after such a big day with her…"

"No. He was very subdued. Concerned about Robin being so weak, but… distant. And he didn't stay with her. He often stayed late, watched her go to sleep."

"But he didn't on Wednesday."

"No."

"And did he come on Thursday?"

"I didn't see him."

"He said he dropped in briefly, but she was sleeping."

Betty shrugged. "He might have. She did spend most of Thursday sleeping."

"Did that surprise you? Were you concerned in any way?"

"She'd obviously had a busy day and been exhausted Wednesday, so… we were concerned that she get enough rest and not catch anything… we were happy she was sleeping. Patients need sleep."

"You didn't think maybe he'd given her something?"

Betty's eyes were wide. "Given her something? What would he give her? He's not a doctor."

"I don't know. Alcohol. Valium. Ambien. Percocet or Oycotin. Or maybe something that conflicted with one of her meds. You must have patients that think they can just take whatever they want without talking to the doctor. Or they know they're not supposed to and sneak something."

"Well… yes. That's true. But I never thought Robin had taken anything. Just that she was worn out."

"You said she'd been in more pain the final few days."

"Yes."

"You didn't think she took anything extra for it? On top of what you were giving her? Lawrence said he was worried the cancer was into her bones."

"We weren't sure why she was in so much pain. But we were managing it, she wouldn't have needed to take anything else."

"And Lawrence couldn't have decided she needed something

more and slipped it to her? Even into her IV without anyone noticing?"

"Anything is possible," Betty said, frustration edging into her voice. "I can't prove she didn't take anything and nobody injected anything into her port. But did I think anything had? No. Do I think anyone did anything to cause her death? No. Ask it as many ways as you like, Mr. Goldman, it was just Robin's time. Nothing will convince me otherwise."

"Did Lawrence get along with Robin's mother and sister?"

Betty's eyes widened. She didn't answer immediately, weighing her answer. "They seemed… civil. Not warm. I think there was a little competition as to who was going to sit with her. Not like some patients where when someone new arrives, the previous visitor leaves to make room."

Zachary tried to envision what the dynamic between Lawrence and Gloria would have been like. Gloria, a strong and outgoing woman and Lawrence, hesitant and uncertain. Would he have stood up to her? Or was the contest between Robin, wanting Lawrence to stay, and Gloria, wanting him out of the way?

"Did you get the feeling there was animosity there? Maybe the family didn't approve of him."

"Well, he was very different than her. But I don't know what they thought of him, they never said anything in front of me."

***

Zachary decided to do some research on Lawrence before approaching him again. He needed to know for sure who he was facing. Even someone who seemed quiet and self-effacing could be explosive when confronted. Zachary was investigating someone he thought might have committed homicide, even if it was just classified as a mercy killing or an unauthorized assisted suicide.

Lawrence Long had a number of social media accounts. He was, it would appear, an artist. He created sculptures and paintings, the kind that ended up getting installed as public art, drawing the ire of a public who wanted to know what the heck it was supposed to be. Big shapes, bold colors, and cobbled-together junk. Too sophisticated for Zachary's artistic sense. He was a photography man to the bone, dedicated to capturing the real world, raw and unflinching. Lawrence's kind of work gave artists a bad name.

But maybe art was a shared interest he could approach Lawrence with. Rather than just showing up and demanding more answers, essentially calling Lawrence a liar, he could come up with a ruse that would put Lawrence more at ease.

So, with a little thought and another phone call, Zachary soon found himself in Lawrence's studio. In other words, his garage.

Zachary was prepared for another studio like Isabella's. She was one of the messiest people he had met, with towering piles of materials that threatened to topple over and bury them both. Zachary had always emulated Mr. Peterson, the foster father he had learned photography from, whose tiny darkrooms were always meticulously organized, with everything assigned a place. It was the one place Mr. Peterson had kept clean and ordered. It had soothed Zachary's anxiety and had kept him from getting distracted. He was able to focus on developing pictures, achieving a sort of a zen state that he didn't get from anything else in his life. So he kept his own darkroom and filing system the same way and tried to apply the same principles in the rest of his life, finding it easier to put things away and clean up after himself immediately than to let himself get overwhelmed by disorder.

Lawrence's studio was something in between. Messy, but with a semblance of order and not filled to the gills with junk he would never use. He had several large sculptures in the center of the room, with paintings on easels and other supplies on benches and shelves around the edges of the garage. Scraps of metal, what looked like car parts, and other items that Zachary wouldn't have expected to be used in art.

"Come on in. Make yourself comfortable," Lawrence invited without inflection.

Zachary didn't offer to shake his hand this time. He looked around and selected a stool that had originally been red, but was speckled with various colors of paint. Zachary looked at it carefully and ran his hand over the surface to make sure that none of the paint was wet, before sitting down.

"So, what was it you wanted?" Lawrence asked. "You were looking for pictures of Robin?"

"I thought it might help Bridget," Zachary explained. "I think that Robin's death was just such a surprise to her, she's really obsessing over it in a way that isn't healthy. I thought that if I could pull together some pictures, maybe put them together in a slide show or a collage, it would give her something to hold on to. Something to remember Robin by. And then maybe she wouldn't be so... at such loose ends about Robin's death."

Lawrence considered this, his expression veiled. He wasn't so sure about meeting with Zachary a second time, even under the new pretense. Did he have a guilty conscience?

"Doesn't Bridget have any pictures of her? Couldn't you get them off her Facebook memorial page?"

"But I want something special for her. Something from those last few days of Robin's life. I was thinking, when you were telling me about the lovely date you had with Robin the Wednesday before she died... that maybe if Bridget could see those pictures, could see both how frail she was, but also how happy she was, right up until the end... maybe that would calm her down."

"It's quite personal," Lawrence protested. "I mean, Robin and I... that was our last time together. I didn't really anticipate anyone... sharing those moments with anyone."

"I don't need anything that's too private. Just maybe... a picture of her on the carousel... smiling. Enjoying that last day."

Lawrence didn't respond right away. Maybe Zachary was giving off some signal that he wasn't sincere.

"Surely you took some pictures," Zachary cajoled. "And you two were out in public, so they couldn't be *that* racy!"

It didn't bring even the ghost of a smile to Lawrence's face.

He sighed, and finally motioned Zachary over to a computer in the corner of the garage. Not a great place for a piece of equipment that could be sensitive to dust or other contaminants in the air from Lawrence's work. But maybe it was just a cheap one that he kept to be able to pull up pictures of models while he painted.

With a few taps and clicks, Lawrence opened up his photo folder and hunted down the pictures from the previous Wednesday. He started to page through them quickly, not giving Zachary a chance to get a good look at any one of them. Robin's thin, wan face. A few smiles, but mostly she was looking away from the camera, pensive or detached. She didn't look like a girl on a bucket-list date. No big smiles. No romance. There were very few pictures that included Lawrence as well. Zachary made a motion for Lawrence to stop.

"Wait, go back. I want to see that one with the two of you together in the carriage."

Lawrence looked unhappy about the request, but backed up until he stopped on it.

"Oh, that's very nice," Zachary said. And on the surface, it was. The happy couple in the fairy-tale carriage, all sweet and happy. But neither of their smiles looked sincere. Though Lawrence had his arm around Robin's shoulders, she sat stiffly, as if he were a stranger instead of her beloved. They held themselves apart, posed for the camera, but exuding no real warmth.

"Could I get a copy of that one?"

Lawrence grudgingly agreed and marked the photo to be copied. He continued to go through the photos that had been taken that day, with Zachary stopping him occasionally to request one of them.

It was all as Lawrence had said. The carriage ride, the picnic, lying in the sun, the carousel, the cotton candy. It was obvious that Robin was exhausted by the end of the batch of photos. She had done way too much. Lawrence had taken one last picture of her at the end of the day, being tucked into her bed at the cancer treatment center, looking directly at the camera with a hard, unfeeling smile.

"Can I—"

"Not that one," Lawrence said. "That's the last picture I have of her. I don't want... I don't want anyone else to have that one."

Zachary wouldn't have wanted anyone else to have that one either. It said too much. Something was wrong. Robin and Lawrence were not happy lovers, back from a tiring day, having done everything Robin had set out to do to make her last day with Lawrence special. Something else was going on.

He waited for Lawrence to copy the pictures to a thumb drive. He didn't want to do or say anything that might antagonize the man until Zachary had the pictures safely in his pocket. He tucked them away and looked at the computer screen, still thinking about that last picture.

"When are you going to tell me the truth, Lawrence?"

"What?" Lawrence was obviously startled by the question.

"It's obvious you're trying to hide what happened that day. It's as clear as the nose on your face. So tell me. Quit trying to string me along."

Lawrence looked back at him, eyes wide and shifting back and forth. He walked over to one of the sculptures in the middle of the garage and looked it over, comparing it to the final product in his mind's eye, touching the cool surface and pretending that Zachary wasn't there to ruin everything for him. Zachary said nothing, letting the silence build. Lawrence knew something and he needed to confess it to Zachary. If he didn't, he would just go on feeling guilty and worrying that one day someone was going to find out his secret.

"It was supposed to be our last date," he said finally. "Robin didn't know she was going to die so soon, but she intended it to be our last date. She wanted to end on a high note, to have a perfect last date, and remember everything that way..."

Zachary frowned, his forehead getting tight as he thought about it. "Are you saying..."

"She broke up with me." Lawrence's voice was rough. "This whole thing was… I don't know whether it was supposed to make me feel good or to make her feel better about dumping me."

Zachary could feel his pain. It cut a little too close to his own heart, being dumped by Bridget when she was going through treatment. There was something terrible about being dumped by someone when they should have needed you more. Something so damaging about being told 'I have to eliminate everything that isn't positive or necessary from my life in order to fight this thing. So you've got to go.' No matter how Bridget or Robin tried to soften that message by surrounding it with special experiences or long-winded explanations, the message was still the same.

I'm dying and I don't want or need you anymore.

Zachary pictured that last photo on Lawrence's computer. Robin going to sleep with a grim smile on her face. Exhausted, but satisfied about having booted a negative force from her life. The Zacharys and the Lawrences took too much time and attention and didn't give enough back, so they had to be jettisoned at the earliest opportunity. Get rid of the drag and the excess weight.

They made up names to make it sound like a positive move. Rid yourself of toxic people. Put on your own oxygen mask first. Self-care. Words that would let them justify their selfishness and forget about the wounded and bleeding they left behind.

Lawrence was looking at Zachary, waiting for his reaction. A long time seemed to have passed since he made his confession. Zachary tried to focus his brain and pull himself out of the past. He'd dealt with worse things than being dumped. He'd dealt with all kinds of pain and abandonment before. Being dumped by Bridget should have been nothing.

"I'm sorry." His voice was weak and gravelly. Zachary cleared his throat and tried to speak with confidence and authority. He wasn't the one who was wounded. Lawrence was. Lawrence was the one who needed reassurance and understanding. "I'm sorry that happened to you. That really sucks."

"Yeah." Lawrence laughed bleakly. "You said it, brother."

He looked back at his sculpture again. Zachary looked at the twisted pieces of metal. It was sharp and raw and dangerous-looking. Zachary wasn't one for abstract art, but he could see the attraction to this one. He could feel the raw emotion and anger when he looked at it. Lawrence was displaying no anger himself. He let it out in his art, but he wasn't opening up that side of himself to Zachary.

Had he shown it to Robin? Had he gone back to see her on Thursday with a plan? Get her to take him back, or else?

"You must have been furious. Her playing with you like that. Acting as if she could make up for the pain with a nice last date. Who does something like that?"

"Robin could be very manipulative," Lawrence admitted. "She did things sometimes… she acted like she was playing by the rules when she wasn't. Not so much manipulating your actions… but trying to manipulate your feelings."

Zachary nodded. "I can see that. You were supposed to be grateful to her for that one last day. You were supposed to remember her as being someone generous and loving, not someone who pulled the rug out from under you."

"Yeah." Lawrence sighed, looking up at the large iron sculpture. "So is that all? You found out my secret. You got everything you need now?"

"I'm sorry. But… I had to know what really happened. I can't complete my investigation if it's all built on lies."

"Well, congratulations."

"I'm not happy about it, Lawrence. But I needed to know."

"I didn't hurt Robin," Lawrence pronounced. "I couldn't do that. I'd never do anything to hurt her. If she died because she did too much on Wednesday… that's not on me. That was all her own plan and her own doing."

9

Zachary had a restless night full of broken sleep and annoying fragments of dreams. He replayed the conversation with Lawrence over and over. He saw the slide show of the photos he had viewed, including the last photo that had ever been taken of Robin while she was alive. Worse than that, he re-experienced being dumped by Bridget, time after time. Feeling again with agonizing clarity the shock and pain of her cutting ties with him. He wanted to be fresh in the morning, so he didn't want to take any pills to help him sleep. That ended up being a mistake. He should have chosen some dopiness and med hangover to looking like a red-eyed zombie in the morning.

He had decided that a visit with Kenzie was in order. Not over the phone or over dinner this time, but in a more official capacity. He put coffee into his travel mug, put an icepack over his eyes for a few minutes to try to reduce the tell-tale redness, and headed off for the police station. The medical examiner's office was in the basement. A lot of the officers knew him and he was no Phillip Marlowe or Magnum P.I., packing heat wherever he went, so getting through security didn't create any great difficulty.

In the basement, Kenzie was at her desk, efficiently dealing with the paperwork and incoming phone calls, tapping away at her computer to look things up or book appointments in. She looked up at Zachary's approach and gave him a little smile.

"Hey. What are you doing here?"

"Just thought I'd come and see how everything was going."

"Right." Kenzie laughed. "This isn't exactly a place that people just drop into for the atmosphere. Not even you, Mr. Zachary Goldman."

"Really? I hear people are dying to get in."

"Shut up."

Zachary couldn't help snickering. "Okay, I know. I've used that one before," he admitted, "but you have to give me a chance to get warmed up. I'm a little stiff."

"Do you want me to find a scalpel and use it on you? Because I will."

Zachary smiled. She studied him, her brows going up. She pressed her lips together as if she had just applied her red lipstick.

"So what's up with you? You look like hell."

"Just one bad night. It's nothing."

"The way you take care of yourself, one bad night could do you in. Have you had anything to eat since I saw you last? You look like the walking dead."

"I've eaten," Zachary protested. And he had. A little of the fruit that Bridget had bought. And he had found the time to go grocery shopping, even though he knew both Kenzie and Bridget would be appalled if they saw what had been in his cart and now resided in his kitchen. Prepackaged snacks and meal replacement bars. Frozen pizza, lasagna, and roast beef with potatoes. Energy drinks to supplement his coffee intake. He needed to clear more of Bridget's food out of the fridge before it went bad. "I told you. I just had a bad night."

"I don't want you ending up in here. No offense, but I don't need the likes of you cluttering up the drawers. And who knows what Dr. Wiltshire would find when he opened you up. Nothing but coffee and pills, I suspect."

Zachary shrugged. "Probably."

Kenzie sat back in her chair, stretching and still watching him. "So? What's up?"

"Robin Salter dumped Lawrence two days before she died."

Kenzie considered this. "How do you know that?"

"He admitted it to me. I told him I knew he was trying to hide something from me about that last day he spent with her, and he admitted that it had all been the build-up to breaking up with him."

"What day? What happened?"

Zachary briefly described the last date. He held up the thumb drive with the pictures on it. "You want to see?"

Kenzie reached for it, her eyes widening. "This feels a little voyeuristic," she confessed, bending down to plug it into her tower. "I don't really need to see them…"

But that didn't stop her from clicking on the drive icon when it popped up on her screen, and scrolling through the pictures. She nodded, her eyes riveted to the display. "Just look at them. They're trying to act like a lovey-dovey couple, but they couldn't be farther away from each other. And their expressions… talk about painful. I can't understand why they would go through this whole charade."

"I don't know when she told him she was dumping him." Zachary watched the pictures scroll over Kenzie's screen. "I think he must have known pretty early on, even if she didn't tell him, that something was wrong. Just look at his face and the way he's holding his head." Zachary felt a stabbing pain through his heart. The pain of breaking up with Bridget was still as fresh and raw as it had been that day. The betrayal. The physical illness of losing her, of her abandoning him as some broken thing, just like his mother had done decades before.

"Zachary!"

The ringing in his ears was too loud for him to hear Kenzie's words. He stared at the couple on the screen with the feeling of a heavy truck gradually sliding down an icy hill, gravity inexorably getting its own way.

"Here, sit down." Kenzie had come around the desk and was shoving a chair behind his knees, forcing Zachary to sit. She put her hand on the back of his neck. "Do you need to put your head between your knees? Do you need to take something?"

"No." He forced out the words. "I'm fine."

"You're fine if gray is your natural color. Take a few deep breaths."

Zachary did as he was told. His vision gradually expanded until he could see Kenzie and her desk and everything around them instead of just the pictures on the monitor.

"Maybe you should turn that off." Zachary motioned to the screen.

Kenzie frowned, but she did as he said. "They're your pictures," she said. "It's not like this is the first time you've seen them."

"I know. I don't know why. Just that I can't look at them right now. I can't... I just keep seeing Bridget."

"Bridget? Why?"

Kenzie knew his story, so he wasn't sure why she couldn't put it together by herself. "Because she broke up with me while she was in treatment too. I just... can't seem to separate the two of them. Maybe that's why Bridget needs to know what happened to Robin. Because they're so much alike, she sees herself in Robin."

"Why would anyone break up while they were going through treatment? I thought that would be when you needed people around you the most."

"Yes. But apparently not *toxic* people."

"Toxic," Kenzie scoffed. "That's what you call someone who won't just go along with everything you say and do. The only way you could be toxic to Bridget is if she ate you, and then only because of your meds. She wanted out, pure and simple. She wanted the freedom to do whatever she wanted."

It was a lot of insight for someone who had said just a second before that she had no idea why Bridget would break up in the middle of chemotherapy.

Kenzie removed the drive and handed it back to Zachary. He shoved it down into his pocket.

"What would it take to get the medical examiner involved?"

"In what? In Robin Salter's death?" Kenzie's tone jumped several notes.

Zachary just nodded. He knew it was going to be an uphill battle. He couldn't just suggest that the medical examiner look at a death that had been deemed to have been a natural, doctor-attended death. He didn't have any standing in the case or in the political structure.

"Good grief, Zachary. You know she had cancer. What proof do you have that it was anything but the cancer?"

Zachary tapped the drive in his pocket. "I have these pictures. Lawrence's confession that she dumped him. His statement and the nurse's, saying that he went back to see Robin on Thursday, after she dumped him. Why would he? If it was you, wouldn't you stay as far away from her as you could?"

"Are you telling me you didn't go back to Bridget and try to convince her to take you back?"

Zachary swallowed. "She said she needed space, so I gave her space. I thought she'd change her mind in a day or two."

"And you never went back to see her to try to talk her into getting back together?"

Zachary suspected she would only think him dishonest if he continued to deny it. "Well... yes. I did."

"And did you poison her?"

"No!"

"Then what makes you think that Lawrence did? If you are so struck by the similarities of your cases, then explain that. You had no intention of killing Bridget, did you?"

"I couldn't. I would never have even thought of it."

"Why would Lawrence?"

"He's... he's suppressing his anger. I can see it in his sculptures. And Bridget didn't die two days after she broke up with me. Robin did."

"What evidence do you have that he had anything to do with her death?"

"Nothing. She was in more pain the last few days. The doctor and nurses were surprised that she died when she did. It would have been easy to put insulin or something else into her IV. You don't think it's enough that she mysteriously died right after they broke up?"

"She didn't die mysteriously. She had cancer."

"But it wasn't the cancer that killed her."

"How do you know that?"

He looked at her. "I guess I don't, without an autopsy."

"You think you have enough to convince Dr. Wiltshire to do an autopsy? When the body has already been transferred to a funeral home? For all we know, she might have been embalmed or cremated already."

"I was hoping that you would talk with Dr. Wiltshire… maybe recommend to him that there was reason to be suspicious."

"It's very irregular. I don't want to get in trouble for getting involved in something that is none of my business."

"Isn't it your business to find out why people died?"

"People who come in here through proper channels. We can't investigate every single death."

"I think there's enough here to at least give it another look."

Kenzie looked at her computer, ignoring Zachary. For a few minutes, they each sat there, Zachary trying to think of what he could say to convince Kenzie to at least present the case to the medical examiner. Kenzie answered several phone calls and processed forms. Eventually, she looked across her desk at Zachary.

"Tell me why you're doing this, Zachary."

"I want to find out what really happened to Robin. If she was murdered…"

"But why? Tell me it isn't because you want to get back together with Bridget."

Zachary felt like she had sucker-punched him. For a minute,

he forgot how to breathe. What could he tell her? Of course he had taken the case because of Bridget. Of course he wanted to get back together with the love of his life. But he couldn't tell Kenzie that. He didn't want to risk losing her too. He focused his gaze just below her eyes, so he didn't have to meet her intense gaze.

"I want to find out the truth." His voice sounded strangled in his own ears.

"Because of Bridget."

"Don't you think Robin deserves justice?"

She just looked at him. Could everyone read him so clearly? Zachary looked down, blinking, not wanting her to see his desperation.

"Bridget isn't coming back, Zachary," Kenzie said firmly. "She's playing with your heart. Using your feelings toward her to get you involved in an investigation is really low. Can't you see how she's using you?"

"Robin Salter was murdered," Zachary said firmly. "She shouldn't be buried without anybody even knowing that."

"What's all this?" A man's voice came from behind Zachary. Kenzie looked up, all color draining from her naturally fair complexion. Zachary turned around to see who was there. At first glance, Zachary would have through him just another lab technician. But the name badge on the man's lab coat gave him away as Dr. Wiltshire, the medical examiner. He was a clean-shaven older man, the hair on his temples gray, a pair of rectangular reading glasses sliding down his nose. He had a couple of files in his hands and had obviously come out of the lab to give them to Kenzie.

"It's nothing," Kenzie said evenly, giving Zachary a glare that was obviously meant to keep him quiet. But it was his one chance to present the case to Dr. Wiltshire and he wasn't going to pass it up.

"It isn't nothing," he insisted. "When a woman dies unexpectedly two days after she dumps her boyfriend, don't you think that is suspicious?"

Dr. Wiltshire pushed up his glasses and looked at Kenzie. A red flush at her neckline was spreading upward.

"Tell the whole story," Kenzie insisted. "Tell him she had terminal cancer and was under a doctor's care. Her doctor said it was natural causes. That's why it never came through here."

"Doctors can be wrong. Everybody says it was too early. She was expected to live for months yet. She wasn't dying. She was still fighting it and it wasn't her time to go."

"It was a doctor-attended death," Kenzie snapped. "It was his responsibility to report it if he thought there was anything suspicious about the circumstances of her death. People die before they are expected to all the time. They're not all murdered."

"She treated her boyfriend like trash. She kicked him to the curb, and not forty-eight hours later, she was dead."

Dr. Wiltshire studied Zachary, head cocked curiously. "Do I know your face? Who are you?"

Zachary thought he should stand up and introduce himself properly, shaking Dr. Wiltshire's hand. But he was still so shaky, he didn't know whether his legs would hold him. Collapsing in the middle of the floor was really not the best way of convincing the medical examiner that he had logical, reasoned arguments with respect to Robin's death.

"My name is Zachary Goldman. I'm a private investigator."

"A private investigator. And you were hired to look into this case?"

Zachary nodded.

"His ex-wife asked him to look into it," Kenzie interposed, trying to sway Dr. Wiltshire from thinking that someone had thought the case had enough merit to actually put the money into hiring Zachary to investigate.

"*Ex*-wife?" Dr. Wiltshire repeated. "And you took the case?" His opinion had clearly been swayed the wrong direction by Kenzie's argument. "I wouldn't take a case from my ex-wife if she was holding a gun to my head!"

They both laughed at the good-natured joke, but Kenzie's glare at Zachary was poisonous. She did not appreciate being shown up in front of her boss. Zachary could guess that the next time he wanted her opinion on a case or an explanation of medical terminology, she was not going to be so eager to help.

"Do we have a file on this case?" Dr. Wiltshire asked Kenzie.

"No, sir. Like I said, the doctor attending said it was a natural death. She was terminal."

"We can't rule out foul play even if she was dying anyway. The timing was unexpected?"

Kenzie looked at Zachary again. "I don't know a lot of the details of the case. You'd have to ask the private *dick* here."

Zachary swallowed. She was definitely not happy with him.

Dr. Wiltshire considered. "Why don't you come into my office," he invited Zachary. "Kenzie, please open a file and bring me the initial intake form. How long ago did this happen? Do we know where the body is?"

"It was last Friday," Zachary contributed. "The funeral home collected her body. I don't think there's been any service yet, but I don't know whether she's still… what state the body is in."

"You know which funeral home?"

"No."

"Find out from the hospital or care center," Wiltshire told Kenzie, "and tell them to put a hold on the remains as a courtesy, until we contact them with further instructions."

Zachary tried not to look at Kenzie as he got unsteadily to his feet to go with the medical examiner into his office.

Dr. Wiltshire looked back when he realized that Zachary wasn't keeping up with him.

"Sorry," Zachary apologized, growing even more conscious of his legs and how they were not moving properly. "I had a spinal cord injury and sometimes it takes a minute to remember how to walk…"

Dr. Wiltshire nodded and waited for him, then walked more slowly to his office to allow Zachary to get control of his gait, which still felt unnatural. They sat down, Dr. Wiltshire behind his desk and Zachary in one of the guest chairs before it. Dr. Wiltshire took off his glasses and laid them down on the desk.

"You're the private investigator who challenged my findings on the Declan Bond case and proved that he was murdered."

"Uh, yes." Zachary nodded, hoping this wasn't going to get him kicked right back out of the office without a further interview.

"How is his mother? My daughter-in-law loved *The Happy Artist*. Is she going to start the show again? Or have they canceled her contract?"

"Her return is going to air in a couple of weeks. It's been a hard time for her, but I think she's looking forward to getting back again."

"Good." Dr. Wiltshire smiled. "Her audience will be thrilled. She has quite the following in these parts."

"She does," Zachary agreed politely.

"And you were the one who was involved in that nasty business at Summit too, weren't you?"

Zachary swallowed. He shifted in his seat and tried not to think about the nightmare that had turned out to be. Clarissa haunted his dreams regularly with her electric shock devices and her sadistic smile. At least the nightmares about Annie were fading.

"And now you're looking into another death in my jurisdiction."

Zachary felt like he should apologize, but he held his tongue. He wasn't trying to discredit the medical examiner. It hadn't even crossed Dr. Wiltshire's desk. Zachary was just trying to find the truth. He was just doing his job.

"What have you discovered so far?" Dr. Wiltshire asked. "Start at the beginning."

Zachary did his best to give a coherent narrative of all that he had discovered so far. Bridget's impressions that Robin was not near death and had not given up the fight. The medical professionals' concurrence, even though they didn't think it meant anything. Robin's symptoms before her death, the availability of insulin and her IV.

Dr. Wiltshire listened carefully, asking the occasional question. Zachary was aware that it didn't add up to much. It was all circumstantial and there was no evidence that anything had been done to harm Robin. But there wouldn't be any evidence unless an autopsy was conducted.

Dr. Wiltshire picked up his glasses from the desk. He cleaned the lenses, scratched his ear with one of the arms, and tapped them against his desk thoughtfully.

"This is unusual," he said eventually. "I have to say, we don't take on the case of every crackpot who walks in off the street or every family member who wants an investigation started. But you do have a track record. And there is enough to suggest that someone might have shortened Robin Slater's life…"

"You'll look into it, then?" Zachary asked, hardly daring to hope.

"I'm sticking my neck out here, so I hope you're right and there is something to it. Not that we ever wish foul play on anyone. But we are in the business of uncovering the truth."

There was a tap on the door and Kenzie entered. She didn't look at Zachary, but approached and put a new folder down on Dr. Wiltshire's desk, looking at him questioningly.

The medical examiner nodded his thanks and opened the folder up to fill out the first form. "You asked the funeral home to hold the remains?"

"Yes."

"Has she been embalmed?"

"No. Not yet."

"Well, that will help. This is going to take a little finessing, Kenzie. It's going to take some work to smooth the feathers we ruffle by getting involved in a case this way. I'll need to file a report with the police department to start a proper death investigation. The evidence has already been compromised."

Kenzie nodded jerkily. Zachary wished he could just sink into the floor. She was going to be furious with him. He hadn't intended to do an end-run around her, but now her boss had overridden her, and if Zachary knew Kenzie, she was truly pissed about that.

"Okay. Let's get the remains scheduled for a post as early as we can. Some of the evidence will have already broken down." He glanced over at Zachary. "Some substances break down after death. Insulin breaks down within forty-eight hours, for example, which is one of the reasons it is preferred by killers. It looks natural, it's fast, and it's almost impossible to detect."

"If it was insulin… is there any way you'll be able to tell?"

Dr. Wiltshire sighed and rocked his chair back. It let out a long squeal. "By starting a death investigation, there will be police involvement. They can get copies of the patient's records and inventory to cross-check them, get surveillance videos, shift schedules, that kind of thing. They'll do interviews and maybe someone will confess."

Kenzie shook her head. Zachary knew she was holding back. She wanted so badly to blast him and tell him how bad they were all going to look when there was no evidence of anything but a natural death. That turned his thoughts in the opposite direction.

"If there wasn't foul play and it was the cancer, will you be able to tell that?"

"Possibly. We may get lucky and be able to see that a mass cut off blood flow to a major organ or shut down liver function. Though the staff probably would have seen signs of that."

"But don't hold my breath."

"The result of my investigation will likely be that there is no evidence to indicate it was anything other than a natural death. I don't want to mislead you. The chances we will find anything are very slim." Dr. Wiltshire smiled at Kenzie. "But I do like a challenge! And you and Mr. Goldman have a history of being able to untangle things."

Kenzie opened her mouth to protest. Zachary looked at her. He hadn't said anything about Kenzie helping him out with previous cases, so anything that Dr. Wiltshire had divined had either come from something Kenzie had said to him, or just from the fact that Zachary had gone to her for help.

"I'm reading between the lines," Dr. Wiltshire said, "but I don't think I'm wrong, am I?"

Kenzie shifted her stance, looking uncomfortable. "It's mostly Zachary," she said. "He's like a bulldog with a steak. I help him a little with forensic knowledge, but… he's the brains behind it."

Zachary was stunned. He had grown up with everyone telling him how stupid he was, how easily distracted and impulsive, how he couldn't ever just focus on one thing and get the job done. He had no schooling past twelfth grade except for what he had taught himself. He hadn't even earned a diploma. Growing up in foster care had meant going straight into the workforce once he was eighteen.

"I'm..." He wasn't sure what to say to this. "I'm stubborn, that's all. I just... stick with it until it's done."

"There's much to be said for being stubborn. And now... Kenzie and I have some fires to light and some to put out. You know how to get ahold of each other?" His grin widened.

"Uh, yes, sir," Zachary agreed, getting to his feet. Though he still felt awkward, his legs had gained some strength, and he was able to walk back out of Wiltshire's office without looking too much like a penguin on crack.

He had accomplished the impossible. A death investigation was going to be opened into Robin Salter's death.

But what were they going to find?

11

Zachary's heart was thumping as he approached the house. It wasn't like there was a restraining order against him. Bridget had threatened to get one in the past, but Zachary had never been served with one and it wasn't like she didn't know where he lived. She was the one who had been coming to see him lately. She had been the one who needed him. He rolled the word around in his mind. It made him feel stronger, more virile. She *needed* him.

He rang the doorbell and in a few minutes, Bridget opened the ornate white front door. She raised her eyebrows, looking at him and then looking behind him as if he might have brought someone else with him. Who would he bring? Kenzie? The police? Lawrence Long?

"Hi."

"What are you doing here?" She didn't know how to react to his presence. She couldn't be angry with him, even though she'd previously told him to stay away, because he was doing what she wanted him to do, and she didn't want to alienate him. She didn't know whether to be concerned about his health and well-being, her usual fall-back position. Or was he there for something else?

Zachary smiled, feeling warm. He had done it. She had needed his help, and he had succeeded. At least with the first step.

"I did it, Bridget. We did it."

"Did what?"

"We got them to open up a death investigation into Robin Salter's death. They looking into it."

"Who is? What are they going to do?"

"A proper investigation. Doing an autopsy to determine cause of death. Interviewing witnesses. Reviewing the hospital records. The whole bit."

She stared at him, stunned. "Are you kidding me?"

He shook his head. "No. They're looking into it. The medical examiner's office has opened their file and requested her remains from the funeral home. They're starting on the arrangements right away."

"I can't believe it."

Zachary wanted to step forward and take her in his arms. He wanted to assure her that it was true and comfort her in the loss of her friend. He wanted to be the one who was there for her again. A partner. Her other half.

He took a step toward her. Bridget took a step back, maintaining the distance between them. Zachary stopped.

"So this is real," Bridget said.

Zachary nodded, though he was uncertain what she meant.

"This is really happening. I wasn't just imagining things."

"We don't know yet whether there was any foul play, or whether she did just die," Zachary clarified. "We have to wait and see."

"But there was enough there for them to look into it. They believed that there might be something wrong."

"Yes, you were right."

Zachary reached a hand toward her to take her by the arm. She seemed a little unsteady on her feet, and he was suddenly worried about her. Maybe he shouldn't just have shown up at her door and announced it without any lead-up. Maybe he should have told her to sit down first.

"Who is it?" a male voice boomed, and in a moment, Gordon stood behind Bridget.

Gordon Drake was not a bad guy, other than the fact that he had moved in on Zachary's territory and was now living the life that should have been Zachary's. For that, Zachary strongly resented him. He knew that it was just an emotional reaction, and not a fair one. Gordon hadn't come into the picture until after Zachary was gone. He hadn't been fooling around with Bridget while she and Zachary were still married. Zachary had checked into his background, and Gordon didn't seem to have any major skeletons in the closet. As far as Zachary knew, he didn't complain when Bridget called or dropped in on Zachary, even allowing their holiday plans the previous Christmas to be delayed while Bridget checked up on Zachary's wellbeing. Gordon was, to all appearances, an all-around good guy. But that didn't mean Zachary had to like him.

"Zach," Gordon greeted cheerily. "What are you doing here? You're looking good." He looked at Bridget. "Anything I can help with, my dear?"

She gripped his arm, which irritated Zachary, as he had been about to take her arm and to steady her, but once again Gordon had stepped right in between them. Gordon looked down at Bridget with an expression of concern. "Are you alright?"

"She might want to sit down," Zachary said. "I was just talking to her about Robin Salter. The developments in her case."

Gordon raised his brows, bemused. "Robin Salter...?" He looked back at Bridget. "Isn't she that woman you were in treatment with?"

Bridget nodded. Zachary was interested to note that Bridget had apparently not talked to Gordon about what had happened. It wasn't immediately apparent whether Gordon even knew that Robin had died. Bridget had not told him anything, but she had gone to Zachary for help.

Score one for Zachary.

"Do you want to sit down?" Gordon asked Bridget. He indicated Zachary with his eyes, clearly not sure what to do about him.

"Yes… come in, Zachary, and tell me about it."

Gordon made a grand gesture for Zachary to enter. For the first time, Zachary was allowed in through the front door. Any other time he had shown up at Bridget's door, he'd been run off the property with threats of the police and getting restraining orders. But things were changing. He was once again part of Bridget's circle.

It was a spacious house, lots of classically beautiful art pieces. Nothing abstract like Lawrence's work. Not the kind of place that you had kids in, so Zachary could only guess that Bridget was sticking to her guns about not wanting to have a family. She had done as the doctors had said to and had her eggs frozen before radiation in case she ever changed her mind about that, but Zachary imagined that ten or twenty years down the line, the eggs would reach their expiration date and be quietly destroyed without anyone ever using them.

He would have loved to have had children with Bridget. He had imagined it from the first day they had met. But she had been adamant that she wanted a career before family. She *didn't* want family almost as much as Zachary *did*.

Gordon and Bridget led the way to a cozy living room decorated almost entirely in white. They sat down together on a long white couch and Zachary chose one of the few pieces in the room that was a deep rich red instead of white. Even though he had put on clean clothes that morning, he would be humiliated if he'd left one smudge of dirt on one of the pristine white pieces of furniture.

"I asked Zachary if he would look into the circumstances of Robin's death for me," Bridget explained to Gordon. She was pale, but each cheek had a red flush in the middle. Or maybe it was her makeup, still tinting the skin that had gone as white as the room's decor.

"Robin's death?" Gordon echoed. "Bridget, what happened? Why didn't you tell me?"

Bridget dabbed at dry eyes with a tissue. "It was... I don't know. I didn't want to tell you about it until I knew what had happened. I wanted to know first."

"And... what did happen?"

Gordon looked at Bridget and Bridget looked at Zachary. Gordon turned his head to look at him as well.

"What did happen?" Gordon repeated.

"We're still sorting it out," Zachary explained. "They've now opened a death investigation, which means they'll actually be collecting evidence and doing an autopsy. Trying to establish the cause of death instead of just relying on what the doctor attending her said."

"But it was cancer, surely."

Bridget shook her head.

"It still might have been," Zachary cautioned, repeating what Dr. Wiltshire and Kenzie had tried to drill into him. "It may be that they do the autopsy and find that it was the cancer, it was just more advanced than the doctor thought. Or a blood clot caused by the cancer. Or some other complication. But they're going to check."

"What did you find out about Lawrence?" Bridget asked. "He didn't do it. I know that. But what did you find out?"

Zachary leaned forward, his elbows on his knees. "I found out that Robin dumped Lawrence the Wednesday before she died."

"What?"

"That was the secret. That's what he was trying to hide. They didn't have the perfect last date because she wanted to do those things before she died or wanted to give him the gift of a perfect day together to remember her by. She wanted to have one last date with him, and then she broke it off. Told him that she wanted him out of her life."

Bridget opened and closed her mouth. "But that's... cruel.

They were always so good together. Why would she even break up with him?"

"I guess they weren't as perfect as you thought." Zachary thought back to their own relationship and how Bridget had jettisoned him once things got to be too difficult. "Maybe she needed space. Maybe he was just dead weight."

Bridget's forehead wrinkled. Zachary couldn't tell whether she recognized herself in his words or not.

"So she broke up with her boyfriend," Gordon summarized, eager to hear the rest of the story, "and then…?"

"That was Wednesday night. Thursday she was very tired from the long day and mostly slept. Lawrence did show up at some point, but he didn't stay long. And the next morning, Friday, the nursing staff found her dead."

Bridget and Gordon both stared at Zachary.

"You think he killed her?" Gordon asked. "You think he put something in her food, or smothered her with the pillow…?"

"He didn't smother her," Zachary said. "I think the nurses and the doctor who signed her death certificate would have noticed if she'd been smothered. But poisoning… I think he might have. It wouldn't even have to be in her food. It could be straight into her blood, through the IV."

"Lawrence didn't do it," Bridget said. Her voice was weak, less sure than it had been the last few times she had insisted it couldn't have been Lawrence. She was starting to see that he was the one who had the most motive and opportunity. "I know how much he loved her. When they were together, he couldn't take his eyes off of her. It was like…" She looked at Zachary and stopped. Was she remembering how besotted he had been with her? How she would look up and find his eyes on her, just drinking her in? "He just couldn't have, Zachary."

"Extreme love can turn quickly to hate when spurned," Gordon said wisely. "It's a story as old as time. If I can't have you, nobody can. If you won't have me, you won't have anybody. Jealousy has turned many a lover's hand against his former mistress."

"Don't, Gordon," Bridget murmured. She looked at Zachary again, as if hoping that he hadn't heard Gordon.

"Anyway…" Zachary decided to fill Bridget in on the few other bits she didn't know, telling her about meeting with Dr. Wiltshire and his agreement to open a death investigation for Robin. "They're going to audit the insulin prescriptions against the inventory to see whether there are any missing doses. I guess they'll do that with any of the medications they think could have been used to kill her. And they'll look at all of her records, and at all of the shift logs and the surveillance cameras. Make sure she wasn't given something she should not have been."

"You're not going to find anything on the surveillance. I don't believe anyone killed her intentionally. She was probably given a wrong dosage, or the wrong medication…"

"I don't know what it was. I told Dr. Wiltshire everything I knew. He couldn't tell from the symptoms what it might have been… she was sick. She was going to die anyway… just maybe not that fast."

"It still doesn't make it right. She should have had more time with her family. I want whoever is responsible for taking her away from her family and friends so soon to pay. They shouldn't just walk away from this. It shouldn't just be an 'oops' like if you added the wrong cells in a budget spreadsheet. We're talking about someone's life here. Her last days were just taken away from her."

Zachary could hear the pain in Bridget's voice. Survivor's guilt? Because she had overcome cancer and Robin had not? Because Bridget still had days and years ahead of her, and Robin was gone?

Bridget still had time to make things up to Zachary and be reconciled with him. Robin would never have that chance with Lawrence. That ship had sailed.

Nurse Betty wasn't nearly as happy to talk to Zachary as she had been on the previous occasions. She gave him a glower that would have curdled cream.

"You sure stirred up a crap-ton of trouble. I thought you were a nice guy. Quiet, not pushy, just a nice guy helping out his wife. But now… we've had police all over this place. I have been run off my feet trying to get them all of the records they want. We have patients to care for. We can't be running around dealing with all of their demands!"

"I'm sorry it's all landed on you. I never meant for that to happen. I didn't realize how much extra work it would be for you."

She looked a little mollified, unsure whether to keep complaining or not. She hadn't expected any sympathy from him.

"It's just that for Bridget and for Robin's family… they had to know the truth. They had to know what it was that went wrong, if anything. What it was that took Robin away from them so suddenly. I certainly never intended to target you or any of the other staff."

"Well, of course we want to know what went wrong too," Betty agreed. "But we've all seen it happen before. Some people just go before you think it's their time. It doesn't mean anyone did anything wrong or anything malicious. Sometimes a person's time just comes before you expect it."

"I'm sure that's all it will be in this case," Zachary soothed. "Can I get you anything? Can I bring you a coffee or a sandwich from the cafeteria? You're probably sick of cafeteria food; is there a restaurant nearby that you like? I can bring you whatever you want."

She blushed and patted at her hair. "Oh, you don't need to do anything like that. I'm just doing my job. These things happen sometimes and you just have to go with the flow."

"I know, but it's been such a burden for you…"

"No, no." She waved his concern away. "It's something interesting to break up the long stretches of boredom. At least being called on to photocopy records means that I wasn't the one who had to take care of Mrs. Groucho's diaper this morning." She rolled her eyes dramatically. "Oh, but that woman can…" She pressed her thin lips together primly. "Treatments can be very hard on the digestive tract, and she is no exception. And the way she starts yelling the second she makes in her diaper, you'd think the woman was on fire! Honestly, some of the patients around here think they are the only one you have to take care of. Believe me, if I only had to take care of one woman, it would not be her."

Zachary chuckled sympathetically. "I can only imagine. It must be very trying to deal with some of the patients."

"They ain't called *patience* for nothing." She shook her head.

"You'd rather deal with someone like Robin?" Zachary suggested.

Betty raised her brows and cocked her head slightly. "Robin Salter?" she said. "No, I should think not!"

"Oh. She wasn't one of the better patients?"

"Oh, no."

Zachary remembered Lawrence confiding that Robin sometimes overdramatized and complained about the care she was getting at the treatment center. Maybe he was being generous. A woman that could string a man along like Robin had, only to dump him hard at the end of the day was probably not the nicest one in the unit.

"I didn't realize. Her boyfriend did say that she often found reasons to complain, but he didn't think she had any reason to. He thought the care here was very good."

"Well, thank you for that."

"I know I never found any reason for complaint when Bridget was here," Zachary said. Which was truthful. He hadn't been around to hear any complaints from her or to have any himself. If Betty thought about it, she probably knew that, but she wasn't about to turn down a compliment.

"I suppose they have a right to be miserable," Zachary said. "But taking it out on the staff… that's not very fair."

"You know, we get some patients through here who are angels on earth. They could be coding and they would smile and apologize for making you hurry. But some people, the women in particular… honey, the sooner they are out of here, one way or the other, the better."

And Robin had been one of those patients. Zachary was glad that the police department was already looking at the staff at the care center. It saved him the trouble of trying to sort out which of them might have had a reason to put an early end to Robin's suffering. It sounded like they all did.

Zachary had decided that he was going to pop over to the cafeteria and pick something up for Nurse Betty anyway. She might have said that she didn't really want anything and that she had been happy to have to do paperwork for the police rather than take care of irritable patients for a while, but he knew he had still inconvenienced her, and that even after that, she had given him more insight into Robin and what it was like to deal with her while she was there. The more he knew about Robin's personality and the dynamics, the better.

"Leave me alone! Just get your hands off!"

Zachary froze at the words. He stopped stock-still in the middle of the hallway. If someone had been walking behind him, they would have walked right into him. Zachary looked around.

"No," the voice repeated. "I said to stop."

The sound came from one of the small visitor rooms that branched off from the main hallway. Small rooms for families to meet in, some with a TV or toys, some with plants, toys, or books; there were different kinds of surroundings to suit different visitor personalities or needs. Zachary stepped into the doorway ready to stop whatever assault was going on.

A man bent over a woman in a wheelchair. He was standing at an awkward angle beside it, as if he had been behind it to push it, but had to step around it to take care of a problem. The problem seemed to be his attempt to sponge off a layer of drool that coated the woman's chin and stretched down to her chest, where she wore a bib to soak it up. Her hands, stiffened into claws, battered at his, trying to make him stop

Zachary didn't know what to do or say at first.

The man avoided the woman's awkward movements and patted at her throat and chest, blotting the spittle with a thin hospital towel. It was obvious from his smock that he was part of the staff. The woman's movements became more frantic, her words dissolving into a sob of protest.

"Leave her alone," Zachary finally worked up the courage to say.

The hospital worker turned around to look at Zachary. He sneered, but he took a step back from the patient as if he had been caught doing something he wasn't supposed to.

"Who are you? This is none of your business." The oft-repeated refrain of an abuser.

"She asked you to leave her alone, so leave her alone."

"She needs help. I'm just taking care of her."

"She said no."

"She doesn't get to say no."

"I say she does," Zachary insisted. He stepped into the small room. He wasn't physically imposing; he was smaller than the man, and yet the man stepped back again, looking around the room to measure his escape.

"You don't work here. You don't have to spend your days carting around people who are so broken down by disease and treatment that they can't do anything for themselves. She should be thanking me, not fighting me."

"She doesn't owe you anything."

"I need to take her back to her room."

"No, you don't."

"I'll call security on you! You don't have any right to be ordering me around. Who are you to walk in here and act like you're my boss?" The man was inching toward the door. It was obvious he was on his way out. He was just using the words to cover himself, like a man caught with his pants down.

Zachary just stood there and watched him retreat. He shifted his body sideways to allow the man to make a swift exit without blocking his way. Zachary wasn't about to get punched in the nose by an animal desperate for escape.

Zachary stood there and listened to the whisper of the man's soft-soled shoes down the hospital corridor.

He turned to the woman. He didn't know if he should apologize to her for interfering or maybe push her back to her unit.

She was younger than he had first realized. The clawed fingers and reedy voice had made him think she was an elderly woman. But he saw that in spite of her boniness and air of frailty, she was younger than he was. Her expression was a mixture of relief and dread. Did she think that he was going to do something to her? That he'd gotten rid of the man just to have her to himself?

Zachary sat in one of the visitor chairs, lowering himself to her eye level. "Are you okay?" he asked gently, "What else can I do for you?"

She gave an odd, choking laugh and tears brimmed up in her eyes.

"They think they have a right to your body," she said. "They think that being in a wheelchair or being weak means they can do whatever they want. But I'm still in here! I still have the right to choose who touches me and how!"

Zachary nodded. "Yes. You do."

"It may be his job to take me from one place to another, but it's not his job to touch me. And even if it was, I can still say no!"

Her voice was getting stronger and more strident.

"I'm sorry," Zachary said. Apologizing not for himself, but for what had happened to her. All of the times people had made presumptions and thought they had the right to control her.

The woman was quiet for a few minutes, breathing and trying to get her emotions under control. Tears brimmed over her lids and down her cheeks, and Zachary made no move to try to stop them or wipe them away. He made a soft, calming noise.

"Sh, it's okay."

After a couple of minutes, she attempted to bring her hand up to her face. Zachary saw that she had a balled-up tissue or cloth in her grip that she was trying to dab at her face with. A way for her to have control over her own spit and tears. Her arms shook and the muscles in her hands and arms grew taut as she tried to perform the simple task. She touched the tissue to her cheek, but that was all she could manage. More tears flooded down her face and soaked into the tissue. Keeping her hand up appeared to be too great an effort for her, and it sank down into her lap until both hands lay there still, side by side.

"You put a person in a wheelchair," she said shakily, "and they suddenly become an object. Something to be acted upon. People grab the wheelchair and push you around without asking, like just because you have some impairment, you no longer have a will of your own. You complain, and they say they are just *helping*." Her hands shook in her lap. "And it doesn't stop there. Some of them say vile things. They touch you without permission. You can't do anything to stop them. They can do whatever they want to and get away with it. Because even to the police or the staff or people out in public, you are just an object. You lose your personhood when they put you in this chair."

"That's…" Zachary couldn't think of language strong enough. He remembered what it was like after the accident that had left him paralyzed and needing to learn how to walk and take care of himself again. People coming in and out of his room, moving him around, transporting him from the bed to the chair, down to physio, or wherever else they wanted him. It wasn't as serious as what the woman was describing; he'd never had anyone take advantage of him. Not really. He'd felt minimized and less than a real person, but he hadn't had to deal with all of the things she was talking about. It was probably worse for a woman, and his convalescence had not been long. "That's not right. I'm sorry. People don't have the right to treat you that way."

She snuffled, snorting back tears and phlegm and swallowing. The choking, gagging noise made Zachary feel sick. He wanted to help her, but he knew there was nothing he could do. Even to offer seemed insensitive when she was so worked up about people treating her as an object.

Zachary felt guilty for his instinct to help. Was he any better than the others? If he had worked there, how long would it have taken for him to stop listening to the objections and asking or waiting for consent? With so many people needing so much help, could they be blamed for moving in and doing what needed to be done, even if the patient didn't want help?

It had been a complaint he had often heard from Bridget, even before she was sick. *I don't need help. I don't need you to do things for me.* He had wanted to do things for her, to be the strong one, the provider. But she was strong-minded and independent and didn't want him to rush in and take over when a jar needed to be opened or the groceries carried in.

How much of a toll had it taken on Bridget to approach

Zachary and ask him for help in finding out what had happened to Robin?

"Who *are* you?" the woman asked. "I don't think I've seen you here before."

"My name is Zachary Goldman. My wife was in treatment here a while back, but right now I'm looking into the death of Robin Salter."

"Robin?" Her head had been sinking down and it bobbed up at his explanation.

"Yes. Did you know her?"

"I know who she was. Didn't know her very well. We weren't in the same unit. Are you a policeman, then?"

He considered whether to fudge his answer. People sometimes felt more comfortable talking to someone they thought was a police officer rather than a private investigator. But his rapid assessment was that the woman had been mistreated by authority figures and was more likely to trust an individual than an official.

"No. I'm a private investigator. Bridget knew Robin and asked me to look into it. The police are involved now, but I'm not part of the department."

She gave a small nod.

"I'm Ruth. Ruth Wick." She lifted her left hand, the one not holding the tissue, and offered it to him, fingers still hooked. Rather than trying to fit his hand into hers in a traditional hand-shake, Zachary folded his fingers around hers to give them a comforting squeeze, then let go.

"Pleased to meet you, Ruth."

"Thank you… for that." She made a small gesture in the direc-tion of the door the hospital worker had left through.

"No problem. You think he's really going to call security on me?"

"Why would he? You didn't do anything wrong. He doesn't have any reason to have you kicked out. It would just backfire and put him in the spotlight. Cowards like him don't want the attention."

"Are you okay now?"

"Getting there. Being like this," she nodded toward her lap to indicate her condition or the wheelchair, "it makes you very vulnerable. You depend on other people for all of your needs. Most of the nursing staff is pretty good, but it's like walking around naked." She gave a short laugh. "I feel like I spend half the day naked as it is. I don't want to feel that way the rest of the time."

Zachary nodded. "I had an accident," he confided to her. "I had a spinal cord injury. Not serious, but enough that I was paralyzed for a few days and had to work to get my mobility back. It is invasive to have other people handling your body and acting like you are a thing instead of a person."

Ruth nodded. "And I've heard them talk about the patients who are worse… ones who can't respond at all or are in a vegetative state… talking about them like they are plants in a garden instead of people. Even if they can't move at all, they are still people," she said explosively. "Talking about watering the vegetables is disrespectful! It's depersonalizing." She sniffled again. "And I'm going to be one of them, one day."

There was a lump in Zachary's throat. "I'm so sorry."

"What am I going to do when I can't even tell them to stop anymore? What am I going to do when I can see and feel what is going, and I can't even say a word?"

"I don't know." He didn't suggest assisted suicide. He was sure that she knew all of the options and had already looked into that. But if she had religious or other ethical objections, or if she was looking at being completely disabled but not considered to be terminal within six months, it wasn't an option.

Ruth took a long, shuddering breath. She swallowed and lifted her chin. "Okay. I'm done feeling sorry for myself now. Enough self-pity. Where were you headed? Were you on your way in or out?"

Zachary shrugged. "Both, actually. I was talking to one of the nurses in Robin's unit, and I thought I would get her something from the cafeteria before doing anything else."

"Ah. Okay."

"Did you want to come with me?" Zachary offered. "Or if you wanted, I could take you back to your unit or wherever it was you wanted to go next. If you don't want to stay here." He was worried about offending her with his offer. She had just been complaining about people moving her around, and he was offering to do just that. He had no idea whether she was capable of getting around on her own. Her hands didn't appear to be dexterous or strong enough to control the wheelchair, which was not one of the electric ones with a joystick. But he could be completely wrong. He didn't know anything about her condition.

"I'd love to go to the cafeteria," Ruth said, brightening.

"Great!" Zachary didn't get up from his seat right away. "Do you want me to push you, or...?"

"Yes, please."

Zachary got up. He positioned himself behind her and checked the brakes on the wheelchair. They had already been released, so he gave a little push and got Ruth on her way. She was very light and pushing the chair was effortless.

Once in the cafeteria, they discussed what the best treat to get for Nurse Betty would be, neither of them knowing any of her preferences. After settling on a chocolate puffed wheat square and hoping Betty wasn't gluten intolerant, Zachary took a look around at the other offerings.

"Can I get you something?" he suggested. "Would you like coffee or a piece of pie?"

"Oh, you don't have to... are you having anything?"

Zachary could see that he wasn't going to be able to get her anything without buying something for himself. Otherwise it would be seen as a pity offering. The last thing that Ruth needed was for him to show her pity. She was trying to be strong and independent, and he needed to support that.

"Hm. I'm thinking maybe... apple pie. You're not going to

make me eat alone, are you? Just me, and my pie, and Nurse Betty's chocolate square?"

Ruth giggled. "I don't know. It could be difficult. I'm really not up to eating by myself."

"I could manage it, if all you need is a steady hand. If you need a tube, we're going to need some help…"

"I'm not quite to tube feeding yet," Ruth said, with an appreciative smile. "But I am on a liquid diet, so…"

Zachary considered the options. "Maybe yogurt or pudding? Would that work?"

Ruth shifted back and forth in her seat, trying to see what was on the higher glass shelves. "Are there Jell-O parfaits?"

"Red or green?"

"Red!"

Zachary added a piece of pie and a red Jell-O cup to a tray and slid it along beside him as he pushed Ruth forward. "Do you mind if I pick up the tab?"

"I seem to have left my purse at home."

"Good." Zachary checked them through and picked up a plastic spoon and fork at the cash register, then found a place for them to sit and eat.

1 3

After a leisurely snack, Zachary pushed Ruth's chair back to her unit, following her directions. They arrived to find the unit in an uproar, with nurses squawking loudly and police officers questioning the man who had been harassing Ruth.

"Ruth! Oh, thank goodness you're okay!" exclaimed one nurse, hurrying over to them. "What happened?" Without waiting for an answer from Ruth, she looked at Zachary. "Where did you find her?"

Zachary waited for Ruth to answer, but before she could, the hospital worker interrupted.

"That's him! That's the man who threatened me!"

"Threatened you?" Zachary echoed, raising his eyebrows.

"Sir, I need you to step back from the wheelchair," one of the cops said, straightening to his full height and moving toward Zachary, hand on his holster.

Zachary wasn't sure whether he was going for a taser, a gun, pepper spray, or something else, but he wasn't going to wait to find out. He released the wheelchair, putting his hands up.

"There's been a misunderstanding," he said, looking at the hospital worker. "I don't know what this guy has been telling you, but I never threatened anyone."

"Step back please. When you are clear of the wheelchair, I want you to lie face-down."

"Seriously?" Zachary took a step backward, and then another. Walking backward was not something he had practiced very much and he teetered, worried for a moment that he was going to topple over before he regained his balance. He put his hands on his head to get down to his knees, and then to lie down. "You're making a mistake listening to this guy."

But the police had to do what they had to do. The cop patted him down and removed the contents of his pockets. There was nothing of particular interest for them to find.

"Zachary didn't do anything!" Ruth protested, her voice high and reedy. "He just went with me down to the cafeteria and we had something to eat. He didn't do anything wrong. *Lucas*," it was the first time she had put a name to the hospital worker, "he's the one you ought to be arresting."

"Nobody is being arrested at this point," one of the other officers said smoothly. "Just tell us what happened and we'll take it from there. No need to get upset."

"I am upset! Zachary was a good Samaritan who came and helped me out, and you're treating him like a criminal. Let him get up and stop being ignorant!"

The police officers exchanged looks with each other. No one looked directly at Ruth. Finally, a heavyset officer nodded, and the one who had frisked Zachary helped him politely to his feet. He looked at Zachary's pocket contents, unsure whether he should be giving them back. The one in charge picked up Zachary's wallet and opened it up to have a look.

"Zachary Goldman," he read. "What is your relationship with Miss Wick?"

"I had dessert with her in the cafeteria. We don't have a previous relationship."

"Zachary Goldman," someone repeated behind Zachary. "Private eye?"

Zachary turned his head and saw Joshua Campbell. Zachary

didn't turn all the way around or make any attempt to greet him, not wanting to alarm the officers who were contemplating him.

"Well, I'll be," Campbell said, grinning. "What's up, Zach?"

"Uh…" Zachary wasn't sure what to tell him.

"You here on an investigation?"

"Mind if I get my stuff back, now?"

Campbell motioned for him to help himself, and Zachary picked up his possessions and put them back in his pockets. Everyone seemed to be waiting for him to say something. Zachary realized he hadn't answered Campbell's question. "I'm investigating the death of Robin Salter."

"The way I understand it, *we're* investigating the death of Robin Salter," Campbell countered.

"The police didn't get involved until after I reported to the medical examiner. I don't give up a case just because the police decide to investigate as well."

"No. Stubborn that way," Campbell agreed. He sighed and looked around at the other police officers. "Nothing left to see. I take it this is the young lady who disappeared?"

Everyone nodded.

"You weren't kidnapped?" Campbell asked Ruth. He was the first of the officers who had deigned to talk to her directly. "You were not held or taken anywhere against your will?"

"No," Ruth said tartly. "I was not."

"Then I'm guessing that all of this alarm was a simple over-reaction."

There was a lot of grumbling from the other officers, and Lucas did his best to avoid answering any questions directly and to brush the whole thing off as a misunderstanding. Campbell remained nearby as everyone dispersed. He cocked his head at Zachary.

"No trouble, Zach?"

Zachary looked at Ruth, wondering how she wanted it handled. Ruth sighed and shook her head. Zachary guessed that she didn't want any additional harassment that might come from accusing one of the hospital staff of acting improperly. Especially when all she had to complain about was that Lucas was trying to mop up her spittle before returning her to her unit. Just doing his job.

Zachary pressed his lips together, considering whether there was anything he could say that would give Campbell a heads-up, but not go against Ruth's wishes.

"Did you run him to see if he had a record?" Zachary questioned, tilting his head in the direction Lucas had been standing up until a couple of minutes before.

"He wouldn't be able to work here if he had a record."

"Nothing?" Zachary persisted.

"I'd have to check to see if there was anything else… dropped charges, a sealed juvenile record. But there's no warrants outstanding and no convictions."

"Might be a good idea," Zachary said.

Campbell looked toward Ruth, wanting more details.

"Just a feeling," Zachary said, not giving him anything else. "Something setting off my alarms."

Campbell nodded. He was a cop. He understood all about trusting those niggling little feelings.

"I'll take a closer look. You're okay now, ma'am?"

"I'm tired."

"Of course. I don't need anything else from you."

Ruth looked at Zachary, then looked around at the medical staff. She indicated one of the nurses with her eyes. Zachary got the woman's attention.

"Ruth would like to go back to her room," he explained. "She's worn out from visiting."

"Well, we'll take care of that, dearie," the nurse said, taking hold of the handles of Ruth's wheelchair. "Time for a nap, Ruth."

Ruth's head wobbled in what wasn't quite a nod. The nurse wheeled her away.

Campbell and Zachary watched them go.

"Another case?" Campbell asked.

"No. Just met her today. I just want to make sure… she's taken good care of."

"They have a very good reputation here," Campbell assured him. "Try not to let your view be colored by what happened to Robin Salter."

"I'm not. She's just… very vulnerable."

Campbell nodded his agreement. "Well, I suppose if I'm not going to arrest you for kidnapping, we may as well get on our way. You're here on the Salter case?"

"Yes. I wanted to talk to a few more of the people who knew her. Maybe some of the other patients might have some insight."

Campbell let out his breath and made a face. "Look, Zach, we know each other. You know I've got no problem as long as you're operating within the law. But remember we're just starting on this case, and you investigating it simultaneously… I just don't want anyone's toes being stepped on."

"You can't stop me from asking people questions."

"Well, I could strongly discourage you. But that's what I'm talking about… we're both professionals. We can work this out so that no one is getting in anyone else's way."

Zachary walked along beside Campbell. It was true; Campbell was one of the cops Zachary had never had to worry too much about. He didn't automatically get his back up whenever he saw Zachary or heard he was involved in one of their cases. There were certainly enough cops around who did, doggedly territorial of their own investigations.

"I've already talked to the main doctor and nursing staff. That's probably who you're focused on, isn't it?"

Campbell nodded. "They have not been happy with all of the questions and extra work we've been making for them, believe me!"

"I know," Zachary agreed, and held up the puffed wheat square. "Peace offering for Nurse Betty."

Campbell chuckled. "Keeping the wheels greased with sugar

and chocolate. Yeah, she's a bit of an old battle-ax, that one. Wouldn't want to be a patient stuck in her care."

"I don't think she's a bad nurse. She's just trying to keep things running smoothly. Hospitals don't run well with cops and private investigators shaking everything up."

They got to the unit. "Bridget was here?" Campbell questioned, looking around. "That's how you got involved in this case?"

Zachary nodded. "Yes. This is where she was, where she got her treatments. Not a place you want to be… but the best place, if you're trying to fight that fight."

"Well, just glad she's in remission, Zach. That's good news."

"You bet."

They stood there for a minute longer, then went their separate directions without further comment. Zachary tracked Nurse Betty down and offered his bribe, and she told him which patients would be able to tell him the most about Robin.

Zachary's first interview was with Chenka Redneslav, Robin's roommate at the time she died. She had been moved to another room so the crime guys could properly process Robin's room and see if there was any evidence to be turned up a full week after Robin's death. Chenka was grumpy about having been moved and let Zachary know she didn't appreciate it.

Chenka was a blonde with classic Russian features and an accent just heavy enough to be romantic. She was slim, but not emaciated like some of the women in the unit. Like Robin, she had retained her good looks. Even in a hospital bed with no makeup on, she was stunning.

"I don't know why you have to come in here and start stirring things up. You're making everybody miserable with all of your questions and bringing the police into this. Everything was fine, I don't understand why you had to stick your nose in and interfere."

"I'm sorry it's been such a problem," Zachary apologized. "But I'm sure that if it was you, you would want people to know the truth. You wouldn't want everyone thinking it was just a natural death when it was not."

"You don't know that."

"No, but it needs to be investigated."

"It's ridiculous." She folded her arms across her chest and looked out the window. She hadn't had a window in the room she had shared with Robin.

"I know. And again, I apologize. I'm just trying to find out the truth. You believe it was Robin's time, I gather? You didn't think she was going to last much longer?"

Chenka pursed her lips. "I didn't think she was going to die *then*," she admitted. "But she had cancer. We all have cancer. Any of us could go at any time."

"Sure. Any time. *You* could go tomorrow," Zachary agreed.

She frowned fiercely at this. "Why do you say that? I am not… I am not going to die tomorrow. They're going to keep giving me medicine, and they will kill all of the cancer. Then I will be well again."

"You could go at any time," Zachary echoed what she had said.

"No, not any time. Those who are ready. Those whose time it is."

"Like Robin."

Chenka looked uneasily over at the call button for the nurse. She wanted to get Zachary out of there, but what would happen if she succeeded? Would it be over, or would he tell people that Chenka had lied to him? Would she be taken to the police station to be questioned, instead of being questioned in the comfort of her room?

"I did not know it was Robin's time. I *know* it is not my time. But I did not know it was Robin's time."

"Robin didn't know it was her time either. My wife was visiting with her just before she died, and she didn't know. She didn't have any idea she was going to die soon. She thought she still had months left."

"Your wife?"

"Bridget Downy. She was a friend of Robin's. They were both in treatment together. You probably know her too?"

"Bridget Downy isn't your wife."

She was the first one to challenge Zachary on the fact.

"Bridget is my ex-wife," he agreed. "But we are still very close. She asked me to look into Robin's death. She doesn't believe it was Robin's time. She thinks something happened."

Chenka chewed on her lip, her eyes fastened on Zachary's. "What happened?"

"You were there. Maybe you need to tell me."

"I did not do anything. I did not see anything. I have nothing to tell you."

"Nothing unusual happened Thursday evening or Friday morning?"

"Nothing. No."

"Robin seemed just like her usual self. No change in her condition."

"Obviously, there was a change in her condition on Friday morning."

"Yes. You weren't aware she had passed?"

"No. She died sometime in the night. I don't know when."

"And the nurses didn't discuss it on their night rounds?"

"They don't go around waking everybody up if they are sleeping. They only give prescribed medications or help if patients are having trouble."

"Did Robin have any trouble?"

"She was restless. But she slept."

"She didn't call the nurse for anything that night?"

"Pain meds. She said she was in a lot of pain."

"Was that normal?"

"Cancer can be painful."

"But for Robin. Had she been in a lot of pain before that?"

"For a few days."

"But not before that?"

"No. Before, she was still pretty good. She had energy and able to get around. But then she got pain in her joints and her stomach and chest. She was afraid it was the cancer spreading. I guess it must have been."

"We'll find that out in the autopsy. After she had the pain meds, she slept okay? Did she talk to you at all?"

"She didn't talk to me."

"Not at all? It would be strange to be in the same room as someone and never to have any conversation."

"I was not her friend. She was only here for treatment, not to make friends."

"But she was friends with Bridget," Zachary pointed out.

"I guess… she only needed one friend, then," Chenka said, shrugging. "She had plenty of family. They came to see her all the time. And that boyfriend of hers. Lawrence."

"But she broke up with him."

Chenka looked at Zachary sideways. "What makes you think that?"

"Didn't she tell you? That she dumped him on Wednesday night, after their big date?"

Chenka shook her head adamantly. "She never told me that."

"She told Lawrence. Was that before they came back? I thought it was after the date, when they were back here."

"I don't know. I don't listen to other people's conversations."

Like with Lawrence, Zachary knew Chenka was lying. Of course she had listened to their conversation. Of course she knew what had happened. Two people couldn't have a conversation like that in a hospital room without someone on the other side of the curtain hearing. Zachary considered. Was she trying to protect Lawrence? Or to protect Robin's reputation? Which one of them was she concerned about?

"Who came to see Robin on Thursday? The nurse said that she had a number of visitors, though none of them stayed very long."

"She was too tired for them. So everyone just said hello and then left again."

"Lawrence came by. Did he think he was going to be able to talk her into getting back together? Did he think she'd only been joking the night before and would have changed her mind?"

"How do I know what Lawrence was thinking?" Chenka scoffed. But her next words belied the assertion. "Lawrence was a nice man. He just wanted to make sure she was okay. He wasn't going to abandon her just because she had broken up with him."

"She wouldn't exactly want him to visit, though, would she? She must have told him they weren't a couple anymore and he should leave." Zachary didn't have to imagine what Bridget would have said to him in similar circumstances. He'd lived it. Zachary had been afraid she was just trying to spare him the horrors of cancer and the treatments. He had vowed to stand by her anyway, to be there as her friend even if she was breaking up their marriage. He had been in denial about just how bitter she was toward him.

Chenka shrugged. "She said she did not want him there."

"Did Lawrence have the opportunity to put anything in her IV?"

"The curtain was pulled across. I could not see."

"What do you think? Was there time? Could he have done it without Robin seeing him? Was she asleep when he got there?"

"Lawrence would not have hurt her. He was a nice guy."

"Even a nice guy can be pushed over the edge when he is treated unfairly."

"He did not do anything to her. He wasn't here for long enough."

Zachary nodded slowly, wondering if it were true. Even if Chenka were telling him the truth, would she have been able to judge if Lawrence had the opportunity to put something in Robin's IV? How long would it have taken? Had Robin been awake or asleep when he arrived? If Robin had been given something Thursday, it wasn't something fast-acting. Any fast-acting drug would have to have been administered by someone at the hospital during the night or early morning.

"Who else was here?" he asked. "Were her other visitors here before or after Lawrence?"

"After. He came during the day. Her family didn't come until late afternoon, when school and work were out."

"Her mother and her sister?"

"And that poor boy."

"Her nephew, Rhys?"

Chenka nodded. "Rhys. Yes. Gloria's son."

"Why do you call him a poor boy?"

She raised her eyebrows at him. "Because of what happened to him." When Zachary continued to look at her blankly, she went on to explain. "His grandfather's murder."

"Murder?" Zachary couldn't pick his jaw up off the floor. "Vera's husband was murdered?"

"Yes, of course." Her eyes were wide. "You didn't know that?"

"Nobody happened to mention it. Did this happen recently?" Even as he asked it, Zachary was running through what he knew about Vera and her family from talking to Vera. Her husband hadn't died recently, but years before. *And Rhys had never been the same.*

"No, when Rhys was a little boy. You don't know anything about it?"

"No. What exactly did he die of? What did it have to do with Rhys, other than that they were close?"

"I don't know all of the details," Chenka lowered her voice as if someone might overhear them. "It was a violent death. Shot or stabbed. Rhys was there. He and his grandfather were home alone."

"Did he see it, then? He knew who did it?"

"They think so."

Zachary cocked his head, puzzled, waiting for more.

"That's when they *lost* Rhys." Even in the quiet of the hospital room, Chenka's words were difficult to make out. He leaned forward to hear better and communicate to her that he was engaged. He wanted to hear more. "The boy was never the same after that. He wouldn't talk. He was sent away for a while, to some institution."

"I didn't know that. So he probably saw, but he could never tell what happened?"

Chenka nodded. "Exactly. He withdrew completely. Like a nervous breakdown. He came back to live with his grandma again after a while, but they couldn't ask him about what had happened without setting him off again, so they had to let it go."

"And he's never talked about it since?"

"He's never talked since."

"Oh. Wow." So Vera was right. He was *special.*

"And now this," Chenka said. "It was bad enough that his aunt was dying of cancer. But now that you've started this investigation… to be saying she was murdered too… I can't imagine how the poor boy—and the others—must be feeling now."

Zachary refrained from pointing out that it wasn't his fault that someone had taken Robin's life. All he was doing was trying to find out the truth.

"We don't know if it was murder," Zachary said. "It might have been an error on the part of the doctor or someone else involved in Robin's care. Or it still might have been the course of her cancer or the chemotherapy. We won't know until the medical examiner has had a chance to complete the autopsy and whatever lab tests they have to order."

"But you made it worse. Worse than if you just let them believe it was cancer."

Zachary gave a helpless shrug. "I'm just trying to uncover the truth."

"Maybe sometimes what is hidden should stay that way."

Zachary redirected the conversation. "Did she have any other visitors? Lawrence, Vera, Gloria, and Rhys? Is that it?"

"I don't know." Chenka closed her eyes and rested her head

back. "I don't remember. She was tired and the nurses discouraged anyone from visiting."

"Any nurse in particular?"

"What?"

"Which nurse discouraged visitors?" Maybe someone had wanted visitors out of the way in order to give Robin something that would ease her pain permanently.

"I don't know. They said she'd be feeling better in a day or two."

"Who did?"

"Nurse..." Chenka trailed off, trying to recall which one it had been. "Was it Rachelle? I don't remember for sure."

Chenka appeared to be getting pretty tired herself. In another minute or two, she was going to be snoring.

"What is she like? Nurse Rachelle?" Zachary tried to remember which nurse that was. He thought she was the heavy redhead he had already spoken with. She hadn't been able to tell him much about Robin or the events of her last day on earth.

"She's a sweetie," Chenka said. "Always very happy and kind, even when she's run off her feet. Not like some of the others."

"Do you have complaints about the care here? Or did Robin?"

"It's a hospital. You can't expect them to take care of you like your baba. It's not an easy job."

Chenka went quiet and Zachary didn't pursue the conversation any further. He'd gotten everything out of Chenka that he was going to.

14

Zachary sat in his car and turned the key again, to no avail. He didn't know much about cars, so he wasn't sure whether he had a dead battery or something more serious. All he knew was, it wasn't starting. He called his mechanic and told him where it was and what it was doing, and Jergens agreed to pick it up and have a look.

Zachary tapped his foot lightly on the gas pedal, considering who to call next. He could try Kenzie or Bowman; either of them would give him a ride if they were available, but both were probably working and wouldn't be free for a couple more hours. He could call a cab, walk, or take the bus.

He took out his phone and instead called Bridget.

"Zachary!" She always sounded surprised and a little disapproving when he called, even though he had been doing his best to help her out. There had been too many times in the past when she'd had good reason to be angry with him, and it was something of a habit. "What's up?"

"My car broke down at the hospital. I'm sort of stranded and I wondered if you'd pick me up. We could go back to the apartment and discuss the case. Kill two birds with one stone…"

"Can't you just have it towed?"

"I am. But then I still need to get home. I don't know how long it will be until it will be fixed."

Bridget sighed, but to Zachary's surprise, she agreed. "Fine. I'll be a little bit. I have some work to do before I head over. Maybe… half an hour? With traffic, that means it might be an hour before I get there. You might be better off getting a cab."

"No, that's fine. I can keep busy for that long. Just give me a call when you're here. You want to pick me up on the east side, the emergency entrance?"

"I never like to pull in there in case someone in a hurry rear-ends me. There's an entrance just south of there, where the elevators are. You know the one with the statue?"

"Sure. I'll head over there and be ready in about an hour."

Bridget acknowledged this and hung up the phone.

Zachary got out of the car, locked it up, and headed for the other side of the hospital. He hadn't picked the east side just to give himself some exercise, but he did think it would help him kill a little time. He strolled along looking at the artwork on the walls, stopping to read plaques, and listening in on private conversations that caught his attention.

The hospital housed not only a small gift shop with the requisite flowers, stuffed animals, balloons, and candy, but it also had a well-equipped pharmacy. Zachary considered the gift shop, wondering about buying something for Bridget to thank her for the lift, but decided against it. She would probably take it the wrong way. She would decide it was a romantic gesture and over-react, reversing all of the ground that Zachary had been able to gain. It was too soon. He'd just have to take it a step at a time and wait until he was sure she was ready for that step. Not wanting to tempt himself, he chose the pharmacy instead.

He wandered up and down the aisles, impressed with the amount of merchandise they stocked. He would have thought that, being a hospital, there wouldn't be a great need for over-the-counter drugs, but they appeared to do a brisk trade.

It occurred to him that it wouldn't hurt to get some kind of immune system booster with the amount of time he was spending at the hospital. Not that he was going to catch cancer, but there were plenty of other bugs and viruses floating around the hospital that could be really nasty. Zachary's diet and sleep habits were not conducive to a strong immune system, so a supplement might be a good idea, even if it were just vitamin C.

He found the supplements aisle and walked along it slowly, running his eyes along the shelves and trying to determine what kind of order had been used to shelve them. The supplements appeared to be arranged by function rather than alphabetically, so he looked over each group. He might get a sleep remedy too. They rarely did anything for him, and he would have to research anything to make sure it wasn't contraindicated by his other medications, but Zachary always had his eyes open for anything that might help him through the long, restless nights.

There was a group of bottles in pinks and pastels, with women's silhouettes on them. Multivitamins for women, herbs to ease cramps or increase fertility. Pregnancy multis, iron, and laxatives. Moving farther along the shelves, he came upon digestive aids of all sorts, then a shelf of various supplements and formulations for balancing emotional issues. Zachary paused to look at them for a moment, but didn't feel like ending up with worse problems, so he continued to look.

There was a big section devoted to boosting immune function as well as treating cold and flu symptoms. The staff had thoughtfully added tissues, wipes, and disinfecting gels to the display. Zachary picked through the various vitamins and formulae, eventually deciding on one bottle of vitamin C and one supplement that was supposed to help protect against cold and flu. He decided to add hand sanitizer as well. He'd use it as soon as it was paid for to eliminate any nasty hospital bugs he had picked up. He had touched a lot of different surfaces during the day. Who knew how many millions of bugs he'd managed to pick up.

Bridget called Zachary to advise him she was pulling up to the statue, and Zachary hurried out to meet her, not wanting to keep her waiting. He sat down in her overly-warm car and smiled in appreciation.

"Thanks so much for the ride, Bridge. Sorry to take you away from your work."

He was curious as to what work she was doing. She'd had a full-time job when they had been married, before she had been diagnosed with cancer. She'd taken a leave of absence for her treatments, then eventually given them notice. Having gotten together with Gordon had changed her financial situation. Instead of pooling her resources with Zachary, whose income was sporadic and, at best, middle class, she could just rely on Gordon to provide her with everything she needed. A big, beautiful home, which Zachary assumed came with maid service so that Bridget wouldn't be run ragged taking care of it, and a life of leisure. She still had the yellow VW she had driven when she'd lived with Zachary. She loved that little car and would probably never give it up until it fell apart. Any work that she was doing was a choice, something that she wanted to do for herself, rather than for survival.

Bridget glanced over at Zachary as he fumbled trying to join the ends of the unfamiliar seatbelt buckle around his coat, which kept ballooning out to block his vision.

"I'd better not find any electronics in that seat or under the mats," she warned. "You put a bug or a tracker in this car, and believe me, you'll never get another rescue from me."

The thought hadn't occurred to Zachary. He was so happy to be sitting in the same car as she was, he hadn't even thought of the opportunity it presented. He could have put some tiny electronic device inside of it. It wouldn't be easy with her watching closely or checking the obvious locations once he was out, but he could still have hidden it pretty well.

After finally clicking the seatbelt into place, Zachary held up his hands to show they were empty. "No electronics," he promised.

"And I had no idea I was going to be in your car in the first place. I don't even have anything on me."

She gave him a hard look, then nodded. "Good." She turned the radio up, which discouraged conversation, and headed back to Zachary's apartment.

"Will you come up? So we can go over the case?"

Bridget considered. "I don't know if that's a good idea. I should probably be heading home. Gordon…"

"He wouldn't let you?" Zachary asked. He knew Bridget wouldn't like to think someone else was controlling her.

"I can go where I want," Bridget asserted. "I was just thinking I should get home soon. I've been out for quite a while today, and he doesn't like—"

Zachary raised his eyebrows.

"It's not like that!" Bridget bristled. "He doesn't like me to do too much. I still get tired faster than I used to. He worries about me."

"Ah." Zachary nodded.

They caught the elevator up to Zachary's apartment, not speaking to each other on the way. Zachary didn't want to get her more worked up. He wanted her to be nice and comfortable and loose. Like they used to be when they were together.

Zachary let himself into the apartment. It occurred to him that Bridget didn't have the keys for the new place. She'd had keys for his old apartment. He wasn't sure he wanted her to have keys, but he wasn't sure he didn't, either. It would be a nice gesture to let her know she was always welcome and that he trusted her. But he'd already called the police once when he thought he had a burglar and it had only been Bridget. He didn't want a repeat.

Bridget heard the distinctive rattle of pills in bottles when Zachary put his pharmacy bag down on the kitchen counter. Her head snapped around.

"What's that?" she demanded. Without waiting for an invitation, she grabbed the bag and opened it.

"Immune system," Zachary explained. "I'm trying to take care of myself. Make sure I don't pick something up at the hospital with all of the time I've been spending over there."

She put the vitamin C down on the counter and examined the other bottle. "What's in this? Are you sure it's safe for you?"

"No, I haven't checked yet. But I will before I take any."

"You know you have to be careful. There could be contraindications with your meds. They could cause a reaction or make something you're taking stop working."

"I know."

She put the second bottle down on the counter. "That's good," she approved, forcing a smile. "I'm glad you're trying to take care of yourself. Good for you for thinking ahead."

She fished the hand sanitizer out of the bag and put it on the counter with the supplements. Crumpling up the bag, she opened the cupboard under his sink, and frowned.

"You don't have a recycling container?"

"Not yet. I'll get one when I'm at the grocery store."

With a scowl, she stuffed the bag beside the garbage can. "I'll just put it here for now, then. Instead of mixing it with the trash." She closed the cupboard door and looked at her watch. "You should have something to eat." She opened the fridge to survey the contents.

"Uh… you don't need to do that, Bridge. I can feed myself. Are you hungry? Can I get you something?"

Her expression as she looked at the food that had been sitting in the fridge for almost a week told him that she was not impressed.

"I don't have a lot of time to prepare anything," Zachary said. "I've been busy with this case. There's frozen meals in the freezer. I did go to the grocery store."

She didn't trust his word, but opened the freezer door to check. Lips pressed tightly together, she closed it again. "So… I gather you had something to tell me about the case?"

"I was at the hospital most of the day today," Zachary said. He hadn't prepared for what he was going to say to her, in spite of the fact that he'd had an hour to wait for her. He should have thought through what he wanted to say while he was waiting. "I talked a bit more to the hospital staff. Some of the patients. Just spent the time going over Robin's last few days, her mood, how she interacted, who was there to visit her…"

Bridget nodded and sat down at the table. "That sounds good. Find out anything interesting?"

"The police were over there today too. They've started in on their investigation. Looks like Joshua Campbell is supervising the evidence-gathering at the hospital."

"Joshua was always nice," Bridget approved. "He wasn't automatically prejudiced against private investigators like some of the police."

Bridget seemed to be able to make friends with everyone, and she and Zachary hadn't been together long before everyone Zachary knew seemed to be friends with her. People he had known for years were suddenly best friends with Bridget, without Zachary ever being sure how they had happened to get to know each other so well.

"Yeah. He was pretty good. Called off the dogs when they wanted to arrest me today…" Zachary grinned.

"To arrest you?" Bridget repeated. "Why would they want to arrest you? Because you were getting in the way when they were trying to investigate Robin's case?"

"No, actually. Campbell headed them off there. Told me not to step on their toes, and they wouldn't step on mine. They were more interested in arresting me for kidnapping."

"Kidnapping?" Bridget's voice shot higher.

Zachary related his chance meeting with Ruth and spending time with her. He kept it light, but Bridget was still frowning, little lines appearing on the bridge of her nose.

"That was very kind of you," she admitted. "You've always been very concerned about other people. The champion of the underdog. That's why I knew you would want to find out what really happened to Robin."

"But…?"

"Nothing. Just that. It was very kind."

"You think I was neglecting Robin's case? Because I wasn't. The whole thing didn't take more than an hour. Even with the police take-down."

"No. I didn't say there was any problem with it."

But her voice certainly did. She definitely had something more to say. Zachary shrugged and waited. Push her, and she would just push back and get angry and defensive.

"I don't know this Ruth, but she sounds very nice."

Zachary nodded again. "She was. She was having a pretty rough time of it."

Bridget's eyes grew distant. She didn't talk a lot about her time at the hospital. She'd rarely said anything to him about her treatments there, what kind of torture she had gone through to kill the cancer and still survive. Zachary knew the doctors pushed as close to the edge as they could. Kill the cancer but not the patient. Kill it so that it would never come back. Zachary lived in dread that it would reoccur. That in a few more weeks or months, Bridget would mention that she was having symptoms. Or she would go to the doctor for her regular scans and they would tell her the cancer was back, and twice as bad. Eventually, Gordon would call Zachary to tell him that Bridget had fought the good fight, but was gone.

"It must have been hard for you too," Zachary offered.

"Of course it was. I wouldn't want to put my worst enemy through what I had to go through. It was horrible. I was so sick. So tired I could barely move or speak. I begged them to stop the treatment and just let me die. But they always talked me back into it. Just two more cycles. Just one more. Another one just to be sure."

Zachary shook his head. "I wish… I'd been able to be there for you."

"I couldn't manage it. I couldn't deal with anybody else while I was going through that. I just needed to take care of myself."

"Of course. I know. I'm just saying. I wish… things had been different."

"I needed all my strength and focus to get through it. There wasn't anything left for anyone else. That's just the way it is. It was the same for Robin."

Zachary thought about Robin and the way she had dumped Lawrence, the same as Bridget had dumped him.

"Was there anything else? What other problems were taking Robin's mind off of her recovery?"

Bridget's eyes wandered around the kitchen as she considered her answer.

"She had some family issues. I told her she should try to resolve them. Get them out of her life so that they weren't pulling her mental energy."

"Resolve them."

"Yes," Bridget said evenly. "If you have all of these toxic people pulling away the energy you need for healing and recovery, you have to cut them off."

"You told her to cut off her family?"

"I didn't say that."

"I'm asking. It's important to the investigation, Bridget. Did you tell her to cut off her sister and mother? Because if she did, they would be suspects too."

"She said her family was too important to her." Bridget's face was stony. "That was her business, not mine. If she thought she was getting what she needed out of the relationships, then that was fine. If they were giving her more benefits than deficits, then maybe she should keep them around her. But… I didn't see her getting a lot out of it. I don't think they were helping her healing." Bridget sighed. She got up and got herself a glass of water. Leaning against the counter to drink it, she added, "Maybe that's why she died."

"You think one of them had something to do with her death."

"I didn't mean it that way. I just think the cancer grew and spread because there was so much negativity in her life. If she had gotten rid of those toxic relationships and only fostered positive, beneficial ones… maybe she could have beaten it."

Zachary nodded. His mouth was dry too. "So… I gather you didn't think much of her family."

"Everybody has good and bad traits."

"Her mother seemed quite nice to me. You didn't think so?"

"I think she was one of the people sucking all of Robin's energy away. She spent all of her time mourning her husband and making sure that everyone around her did too. He died ten years ago, and she still walks around making sure that everyone knows that he died. Her poor murdered husband. Her poor family, losing him like that for no reason. Her poor, damaged grandson. Some people always carry a cloud around with them. The negativity clings to them. You can't be around them without feeling worried and depressed."

Zachary figured that was pretty much how Bridget saw him. Now that she was getting her health back, she could afford to put a little energy into being decent to him. But she still saw him just the same way. As someone who always needed support and extra time and energy. Someone hopelessly negative and toxic. If he was going to win her back, he needed to show her he could change. He could be upbeat and give her back positivity instead of negativity.

"And her sister…" Zachary said, moving through the people in Robin's family, "…I got the feeling she was pretty stubborn and single-minded. She and Robin were probably always competing and butting heads."

Bridget nodded. "Good guess. Yes, they always seemed like they were on opposite sides of everything. If one of them said the sky was blue…"

"Yeah. And from what Vera said, I gather Gloria hasn't always been there. They raised Rhys, rather than Gloria having full-time custody of him."

"Robin always talked about Gloria like she was the bratty baby sister. The one who always wanted to take the spotlight and got away with whatever she wanted to because she was the baby in the family. Robin said that if she'd been the one who had gotten pregnant, she would have been out on the street. But instead of kicking Gloria out, they took her back in. Coddled her and took care of the baby and let Gloria get away with leaving him there all the time and going out to party or do drugs."

"I would think that was better for the baby than letting Gloria try to take care of him on her own."

"Maybe. Or maybe that would have forced Gloria to take some responsibility for her actions and grow up."

"Seems like she did, eventually."

"Not until it was too late. Not until after their father was killed and Rhys was in an institution."

Zachary closed his eyes, fighting back images of his own institutional stays. How many times had he daydreamed about his mother changing her mind and coming to get him and put their family back together again? But it had been too late for his family. There was no going home.

"Zachary."

Her fleeting touch on his hand, so familiar and comforting, and then it was gone. Zachary forced himself to breathe, drawing air in and pushing it out. He opened his eyes, swimming through the memories and emotions to get back to her.

"Sorry. So…" He cleared his throat and tried to get back on track. "Was there more bad blood between Robin and Gloria, or just some leftover sibling resentment?"

"I think they were pretty good. They didn't generally fight when Gloria came by. I didn't hear a lot of sniping between them. But then… I always left when the family arrived, too. Sometimes I'd stay for a few minutes, if Robin asked me to, but not any significant length of time."

"Did Robin resent her mother? Because of the way Gloria was favored? Because she spent more energy mourning her dead husband than she gave to Robin?"

"Robin kind of did, yeah. But that's pretty normal." Bridget spoke in a light tone. "Relationships get strained when you're sick like that. Some people get closer to each other, but if there are problems with the relationship, a stressor like cancer, it magnifies them. Splits people apart."

Zachary nodded. He didn't need to draw a line to connect Robin's issues with her family to Bridget booting Zachary out of her life.

"I'd like to talk to them more in depth. But I think that's going to be harder now that the police investigation has started up. Do you think you could talk to them and get them to meet with me?"

"I don't know. I can try, I guess. What do you want to talk to them about?"

Zachary tapped the pads of his fingers on the table, working through what he knew so far and what his next step should be.

"I don't want to wait until we get the results of the autopsy back. Who knows how long all of the lab work will take and if it will show anything significant. I feel like we're already behind. If we wait until we know whether it was cancer or an accident or euthanasia, it might be too late to find anything out. Especially if the police scare everyone into being quiet. I want to get a better feel for the family and to find out if anything important happened the last couple of days of Robin's life."

"Are you saying they're suspects?"

"I'm not saying that they're *not*..." Zachary scratched the back of his head. "Just tell them... I need background, Robin's history, to talk to them about anything that happened at the treatment center."

"They're not going to like it."

"Tell them... that I think it was just the natural course of Robin's illness, and I won't believe you that it might have been medical error."

"Make it look like I'm the bad guy and you're on their side," Bridget said baldly.

"Uh… yes. They're more likely to let me talk to them if they think I'm trying to prove their case rather than yours."

Her eyes snapped. "You *are* on my side, though, aren't you?" she demanded.

"Yes." Zachary nodded. "I'm completely on your side."

15

Late in the evening, there was a sharp rap on Zachary's apartment door that had him jumping to his feet, heart thumping, before he even thought about it. He tried to slow his breathing to get the wild thundering of his heart under control, and went to the door.

No one had his address. Only Bowman and Bridget. And Kenzie. Maybe a few other people who needed to know where to direct his mail or new furniture. And the landlord. Maybe he wanted to discuss the damage to the wall and doorframe the movers had caused and when it was going to be fixed.

He applied his eye to the peephole and looked out. The lighting in the hall wasn't great. Something he would have to address with the landlord to ensure that he knew whether it was safe to open his door to visitors. Maybe Zachary would install a discreet surveillance cam in the hallway so he could get a proper look at anyone at his door. But as it was, he didn't need much more than a glance at the shadowy figure in the hall to tell that it was a police officer or security guard.

He opened the door even as his brain rang alarm bells that anyone could get a security guard uniform and it didn't mean that his visitor was someone who could be trusted. But the door was open and it was too late to change his mind.

"Zachary," Campbell greeted with a booming voice. "Glad you're still up."

As if Zachary could have slept through the loud knocking on the door.

"Hey. Come on in."

Zachary ushered Campbell into the apartment and shut and locked the door behind him. They went to the living room, where there were at least two places to sit even if there was still an empty hole where the couch should have been. He was going to have to find something sooner or later that would actually fit through the door without being cut into pieces. They each selected an easy chair and sat down.

That eased Zachary's mind a little. He had been sure that Campbell was going to tell him he was off the case and to stay out of the way. He'd been warned away from too many police investigations in the past; he knew that was how such things were handled. If Campbell wanted to warn and threaten him, he wouldn't have sat down. He would have wanted to stay in a position of power over Zachary, using his greater height and heft to intimidate.

"Nice place," Campbell said without sincerity. "I gather you've just moved in?"

"Yeah." There were still a few moving boxes around, so even if Campbell hadn't heard that already, it wouldn't have taken a genius to figure it out. "You probably heard the last place got burned down…"

"Yeah, seems to me something like that might have come across the desk at some point." Campbell's smile made it obvious this was a joke. He settled into the chair with a tired sigh. "Don't happen to have any beer, do you?"

"Uh… no, sorry. A glass of water…?"

"No, I'll get something when I get home. Just on my way there now, but I thought I'd give you a little heads-up on the case."

"You found something already?"

"No, no evidence that points to any medical malpractice or foul play. Just… background."

Zachary leaned forward. It was rare for the police to be so forthcoming. They had privacy policies that prevented them from telling certain things to members of the public.

"I heard today that Robin's father was murdered ten years ago," Zachary said. "Is it something to do with that?"

Campbell nodded. "That was one of the things that came up," he agreed. "An interesting coincidence, but it doesn't appear, on the surface, to be related."

"Did they ever catch the murderer? What exactly happened?"

"The man was attacked in his home. Appeared to be a burglary gone wrong. The thief thought the house was empty, or maybe they had the address wrong and were looking for something else. He was shot. Killed instantly. Turns out there was a child in the house as well, the grandson. But he was unable to testify as to what he had seen."

"Rhys. Yeah, I heard about that."

"They never found the perp and the case went cold. I'm having the boys review the details just in case there is any connection, but I don't think there's anything there."

"Any chance I could see the file?"

"Go through normal channels. I won't block any request."

"Is that it, or was there something else?"

Campbell grinned. "You haven't done a full background, then."

"Uh… no. Just some interviews. Checking to see whether there was anything to the claim that Robin's death might not have been natural causes. What did I miss? One of the hospital employees? Lawrence Long?"

The policeman shook his head. "Nope. Although we haven't finished backgrounds on everybody who might have had access to her at the hospital. That will take a while. But there was a history of domestic violence."

Zachary mentally berated himself for not doing police and courthouse searches of all of the individuals close to Robin. "Lawrence? He certainly didn't seem the type."

"It wasn't Lawrence. There were several police incident files and a protective order. You'll have to search them up yourself, I can't divulge any details."

"I was so focused on medical error or euthanasia, it didn't even occur to me to look at domestic violence."

"They are probably completely unrelated," Campbell said. "More than likely, you're right. You don't usually see domestic violence turn into poisoning, or whatever else happened here. It's just not the natural progression. But... things may turn out to be different in this case."

"Yeah. It's been a curious case from the start. Bridget getting so wound up over Robin dying when she did... it's not like her. She has pretty good intuition, so I had to check it out."

"What are you onto tomorrow?"

"I'm hoping to talk to the family again. But maybe I should search up these cases first, so I have the background..."

"No. I'd go ahead and interview the family members first. The public records can wait. It's not like they're going anywhere, and like I said, they're probably not related at all."

Zachary was baffled. "You're not going to tell me to stay away from the family until your officers have had a chance to talk to them?"

"No. You're a good investigator. If you find anything suspicious, you can pass it on to me. If my officers go in there asking questions... the family's backs will be up before they even start. They'll be guarded. They might have to be Mirandized at some point. But a private citizen doesn't have to worry about Miranda warnings. Things can move more naturally and might leak out. I know you're good at worming your way in." Campbell cleared his throat. "My officers will still need to interview them, but they might just have to be busy with other things tomorrow. You'll tell me if you find anything significant?"

Zachary did report to the police when he had to, but normally he kept information to himself. Robin Salter's case was not a collaboration with the police, and he needed to make sure that was understood.

"If something is reportable," he hedged.

"Come on, Zachary. You can do better than that."

"I can't promise to tell you everything I find. I don't know if anything will be relevant to Robin's case. But if I find evidence of a crime, I'll let you know."

"I came here tonight, without any prompting, to let you know what was on my radar. You wouldn't have found out about this history otherwise. I scratch your back, you can't return the favor?"

"I appreciate the information. I'll follow up on it after I interview the family." Unless, of course, Campbell was trying to push Zachary into interviewing the family while he followed the case in another direction, like wherever those domestic violence charges led. He might have to pursue them both simultaneously, splitting his time and attention in two different directions. "I'm just saying that I'm a private investigator. Not one of your cops. You can't expect me to report back to you like that."

Campbell wrinkled his nose and made a sour expression. He pressed his hands to the arms of the chair to push himself up. "That's not being very cooperative, my friend. I expected a little more gratitude from you."

Zachary stood up as well. "I'll do what I can," he hedged. "But I don't work for you."

***

Zachary always dreaded car problems. Having no real understanding of anything other than the basic maintenance required to keep the metal beasts running, he was always worried that the mechanic's bill was going to run to the thousands and something huge like the engine or the transmission would need to be replaced. Maybe he should have had Ray-Ray take a look at it for him. At five years old, Ray-Ray's knowledge of the inner workings of cars far outstripped Zachary's, and probably that of a lot of mechanics too.

So in the morning and with a tight knot of dread in his stomach, Zachary called Jergens to see when he was going to be able to get his car back and what the bill was going to be like.

"Oh, Zachary, I was going to give you a call." Jergens always sounded hoarse and secretive, like he was doing something dishonest and was afraid someone was going to overhear him. But he was as honest as the day was long, and Zachary trusted him not to run up the bill despite Zachary's ignorance of all things automobile related.

Was it a good thing or a bad thing that Zachary was already on his list of people to call? It couldn't have taken too long to figure out what was wrong with his car. That could mean the engine or transmission was totally wrecked.

"Uh-oh. Is it bad?"

Jergens chuckled. "Oh, yeah, Zach. We're going to have to completely replace your... spark plugs."

Zachary let out his breath. Even he knew that replacing spark plugs was not expensive or complicated. "Whew. I was really worried about it. What's wrong with the old ones? Are they just... worn out?"

It was a pretty new car, and while he had bought it used he hadn't expected to have any big bills in the near future. It seemed odd that the spark plugs would be worn out already.

"They're missing."

"Missing? How could they be missing? It was working earlier yesterday. They can't just... fall off, can they?"

"No. Definitely not. Somebody would have had to remove them. Someone sabotaged your car."

Zachary swore under his breath. He started considering the possibilities. It wasn't just random vandalism. Someone who didn't know him and was just out to commit mischief might key his car or slash his tires, but they wouldn't go to all of the work to get his hood open and remove his spark plugs. That was targeted. Someone sending him a message. Somebody was telling him that they didn't like what he was doing and wanted him to get lost.

While he always had several cases on the go, and it could be any number of disgruntled husbands, employees, or insurance claimants, there was really only one that prominent. Cheating spouses rarely went after the private investigator, rarely even knew who it was. And if they did, it was yelling, a slap in the face, something confrontational.

Spark plugs pulled from his car while he was doing interviews meant someone was unhappy with the Robin Salter investigation. One of the hospital staff? One of the police officers who didn't like him being involved? Lawrence Long or someone from Robin's family?

"Zachary?"

Zachary looked at his phone, disoriented for a moment. "Oh, Jergens. Sorry, I spaced."

"I said if you can catch a cab or bus over here, it can be ready for you this morning. I just don't have time to drop it off to you."

"Yeah, that would be great. I can find my way over there."

"Great. I'll see you later, and you can tell me about the case you're on."

It was Gloria who answered the door, her mouth an angry red slash across her otherwise stony face. It was a pretty good indicator right from the start that they didn't want Zachary sticking his nose into their business.

"Mr. Goldman," she greeted stiffly, and motioned him into the living room, where he had visited with Vera before. "My mother will join us in a moment. She's just getting Rhys settled."

It seemed strange to be talking about getting a teenager settled like she would a fractious baby or toddler. From everything Zachary had heard, Rhys was emotionally traumatized, not mentally handicapped or developmentally delayed. But Zachary had yet to meet Rhys face-to-face, so he wasn't able to make any judgments.

Zachary browsed over the pictures on the mantel again. This time, he wasn't trying to identify the members of the family and their relationships to each other. He was looking for bruises or any other signs of abuse. He was looking for the way they stood together, touched, and looked at each other, searching for subtle clues showing who had been afraid of whom. Who had been abused and who had been the abuser. He saw no bruises on either Robin or Gloria. None on Rhys either, for that matter. Zachary was a good observer, but he didn't spot anything out of place in the pictures.

Vera came into the room, her head slightly down, feet shuffling across the floor.

"I really appreciate you seeing me again," Zachary told both women. "I know this isn't easy for you."

"I don't know what you're here for," Gloria complained. "I don't understand why the police are getting involved. All of this is just nonsense. Robin died of cancer. They can't go around exhuming everyone who has died of cancer, complaining that someone must have done it on purpose. People die. Especially people who are as ill as Robin was."

"I know," Zachary soothed. He kept the role he was playing planted firmly in his mind. He was supposed to be supporting their position, trying to prove to Bridget that there was nothing to be concerned about. No accident. No intention to kill. Just a woman who had come to the end of her natural life. "I'm sorry for disturbing you again like this. If we can just work through a few questions, I'm sure this will be the end of it and you can just go on with your lives and getting through the grieving process."

They all sat down. Zachary looked for a natural starting point.

"You've been talking to the police?"

"No, not yet, but I'm sure that's coming," Gloria declared. "They've been talking to the staff at the hospital. We've had reporters calling here. Reporters!" She said it like it was the most incredible thing she'd ever heard. "Calling here and asking questions about why the police would be opening an investigation into Robin's death. We had to keep telling them that we had no idea. Why would the police be looking into the death of a cancer patient?"

He wasn't about to tell them that he was the one who had prompted them to open a death investigation.

"One of them asked me if Robin had committed suicide," Vera said, shaking her head in confusion. "Why would they think that?"

"It's probably just a natural conclusion. She was terminally ill and she died before the doctors expected her to. Some patients do choose their own exit time."

"Robin would never have done that," Vera insisted.

"Even if she did," Gloria said, "it wouldn't be anyone's business but the family's. It's legal in Vermont. There wouldn't be any need for a police investigation into something legal."

"No, of course not," Zachary agreed. "If Robin had applied for physician assisted suicide, there would be a paper trail. The doctor would just show the paperwork to the police."

"That isn't what happened," Vera insisted.

"No," Zachary agreed. "I know it isn't."

"Your wife thinks it was a medical error." Gloria leaned forward, looking at Zachary intently. "She said that's what you're trying to find out. But that you don't believe it was."

"I don't know…" Zachary rubbed the back of his neck, attempting to look sheepish. "I don't like to second-guess my wife. She's the one who knew Robin. She's the one who lived at that hospital like Robin did… but," a regretful head shake, "I just don't see it. I think she's jumping at shadows."

"Exactly," Gloria agreed. "If Robin had decided to end her own life, she would have told us. She would have said something. And the doctors and nursing staff doing something to her…? They were nothing but gracious and helpful. Heaven knows Robin could be difficult!"

"Gloria," Vera objected. "Don't talk about your sister that way."

"It's not going to change anything now, is it? It's true. The way she complained and ran those nurses off their feet sometimes! But they were very kind and patient with her."

Zachary nodded. "They all seemed very professional there. I don't imagine it's an easy place to work."

"Not a job I would want," Gloria agreed.

"Especially a unit like that, with terminal patients. I don't think I'd be able to function, knowing so many of them were going to die. Unable to do anything to stop the progress of their disease. Not able to do anything for their pain, in the end."

Vera dabbed at watery eyes. "Even just having Robin there was so difficult. Seeing so many other people, some of them whose disease was even more advanced than Robin's, knowing she was going to go through that... it was so difficult."

Gloria sent a warning look toward her mother. "I imagine you would get used to it if you worked there," she said briskly.

"Maybe," Zachary said. "I'm not sure if I ever could."

Vera sniffled. "You wife is lucky that she went into remission. She might have still had to go through the pain of treatment, but she didn't have to face death the same way as Robin did when she was told the cancer had metastasized."

"Ma," Gloria warned again.

"You didn't ever wish... that there was something you could do to make Robin feel better?" Zachary ventured.

"Of course, all the time," Gloria said. "Who wouldn't? But there wasn't anything we could do. The doctor could give her pain prescriptions and stuff to help her sleep, but they couldn't take away the cancer. And if they couldn't do that, she knew she was going to die sooner or later."

"None of the staff ever suggested that they could give her higher doses of painkillers or sleeping pills? Or that you could?"

"No." Vera spoke the word sharply, almost making Zachary jump with her sudden vehemence. "No one ever said anything like that."

"Okay." He made a calming motion with his hands. "Sometimes it is done that way. Making a patient comfortable, even at the expense of their body's ability to keep functioning."

"No. We would never do that."

Zachary nodded that he understood.

"Gram?"

Zachary startled. He whipped his head around to find Rhys standing there, looking at them. Vera stood up immediately

"It's okay, sweetie. It's okay, it's nothing you need to worry about," she soothed. "Come on, why don't you show me your homework? You didn't get everything done that fast, did you?"

He shook his head. Zachary watched the skinny, sad-looking boy until they were back out of sight. He turned and looked at Gloria, trying to control his shock.

"It's a school holiday," Gloria advised, misinterpreting his surprise.

"I thought he couldn't speak."

"He can, physically," Gloria said. She took a deep breath and let it out. She rubbed at the fatigue lines on her forehead. "Obviously. He'll often go days without a word, and when he does, it's usually like that. Just a one- or two-word request. If you push him for more, he'll just shut down. They call it selective mutism, but that doesn't mean he can choose to talk or not. There are times when he is able to talk and times when he is not. Some kids with selective mutism are little chatterboxes at home but then can't get anything out at school. For Rhys, it's not like that. One word or phrase, or no words. Usually."

"How does he communicate with you? Does he sign? Write?"

"No. He... doesn't usually attempt any kind of direct communication. He is capable of speech, writing, gesture... but he just withdraws into himself. It's been like that ever since my father passed."

"How does he do his homework, then?" Zachary indicated the direction Rhys and Vera had gone with a jerk of his head.

"It depends what kind of work it is. He's best at math. No need for words, it's just like solving a puzzle. In other subjects, he's pretty good with short answer or multiple choice. Long answer..." Gloria shook her head. "He just can't seem to be able to tell us what's in his head, to communicate what he's thinking. He does modified assignments in place of essays or creative writing."

"Poor guy," Zachary said. What had happened ten years before that had traumatized him so much that he couldn't share his own thoughts, even about completely unrelated subjects? "It must be very difficult to parent a child you can't communicate with or understand."

He was thinking about the children he had met at Summit Learning Center, autistic or non-speaking, and how difficult it was for their parents to know what was bothering them or what else was going on in their heads. He had heard stories of children who were non-speaking and had no way to communicate more than the most basic needs for the first twenty years of life, but when introduced to alternative communication or assistive devices, were discovered to be capable of complex reasoning and deep self-reflection.

"I can communicate with him," Gloria disagreed. "He understands everything I tell him. That doesn't mean he listens to me all the time. Just like any teenager, he's got a mind of his own and he doesn't always want to do what mom tells him to. I can communicate with him just fine."

"But just because he understands you, that doesn't mean that you can understand what he is thinking and would want to tell you, if he could."

She shook her head in irritation. "You don't know anything about my boy, Mr. Goldman. Just because *you* don't know what he's thinking, that doesn't mean his own mama can't. I know what's going on in his head. I know my own boy."

But she wasn't the one who had responded to Rhys's call and left the room to help him. She wasn't the one who had been 'settling' him at the beginning of their interview. Zachary didn't want to antagonize her, so he shifted the conversation.

"How has Rhys been handling Robin's illness and death? It must be pretty hard on him."

"Why?" Gloria demanded.

"She's his aunt... part of his family. You all lived here together, before Robin got sick, didn't you? She's always been part of his household."

Gloria snorted and rolled her eyes. Zachary was taken aback by her response.

"They... weren't close, then?"

"My mother is close to Rhys. He idolized Papa. But Robin? No. She didn't have much use for him and he didn't have anything to do with her."

"You took him to the hospital to visit her, didn't you?"

"Yes, of course. That was the right thing to do."

What had Rhys thought of that? Had he been happy to go see her? Had he understood that she was dying? There was no indication that he was slow, so he must have understood that she was dying of cancer.

"That wasn't difficult for him? He didn't object to going?"

"Of course he didn't want to go. But that doesn't mean he was going to get away with not going. If I told him he had to come to the hospital with us, he had to come to the hospital with us. Sometimes he had homework or other things he had to do and I'd let him off, but most of the time... he came with us. He could sit quietly and patiently and visit like a grown-up."

"He could visit with her?" Zachary was getting more confused about Rhys's condition and abilities rather than less.

"He could sit with her. Hold her hand. Get things for her. Answer basic yes or no questions. I expected him to do his part, just like anyone else."

"I'm sorry for acting like a dunce," Zachary apologized. "I was told that he couldn't talk at all, and I had formed this picture in my mind about what his capabilities were... I don't mean to insult either of you by asking stupid questions."

Gloria's expression softened a little and she attempted a reassuring smile. "Of course not. They're not stupid questions. You're just trying to understand. Think of any teenage boy. You know how they tend to give closed, one-word answers to everything you ask? How was your day? Fine. How was the math test? Good. Did you do your homework? Not yet."

Zachary had to smile. "Yes."

"Well, Rhys is just the same, except most of the time he doesn't bother with the answer. You know what it is anyway. Just like you know that the average uncommunicative teenager is going to say 'fine' when you ask him how his day was. But you ask it anyway."

"Does he understand why Robin's death is being investigated?"

Gloria shook her head slightly, scowling. "I'm not sure *I* understand why it's being investigated. We haven't talked to him about it."

"I'd like the opportunity to talk to Rhys, if I could. I'd like to see what he thinks of all of this."

Her expression was immediately closed. "I don't see what good that would do you. How would talking to Rhys help you? He can't tell you anything. He doesn't know anything about what's been going on. No. There's no reason for you to talk to him."

Vera shuffled back into the room.

"Is he okay?" Gloria asked. But she didn't, Zachary noted, make any sign she would check in on him.

"He'll be fine," Vera assured her. She looked at Zachary. "It's all been very hard on him. He's already had to deal with one murder in his young life, so all of this is very disturbing. He doesn't like everything being so disrupted."

"Nobody *likes* it," Gloria snapped. "I wish they would just say everything is fine and send her back to the funeral home, so we can have her cremated and have the funeral. At this rate, who knows how long it will be before she's released? It could be months or years before we can lay her to rest." This comment was aimed at Vera, obviously intended to get her wound up.

"Years?" Vera reacted immediately. "How could it take years? They can't just keep her for that long. That's not right! How are we supposed to deal with this if we can't move on?"

"It won't be that long. Probably just a couple of days. The medical examiner is doing the autopsy right away," Zachary reassured her. "They'll release... her remains back to the funeral home very quickly."

"Can you guarantee that?" Gloria challenged. "You're not in

charge of the police department or medical examiner's office. They don't answer to you."

"I'm just telling you what's likely to happen. They don't keep bodies for that long."

"But they *could*."

Zachary squared his shoulders and didn't argue with her any further.

"I wonder if you could tell me some details about your husband's murder," Zachary said to Vera.

"His murder?" She looked confused, peering at Zachary and then looking uncertainly over at Gloria. "Why would you need to know that?"

"I know there probably isn't any connection between his murder and Robin's death, but it's just one of those things that I try to explore. You don't want there to be any loose ends."

"Robin was not murdered," Vera said.

"I didn't say she was. I just want to know the history. The big picture. Then I can tell Bridget that I've looked at everything. I haven't left any stones unturned."

"I don't know." Vera again looked at Gloria, trying to determine what she was supposed to do. "It was so long ago, I don't see how it could help you."

"I'm sure there's probably no connection," Zachary repeated. "I just want to cover all of the bases."

"Well… Clarence… that was my husband… he was home one night with Rhys. Just the two of them. Gloria and I were out. Clarence was babysitting. I mean, not that it's babysitting when it's your own grandson. When we got home… well, it was Gloria who discovered Clarence… Clarence's body."

Zachary looked over to Gloria to see what she had to contribute. She shook her head.

"It was the most awful thing I've ever seen," she said, her voice flat and unemotional. She could have been announcing the weather or the moves in a chess match. "He was there, at the kitchen table. He'd been shot at close range. The police said that he was probably startled by a burglar who thought the house was empty."

"Sitting at the table?" Zachary repeated. "No struggle?"

"No." Gloria shook her head. "Papa didn't hear too well. They were probably in the house and he never heard them… until they walked in on him."

"And Rhys? Where was he?"

"He was in his bed. He didn't see what happened."

Zachary frowned. If Rhys hadn't seen anything, then why had he been so deeply affected by it? And how did Gloria know if he saw anything or not if he had been uncommunicative since then and withdrew any time they asked him about it?

"Just stop it," Vera said. "That's all Rhys would say for days after it happened. *Just stop it. Just stop it.* Any time anyone tried to ask him about it, that was all he would say."

"But eventually, he stopped saying that too," Gloria sighed.

Zachary let a few moments of silence pass, waiting to see if there was anything else Vera or Gloria might have to offer. He let out his breath slowly. He wasn't sure he'd made any forward progress.

"There was one other thing I wanted to follow up on." He looked from one face to the other, watching them for any change. "I understand there were some domestic violence reports and a restraining order."

Their eyes widened and they turned toward each other simultaneously. Fear and anxiety. This was not something they had been expecting. Gloria recovered first.

"That was a long time ago," she said. "Ancient history."

"I see."

"I don't know why you're bringing it up. It doesn't have anything to do with Robin's death."

"Maybe not," Zachary said. "Just covering all bases. Was Lawrence abusive toward Robin?"

"Lawrence?" Gloria was incredulous. "No, no, certainly not

Lawrence. All of that business… that was when she was dating Stanley, not Lawrence."

Zachary remembered the family picture with Stanley in it. "Robin's fiancé."

"Yes. They were engaged, but then they broke up. Probably a good thing."

"Was that before or after Clarence's death?"

Gloria frowned in concentration. She looked over at Vera. "Ma, do you remember? It was after, wasn't it? Stanley was still around when Papa passed."

Vera's eyes were vague and misty as she searched the past. Eventually, she nodded. "Yes. It was after Clarence died."

"Was there something particular they broke up over? Was it because of abuse?"

"People change," Gloria said obliquely. "Robin wasn't the same person before she died as she was… ten years ago when she was with Stanley."

"A lot of women keep picking the same kind of men over and over again. They get rid of one abuser, only to pick a new one. But Robin straightened things out? She didn't pick another abuser?"

Gloria and Vera again exchanged a look.

"No, Lawrence wasn't abusive," Vera assured Zachary. "He's gentle as a kitten. He would never have hurt anyone. He is an artist."

"Sometimes people hide their real personalities, bury them deep down, so you don't see it unless you do something that triggers them. They might seem perfectly normal and reasonable on the surface, and it isn't until you're close to them that you discover their demons."

Zachary should know, he'd been there enough times.

"No. Not Lawrence. He doesn't get angry."

"What about emotional abuse? A woman might move from someone who is physically abusive to someone who is verbally and emotionally abusive and not understand that they're living with someone who is unreasonable and just perpetuating the cycle of abuse. Because he doesn't hit her, she thinks he's different, and that she's just not adequate."

Vera and Gloria shook their heads. Zachary watched them closely. They were hiding something. Those looks had meant something. But if Lawrence had been abusive, why would they hide the fact? If there were any chance she had been killed by an abuser, wouldn't they want it to be known? Wouldn't they want him to be put in jail?

Abusers could be charming to everyone outside their immediate family. They could fool everyone into thinking that the victim was lying or exaggerating about the abuser's behavior. Vera and Gloria might think that Lawrence was perfect, but the chances that he had never lost his temper were slim. Just because they hadn't seen it, that didn't mean he had never gotten angry and physically or verbally abusive.

"That all happened a long time ago," Gloria repeated. "It doesn't have anything to do with Robin's death."

Maybe. Or maybe it was a pattern. But Zachary agreed in order to put their minds at ease. "I understand. Sorry, I just have to make sure everything has been investigated. I want to be able to tell Bridget conclusively that Robin died as a result of the cancer, there was no outside interference. That's what you want too, isn't it?"

They both nodded, relaxing as he abandoned the topic.

"Those last days in the hospital… have you thought of anything that happened that was unusual? Any little thing that concerned you, even if it was just for an instant?"

Vera shook her head, staring vaguely into the distance. Gloria gave an exaggerated shrug. "Nothing. Don't you think we would have told the police?"

"Sometimes the things that bother us can be so small that we think they're not of any value. Or we think that no one will believe us or will think anything of it. So we just brush it off." He looked at both of them carefully, looking for any flicker of doubt.

"No," Gloria insisted.

"None of the nurses did anything that concerned you? None of them treated you like they didn't want you there?"

"We would have told the police."

Zachary nodded his understanding. He prepared to get up.

"Do you mind… could I use your facilities before I go?"

Gloria scowled and seemed to be about to deny him access, but Vera nodded, always the gracious host. "Of course you can. The bathroom is just in this hallway," Vera gestured, "to the left. Last door."

"Thanks. Too much coffee today, I'm thinking!"

Zachary headed for the bathroom before Gloria could try to override her mother and tell Zachary he'd have to find a public restroom on his way home. He found the bathroom, shut and locked the door, and turned on the exhaust fan to help muffle any noise.

He opened the medicine cabinet behind the mirror and scanned the rows of bottles of liquids and pills. It had occurred to him that even if all of the hospital's insulin was accounted for, Vera or Gloria could be diabetic and have their own insulin prescriptions. A few bottles had prescription labels, most of them in Vera's name, but he didn't see any insulin. Zachary had no idea if any of the prescriptions would be poisonous in the wrong dose. He had to assume that they would be.

He turned a few of the bottles so that all of the labels were facing out, then used his phone to take pictures of a few at a time. There were some nonprescription sleep aids, painkillers, vitamin and mineral supplements, and one of the same immune boosters as Zachary had picked up from the hospital pharmacy. Nothing unusual. Nothing he wouldn't find in any other medicine cabinet in any other home. Zachary closed the cabinet quietly and turned on the water.

While he ran the tap, he opened and closed the drawers of the vanity. Bandages, tweezers, toothpaste, razors, feminine products. Nothing unexpected or unusual. Not that he'd expected to find a prescribed lethal dose or anything with a skull and crossbones on it. There was no sign of rat poison, household cleaners, or any chemicals that would have made more sense stored in a garden shed.

He hadn't expected to find anything, but he was still a little disappointed. It would have been nice to turn the murder weapon over to the police. A big ego boost.

But that wasn't going to happen.

17

Zachary checked his voicemail as he got back into his car to see whether Bridget had called. He was also hoping for a call back from Bowman. Zachary had left a message for him early in the morning before he actually got on shift, asking him about the police incident files on Robin. If the records went back ten years, they would have to pull files back from storage. They wouldn't still be on site. There were computer files, or Campbell wouldn't have known any details. Hopefully, Zachary could get printouts of those. But he wanted the physical file too. He knew from experience that there could be important reports or notes on the file that hadn't made it to the computer. A computer record from ten years before would only be a summary, not the full documentation.

There were no messages from Bridget or from Bowman. But there was one from Kenzie's work number. Did they already have preliminary results from the autopsy?

Zachary got comfortable in the car, then listened to the message, which only told him to call Kenzie back, with no hint of what she wanted to talk about.

Zachary tapped to call back, and Kenzie answered in a couple of rings, obviously not in the middle of assisting with an autopsy.

"Hi, Kenz. It's Zachary."

"Where've you been?"

"Uh… interviewing witnesses. Joshua Campbell visited last night last night and—"

Kenzie cut across him. "I was trying to get ahold of you."

"Did you find something?"

"Well, we can't be sure yet. There are still plenty of slides and fluids to be tested. We didn't identify anything that confirmed foul play on gross visual examination. There are some organ abnormalities; we have to test to see whether it is cancer or something else."

"Okay. I guess we didn't really expect to find anything until the labs are done. But insulin wouldn't show up, right?"

"No. For that, you'll have to wait for the results of the hospital inventory against the charts."

"I checked in the family's medicine cabinet in case they had insulin." Zachary was proud of himself for thinking of this. "But there wasn't any in the cabinet."

There was silence for a few seconds from Kenzie before she broke the news to him. "Insulin wouldn't be in the medicine cabinet. It would be in the fridge."

"Oh." Zachary's face grew warm, and he was glad she couldn't see him. "I didn't realize that." He looked at the house. Did he dare go back and say he needed a drink? Even that wouldn't get him access to the fridge. He'd need some other ruse, and he couldn't think of any that would work. "I guess we'll have to wait to see if the police can get a search warrant."

"Yeah," Kenzie agreed. "But so far there isn't any reason to suspect the family of anything, so I doubt they will."

"So that's why you called me? Just to let me know the autopsy was done and you were waiting on the labs?"

"Yes… and I wondered if you wanted to do something. Maybe take in a movie…?"

Zachary was startled. Usually, the most he could get Kenzie to do with him was to go to dinner. And then only when he had medical documents to go through with her. It seemed that it didn't rain, but it poured. On one hand, he had Bridget back in his life, however peripherally, and the chance that he might somehow be able to get her back, and on the other he had Kenzie, suddenly interested in more than just a free meal and friendly chat. He was reluctant to lead Kenzie on, in case he could work things out with Bridget.

"I'm not sure when I'll be free. I've got this case to work, and I still have some other surveillance and insurance jobs I need to put some time into."

"You still need to eat."

"Well, yes, you just said… a movie."

"If you don't want to do a movie, we can do dinner, like usual. That would be okay, wouldn't it?"

"Uh…"

"What? Come on, Zachary. You're breaking for dinner at some point."

"No, probably just grabbing something on the run. I have a lot of work to be done."

"Fine. I get the message. I guess we'll talk again when one of us has something to say." Her tone was hard and brittle Zachary couldn't fail to hear her disappointment and confusion over being turned down.

But he couldn't lead her on when he might still have a chance to get somewhere with Bridget.

Having told Kenzie that he had a lot of other investigative work to do, Zachary decided he'd better do it. He didn't want to get too far behind on his other cases, especially when he wasn't getting paid to investigate Robin's death. If he wanted to be able to pay for his apartment, he needed to be making money. So he went home and tackled the mountain of paperwork he'd been ignoring, did some background searches, and filled out some final reports and invoices on cases he had completed but not yet been paid for.

After a couple of hours, his brain was feeling wrung out.

Zachary pushed the pile of paper aside and logged into one of the social networking sites he had an account on. He told himself he was only there to work background on the subjects of his current investigations, but his eyes were caught by a red-flagged icon. A connection request. He clicked to see who it was, and stared at Rhys Salter's name and photo.

It would seem that Rhys was a little more communicative than Gloria had led Zachary to believe. True, Zachary hadn't asked whether he was active in any online communities, but he'd assumed by her description of his communication abilities that he wouldn't be interested in messaging with friends.

Zachary accepted the request, and once he was connected with Rhys, clicked through his profile to see when it had been set up, who he was friends with, and what he had posted on his timeline recently.

Was it really Rhys? Or was it someone masquerading as him? Anyone connected with the case could have set up a dummy profile for the boy, working on the assumption that Zachary would want to talk to him, which of course, he did.

Everything seemed to be real. The profile was a couple of years old, and most of the friends who had connected with Rhys were boys his age, some at the school Rhys would attend, and some international, who maybe he had met through online gaming or some other shared-interest group. He posted to his timeline sporadically. Nothing with verbose introductions. Usually, just sharing someone else's material, sometimes with a keyword or a friend's name.

There was a colored tag on Rhys's profile that indicated he was currently online. Whether he really was, or whether he had just left his phone or computer on with the app running, Zachary didn't know. He clicked on the chat icon.

"Hi, Rhys, thanks for connecting with me."

There was no immediate reply. Zachary left the tab loaded and switched to another site, forcing himself to work instead of staring at the chat window with Rhys waiting for an answer. When he allowed himself to switch back for a look, he saw a picture of a dog.

"Is that you? He looks sad." Zachary included an arrow pointing up to the basset hound, who did look worried and seriously depressed.

Rhys responded faster this time, with a sad face emoticon.

Zachary typed back, "I'm sorry about you losing your aunt."

There was another long delay. Zachary decided to tackle his paper filing, which he could do while keeping an eye on the screen so he would know the next time Rhys posted. When he finally did, it was a picture of the three women with Rhys. Vera, Gloria, and Robin smiling, arms around each other, with Rhys in front of them. He had been younger in the picture. Below the women's chins. Now, he was probably at least as tall as his grandma, maybe taller than his mom too.

Zachary studied the picture. As with the ones in the photo album Vera had shown him, Rhys was not smiling. Maybe he was incapable of smiling. Zachary could only imagine how many photographers might have told him to smile for a picture. And still, Rhys didn't. He just stared at the camera. Though the women were all smiling, Zachary wasn't sure they were genuine. Their stances looked awkward and separate, even though they were holding each other. Like they had just been posed that way and wouldn't have touched each other otherwise.

Or was he just reading what he wanted to into the picture?

"She was pretty," Zachary posted. "You must miss her a lot."

There was no response from Rhys.

It was almost the end of the day when Bowman called Zachary back.

"Running into some problems with these incident reports, Zach."

Zachary stopped what he was doing on the computer to give

the phone his attention. "What kind of problems?" he asked, thinking of failed searches or database corruption. Bowman knew his way around the system and didn't usually run into any problems.

"I've got brass that don't think you need access to these records."

"What? Campbell said I should have a look at them. He said he wouldn't block them."

"Then it must be someone further up the food chain. I'm not sure who it is, but I'm getting a lot of push back. They want the death investigation closed and they want you shut down."

Zachary swore under his breath. Up until then, he'd been pleasantly surprised at how well the police investigation was going. He hadn't dared expect that they would think he had enough to open an investigation in the first place, and then having Joshua Campbell running the investigation at the scene meant he could continue to investigate without fear of running into cops who thought they had the exclusive right to investigate and to use Zachary as a punching bag.

"I should have known it was going too smoothly."

"Yeah, it should never be easy," Bowman agreed with a laugh. "If it's easy, we obviously aren't doing our job. So what do you want to do?"

"What are my options? Are you telling me you won't give me the information? Were you told to turn down my request?"

"I was told to put you off. Stall you. Make it take longer. If they can close the death investigation and stall you for long enough, it will all just go away."

"How can they shut down the death investigation? There hasn't been a determination yet."

"They're rushing the medical examiner. Don't ask me, I'm not privy to all of the details. They're saying if he hasn't found any evidence of foul play, they should close the file."

"But all of the evidence hasn't been processed. They're still waiting on lab results."

"It's obviously political, Zach. My guess is that the family has reached out to someone and is threatening to go to the media. Not everybody is of the opinion that there was enough evidence to recommend opening an investigation in the first place. They don't like seeing your name on a case."

"Incredible," Zachary growled. "Well, they can't close it without the agreement of the medical examiner, so get me my files. Or I will go to the press myself with how the police department is participating in a cover-up."

He could hear the grin in Bowman's voice. "I'll see what I can do, Zachary. We certainly wouldn't want any bad press."

"Thank you."

"Just remember, there is a family out there who can't bury their dead yet, and that doesn't play well either. They're not going to stay quiet for long, and they want her cremated."

"Which means we can't exhume her later to finish what we started."

"There's only so much you can test for once the body's been burned."

18

It had taken Zachary some time to track down Stanley Green, Robin's ex-fiancé. There were too many Stanley Greens around, too many of them the right age or race. But eventually, he was able to whittle the list down and identify the correct Stanley Green.

Zachary anticipated that Stanley would not want to set up a meeting with him, so he hung around at the building that housed the offices of the copper mining company Stanley worked for and watched for him to come out. It was getting late, and he wondered whether he had missed Stanley or maybe he hadn't been scheduled to work that day, when he finally spotted the face that he had memorized.

"Stanley Green?"

Stanley turned around and looked at Zachary. Maybe it wasn't the best idea to be coming up on a man unexpectedly in the gathering dusk, but Zachary was sure that when Stanley Green compared his height and bulk with Zachary's, he wouldn't be concerned. Stanley looked him over, tried to place him, then shook his head.

"Do I know you from somewhere?"

"No. I just wanted to talk to you for a few minutes. I'm taking part in the investigation of the death of a woman you used to be engaged to." He saw comprehension starting to form in Stanley's eyes. "Robin Salter."

Stanley shook his head. "Robin died? How did that happen?"

"Well, the how is what we're currently trying to figure out. She was in hospital. She had terminal cancer. But as it turns out, someone might have hurried the process along a little." It was a stretch, but the main points were correct, so Zachary didn't worry about it.

"Who would do a thing like that?" Stanley shook his head. "Well, I haven't had any contact with Robin for a long time. I don't think I can help you."

"I'll buy you a drink. Just a short chat and then you can get on with your evening."

Stanley considered this. Zachary was surprised he was so reluctant, given his size. He could probably break Zachary in two. It wouldn't be much of a fight, even if Zachary had been inclined to show off his rather limited physical prowess.

"Alright," Stanley finally agreed. "There's a bar about six blocks down this street." He pointed. "Big orange sign outside. Meet me there."

Zachary couldn't be sure Stanley was going to meet him there, he might just as easily be giving himself an opportunity to skip out and avoid the talk. After watching Stanley head into the employee parking lot to get his car, Zachary hurried to his. He rolled up to the Farmhouse Tavern at about the same time as Stanley, and hurried to catch up with him, feeling like a toddler on his short legs when compared with Stanley's.

They got a table and Stanley took a careful look at Zachary. Apparently unworried by his interrogator, he leaned back, relaxing after a long day of work. A waitress came by and they ordered their beers. Zachary didn't try to talk to him until they both had their drinks. Zachary took a sip of his. It had been far too long since he'd had beer. He would have to limit his intake to one, and that wouldn't be easy. He took another swallow and put it down, a few inches farther away than was comfortable. Stanley's eyes took this in, but he wasn't concerned by Zachary's strange behavior.

"What was your name? Who are you?"

Zachary slid a business card across the table to Stanley. "Zachary. Goldman Investigations."

Stanley looked at the card and considered it for a while before sliding it into his shirt pocket. "How did Robin die?"

"That's under investigation. She died in her sleep at the hospital, but the timing was unexpected. It looks like something might have been administered to her IV." Not strictly true, maybe, but it was enough to hook Stanley.

"Somebody gave her something in her IV? That seems rather…" Stanley searched for a word. "Brash."

Zachary nodded. "It's a strange case."

"And what do you want me for? Like I said, I haven't seen her in years. I wouldn't have any reason to track her down after we were both out of each other's lives."

"Well, from what I hear, there was a restraining order. It seems like you did need something to keep you apart back then."

"Restraining orders don't last forever. If I remember right, it was only for six months. And it was never violated. We *were* able to go on with our lives."

"Good for you. Well… I didn't come here because I thought you did anything to her. I mean, it's always a remote possibility, but I don't think anyone seriously thought you might have something to do with it. I think you would probably have drawn attention at the hospital, and no one claimed to have seen you there."

"That's because I wasn't."

Stanley took a long drag on his beer. He eyed it, probably wondering if he should just down it all at once and then get out of there, saying nothing more to Zachary. But his curiosity kept him there.

"Then what are you looking for from me?"

"Background. You knew Robin back at a very difficult time in her life. You were accepted as a member of her family. Who better to talk to about the personal dynamics?"

"Her family."

"You knew her father before he was killed?"

"Yes. He was still alive when we got engaged." Stanley stopped and said nothing more, even though Zachary gave him plenty of time.

"What was he like?"

"He was… the patriarch… he dictated how things were to be run in the family. No one ever really challenged him."

"What kind of things?"

"Pretty much everything. He's the one who decided to take Gloria and her baby in. He set the house rules. Mealtimes, curfew, bedtimes."

"Robin would have been in her twenties, wouldn't she? He gave her a curfew and bedtime?"

"Look what happened to Gloria. He had to be sure."

"What happened to Gloria…?"

"Her pregnancy."

"Oh." Zachary nodded. He'd lived in his share of homes with seemingly bizarre, arbitrary rules. He never did understand how they were supposed to keep him from getting into trouble. He got into trouble for not being able to follow the rules. It seemed like the only reason they were imposed was so that families would have a good excuse to punish him or to send him on to the next place. "I've noticed they're somewhat… religious."

Stanley shrugged.

"And I have met Vera," Zachary said. "Seems like she might be getting a little forgetful. Or is that just part of her personality?"

"Forgetful? No, I don't think so. She never seemed to have any trouble when I was around. But that was a while back, now."

"How did you and Robin meet?"

"She was temping at the company I worked for. Not Copper," Stanley jerked his head the direction of the building they had come from. "Another company. We saw each other a few times…. I asked her if she wanted to go out… things progressed."

"What was she like? I've heard descriptions from a few different people, but I never knew her myself."

"She was a strong woman. I found that attractive. Good-looking and well-dressed. Not wishy-washy like other women I had dated. You ask them what they want, and they ask what you want. Can't answer a question or express an opinion. Robin wasn't like that. She had definite opinions and she wasn't going to keep quiet because she thought someone else might be of another opinion."

Zachary thought about Bridget. "It can be exhausting to have to make all of the decisions for two people. Having someone who is willing to take charge and not just be blown around… that can be a big relief."

"Yeah. Robin did everything well. I thought she was an amazing person."

"I heard from the hospital staff that she sometimes complained. She was irritated by things that weren't quite the way she wanted them. Does that sound like the way she was when you were together?"

Stanley took a pull at his beer. "Robin was never afraid to lodge a complaint. If we were at a restaurant and the service or the food wasn't top notch, you can bet she would have something to say about it. She knew what she wanted. And she knew how to persuade other people around her to do things the 'right' way."

"And after a while, that started to get old and to grate on you." Zachary knew how relationships worked. A difference that initially brought a couple together could quickly turn into a rift that separated them. Stanley had been attracted to a strong, opinionated woman, but then he had started to dislike the fact that she was so strong and opinionated all of the time. He started to crave someone who was softer and more moldable.

Stanley frowned at his beer. "She got more extreme. More… angry."

And it had become a power struggle. Robin getting angry when she didn't get exactly what she wanted, Stanley trying to change her mind and bend her to his will. The anger had escalated. The violence had escalated and that was how they had ended up with their names on multiple domestic violence complaints and a protective order.

Zachary backed off. He didn't want to make Stanley defensive.

"And Gloria? She was another hard-headed woman?" he suggested.

Stanley shook his head. "She was messed up. She could clean up nicely, put on a good show for a few hours, but she was an addict. A party girl. She was living at home most of the time, but she hadn't settled down. Vera and Clarence were mom and dad to Rhys. Gloria wasn't there most of the time. She didn't know how to be responsible and take care of her baby."

"That must have been hard on them. You don't expect to be raising a child again at that age."

"Plenty of people do, though. They loved Rhys, just adored him. And he loved them right back. They'd only raised girls, not boys, so they could suddenly do things that the girls had never been interested in. Woodworking, hunting, fishing. Guy stuff. Rhys was the little man of the house."

And now Rhys was surrounded by women, his voice literally silenced. Did he pursue any of those interests at school? So many school programs were getting cut, Zachary didn't know if they had shop anymore.

"When Clarence died, Rhys was about five?"

"Yeah. About that."

"And you were still together with Robin for a while after that. So you saw how it affected Rhys? How it affected the different members of the family?"

"Poor little guy." Stanley stared intently at his beer. "Rhys just worshiped Clarence. He loved him to bits. After the shooting…he became like a different person. He went from a smiley, fun-loving kid to being… broken and withdrawn. No one could reach him.

And I tried. I really did. I was the only other man around, not counting Gloria's one-night-stands. I tried, but I couldn't help him."

Zachary nodded. Rhys was still suffering ten years later. That wasn't something that a sometimes father-figure could have fixed with a few visits.

"Do you have any idea what might have happened to Robin? I know you haven't seen them, I just mean as someone who knew the family dynamics at one time… could you see anyone stepping in and… intervening? For any reason. It might have been a mercy killing or assisted suicide. I'm just wondering if anything like that made sense to you."

Stanley raised his glass to take a drink, blocking Zachary's view of his face for a few seconds. He set it down firmly on the table. "I was lucky to get out of there when I did. There were things happening in that family… it was very unhealthy. People… are not always what they seem. Relationships that look healthy from the outside… sometimes they aren't."

Zachary thought about Clarence. He seemed to be at the center of everything. The patriarch set the example for the home. He was the one Rhys had been so attached to. He was the one who had been murdered. If he had been abusive, it would explain Gloria's rebellious years and Robin choosing an abusive partner. Both behaviors were common patterns in abused children. Had he been physically abusive? Verbally? Sexually?

"Clarence's murder was never solved," Zachary said.

"No? I didn't follow it after Robin and I broke up. It's too bad they never caught the killer."

"Did you have any suspicions at the time about how it might have gone down?"

"No. An unknown intruder. Burglar, they speculated at the time." Stanley shrugged.

"You don't think it was anyone in the family?"

Stanley just stared at Zachary.

"The wife is always the prime suspect, isn't she?" Zachary

suggested. "If the family dynamics were toxic… maybe someone decided to take matters into their own hands."

"Why don't you ask the police that? That's their job, isn't it?" Stanley picked up his glass, drained the last of the beer, and stood up as he put the glass down. "You want my advice?" he asked, leaning aggressively into Zachary's personal space. "Get out of this case. Don't walk; run away. Get as far away from it as possible, because nothing good can come of you sticking your nose into it."

Zachary sat there, frozen, for several minutes after Stanley was gone.

He should have expected the intimidation tactics. Stanley was a big man, used to throwing his weight around. He'd been violent with Robin. If Zachary looked into Stanley's background, he'd probably find a long line of abused girlfriends.

Stanley Green would be a dangerous man to cross.

When Zachary got home, he threw a frozen dinner into the microwave to heat and sat down at the computer to check his email. He'd have to be sure to check his social networks for anything further from Rhys. He didn't want to push the boy, but he was really hoping that if Rhys had something to say, he'd make contact again.

Thinking back to the conversation with Stanley, Zachary shuddered. If Clarence had been abusive, then maybe it hadn't been a chance burglary. Maybe it was just set up to look that way. Was Rhys really so traumatized by his grandfather being killed while he slept? Or had he actually seen what had happened? Vera and Gloria could be lying through their teeth.

It was even conceivable that Rhys had been the killer himself. Gun accidents happened. It seemed like not a week went by that Zachary didn't hear some horror story about a two-year-old shooting his mother in the back of the head after taking her gun out of her purse. Something like that was far more likely to cause

Rhys's trauma than just being asleep in his bed. If he hadn't seen or heard or been a part of what had happened, then why was he so damaged?

Zachary took a quick glance at his direct messages, but he didn't have anything there from Rhys. The boy hadn't posted on his own timeline either. Maybe he'd been grounded from using the computer or had been too busy with homework or extra-curricular activities to check in. Or maybe he was dealing with the emotional fallout of Robin's death.

Zachary retrieved his dinner from the microwave before checking his email. Way too many times he just left a dinner in the microwave, completely forgotten, until it started to stink or he opened the microwave to warm something else up. He sat down at the computer and opened his email inbox.

There was an email from Kenzie with a red flag beside it. Zachary opened the message and scanned it quickly.

"You're not answering your phone again. Found something. Call me."

His heart started pumping twice as hard and fast. Zachary put his hand on his pocket, but his phone wasn't there. He looked quickly over his desk and nearly flipped his dinner right off looking under papers for his phone. He jumped up and carried the dinner with him back into the kitchen. There his phone lay on the counter waiting for him. He turned on the screen and saw missed calls and a voicemail from Kenzie. The voicemail would say the same thing as her email. *Call me.* She wouldn't tell him in a voicemail what they had found. Zachary stabbed his finger at the screen to call her back, and decided abruptly it was time to sit down. His legs were shaking so badly that if there hadn't been a kitchen chair right there, he would have ended up sitting on the floor. He put the phone to his ear and waited for Kenzie to answer. It rang through to voicemail. He looked to see which number he had called, and switched to her cell phone instead. It too went to voicemail.

"Come on," Zachary urged. "Come on, answer!" He tried the

call again, praying she would notice her phone ringing and pick it up. It wasn't late enough for her to be in bed yet, but she could be having a bath to relax or be out with friends for dinner. She hadn't asked him to dinner; but then, he hadn't answered her calls.

"Zachary."

"Kenzie, hi! I'm sorry I missed your call. I was in the middle of an interview. I didn't even notice it ringing. It was pretty intense…"

"Well, maybe it doesn't matter to you what we found out. I mean, the woman is dead, after all."

"No, of course it matters. I was continuing my investigation. Bowman told me Dr. Wiltshire was getting a lot of political pressure to close the case. I know he's not going to do that prematurely, but I want to make sure that I've done everything I can to—"

"You really run off at the mouth when you're in trouble, did you know that?"

Zachary closed his mouth and tried to stop giving her excuses. He needed to be businesslike. He wasn't a fourteen-year-old trying to explain why he didn't have his homework assignments to hand in yet again. He was a professional. He hadn't been neglecting the case. He wasn't sure why Kenzie was so pissed at him, but he was just going to have to deal with that. Like a professional.

"That's better," Kenzie snapped, though she sounded irritated that he had stopped talking. He just couldn't win. "We had something show up in the labs that may be cause of death."

"What kind of thing?"

"I told you that some of the organs had irregularities that needed to be checked out. We prepared a number of slides of the pancreas, heart, and liver. And of course, we ordered whatever we could think of to test the blood for."

"Uh-huh."

"It isn't unusual for a cancer patient to have irregular results in their blood tests. Low white blood cell count, red blood cells, platelets, anemia…"

"Right. And blood sugar. Nurse Betty said that Robin's blood sugar had been high. That's why she was getting insulin."

"Who's telling the story here, you or me?" On another day, Kenzie would have said it in a flirtatious, teasing voice. But her cutting tone told Zachary that he was treading on thin ice and had better shut up.

"Sorry. I didn't mean to interrupt."

"She had diabetes because most of the insulin-producing cells in her pancreas had died," Kenzie told him.

"Ouch."

"The whole point of chemotherapy is to kill cells. We just want to kill more of the cancer cells and fewer of the body's healthy cells. It's a delicate balance."

Zachary made an encouraging noise, determined not to interrupt her flow again.

"So it's not unusual to cause something like this. It's one of the risks that patients are warned about. There's probably a waiver somewhere that Robin had to sign saying that she understood all of the risks."

"Right." Zachary tried to demonstrate that he was listening and fully engaged. "Is that what happened to the liver too?"

"The liver is a really important organ. It performs a lot of functions that we don't know how to replicate artificially. With other organs, even though they are vital for survival, we can replicate artificially for some time to prolong life. We can pump blood through a bypass machine, clean it with dialysis, inflate the lungs with a respirator. But liver function is very complicated. We can't replace a liver artificially. Once cancer reaches the liver, the patient's days are numbered."

"Robin's cancer had gotten into her liver?"

"No. Dr. Wiltshire knew there was something off with the liver when he examined it, but it wasn't cancer. There were no masses and the slides didn't show any cancerous cells."

Zachary held his breath, not sure whether he should prompt her to go on, or just wait for it.

"What the liver showed us was iron overload," Kenzie finally finished.

"Iron?"

"When there is too much iron in the blood, the liver tries to store it. But it can only store so much before it becomes overloaded. The stores of iron damage the liver, and if the iron is not removed from the body quickly enough, it results in death."

"How would she get too much iron in her liver? Or her blood? Was that because of her cancer?"

"No. Cancer often causes anemia, which she had been diagnosed with, but that is too little iron, not too much."

"And it's treated by administering iron?" Zachary guessed.

"Bingo. It's going to be harder to figure out if they overdosed her with iron than with insulin. It isn't controlled the same way. I'm not sure there will be any way for them to tell if she was given the wrong dosage or concentration."

Zachary let his breath out in a slow stream. "So it *was* medical error."

"Looks that way."

"Was liver failure the cause of death?"

"Maybe. She also had damage to her heart. Cardiomyopathy was observed. She probably tired quickly with exertion. She may have had chest pain or skipping beats."

"She did. I remember that." It was her roommate, Chenka, who had mentioned chest pain. Surprisingly, her family and the medical staff hadn't been specific about the kind of pain she was having. "Does that mean she might have had a heart attack?"

"Hard to tell whether her liver or heart failed first. They were both in bad shape."

"What other symptoms would iron overdose have?"

"Joint pain. Stomach and digestive issues. Bronzing of the skin, but that's difficult to discern on someone who is already dark-skinned. Diabetes."

"The iron caused the diabetes?"

"Possibly. We can't really tell whether it was the chemo or the iron. We didn't find any cancerous cells in the pancreas."

Zachary's brain was churning through the possibilities. "How long does iron take to kill? It must have been given to her before that Wednesday."

"Two to five days. That matches up with her chart. There was a significant increase in her pain meds beginning the Monday before she died."

"And was the hospital giving her iron then?"

"They started her on an iron protocol the week before."

"Doctor error," Zachary repeated. "Bridget was right all along." Kenzie sniffed.

"I'll have to give her a call." Zachary looked at the time on his phone. "I'll call you back, okay? I'm going to see if I can get her before bed."

Kenzie didn't even say goodbye before cutting the connection.

Zachary dialed Bridget's number. He tapped in the numbers manually, not looking up her contact record. He knew all of her contact details by heart. It was satisfying to punch them in one at a time. He savored the moment. He was no knight in shining armor, but he had accomplished what he had set out to do. He had fulfilled her quest and earned her gratitude.

"Hello?" Bridget obviously answered without checking the caller ID beforehand. "Oh, Zachary. Can I call you back? I was just going to—"

"No. No, this will just take a second, but it's important."

"Well?" She was impatient. "What is it?"

"Robin Salter didn't die of cancer. You were right. She died of iron overdose."

"Iron? I thought iron was good. It can kill you?"

"I guess more isn't always better. Your body can only handle so much, then the liver starts to store it. If there's too much for the liver to store, it can result in death."

"Wow. I remember they gave me iron when I was there. They said I was anemic from the treatments."

"Robin was too. But it looks like they gave her too much."

"Is this official? Does that mean they change her death certificate?"

"I… guess so. I just got this from the medical examiner's office—"

"From Kenzie, you mean."

"Kenzie is at the medical examiner's office."

"Yes, luckily for you." There was a hint of a sneer in her voice.

"Lucky for you too," Zachary countered. "I would never have gotten the death investigation opened without her."

There was a call waiting alert. Zachary pulled his phone away from his ear to look at his screen. It hadn't been his call waiting, but Bridget's.

"I have to take that," Bridget said. "Can we talk later?"

"Sure. Of course. You know how to reach me—"

But Bridget had already hung up.

19

Zachary decided the next morning that a courtesy visit to the Salter family was probably in order. The medical examiner's office or the police department would undoubtedly contact them at some point, but Zachary's investigation had started everything and he wanted to be sure that they were told what had been discovered, rather than waiting for the information to get to them through the grapevine or at some press conference.

Vera was the only one home. Still in a bathrobe, she looked at Zachary blearily, as if she'd just gotten out of bed and wasn't sure who he was.

"Zachary Goldman," Zachary reminded her. "I'm the investigator who has been looking into Robin's death."

"Oh, yes," Vera nodded and motioned Zachary into the house. The front entryway and living room were somewhat in disarray, as if caught between a weekend binge and Monday cleanup that had never been completed. Zachary detoured around what appeared to be Rhys's book bag and a chip bowl and sat down with Vera.

"Are you here by yourself?" He was a little concerned about her being left to her own devices. Presumably she could be trusted on her own, but Zachary was uncomfortable with how distant she appeared to be.

"Yes. Gloria had to take Rhys…" Vera trailed off, clearly unable to remember the details. To school, probably, or maybe a therapy appointment, and then off to work herself. There wasn't really anyone available to keep an eye on Vera if Gloria had to work during the day.

"Are you okay here on your own? Is there anything you need?"

"Oh, of course. I've been on my own for years. I can manage. The kids will be home after school."

Zachary took a quick look at the time on his phone. That wouldn't be for hours yet. But that was presumably the same every other day, and if Vera were unable to take care of herself, they would have found other arrangements for her.

"I wanted to let you know that I heard back from the medical examiner's office with preliminary details of what they had found in the lab work they did for Robin." He intentionally did not use the word 'autopsy,' which would probably just upset her. 'Lab work' sounded much less invasive.

"For Robin?" Vera repeated. "Why?"

"To find out why she died."

"It was the cancer, wasn't it?" She seemed confused, as if she'd been unaware until then that there was any question of Robin's cause of death.

"That was what the doctor thought initially," Zachary agreed. "But we have looked into it further and done some testing, and it turns out that there were actually some other issues to be considered."

"Oh?" Vera cocked her head.

"When will Gloria be home?" Zachary looked down at his phone again.

"I don't know. She usually gets home after Rhys."

"Maybe I should wait until then. So there's someone here with you."

"What is it? What did you find out?"

"Well… it looks like the medical staff made a mistake on the amount of iron she was to be given. I don't know whether the wrong amount was prescribed, or if they gave the wrong dosage. But Robin died of an overdose of iron, not the cancer itself."

"Iron?"

"Yes. Her liver couldn't process the amount that was given to her, and she…"

"She was anemic," Vera said, demonstrating that her grasp of the situation was better than Zachary had anticipated. "They had to give her iron for her anemia."

"Yes. But it looks like they might have given her too much. They *did* give her too much."

"She needed iron."

"Yes, she did."

Vera shook her head. "Gloria should talk to them."

"I'm afraid it's too late. They already gave Robin too much. You remember… she passed away, don't you?"

"How could I forget?" Vera demanded.

"Okay, I just wasn't sure. Yes, maybe Gloria should talk to the medical examiner's office. They can confirm their finding and give her the details."

Vera nodded. She looked around. "Where are they? When is she going to get home?"

"After school." Zachary refrained from looking at his phone again. "Is there anyone who checks in on you during the day?"

"No. I'm fine here by myself. I've looked after myself all my life."

Zachary was still uncomfortable leaving her there alone. He turned on his phone and pressed redial on Bridget's number. Bridget knew Robin's family; maybe she would want to visit with Vera for a while and make sure she was okay. Or maybe she knew someone who could be called to deal with it. It was outside of Zachary's usual experience.

He waited for Bridget's impatient answer, but it went instead to voicemail and Bridget's light, pleasant greeting. Zachary hesitated, then suggested that she call him back. He hung up and looked at Vera again.

"Just one more call," he promised.

This time, he called Joshua Campbell. He might not be exactly the person to contact, but he could probably put Zachary on to the right person.

Campbell picked up after a few rings. "Campbell."

"Hey, it's Zachary. I'm at Mrs. Salter's house, and—"

"What the hell are you doing there?" Campbell demanded. "Didn't you get the message that the case is closed?"

"Well, not exactly… Kenzie told me the preliminary findings—"

"Then you know it was medical error and the file is closed. Why are you still questioning the family? It's no wonder I've got the brass on my back! You never know when to leave things well enough alone!"

"I… wasn't questioning them. I just came over to make sure they knew what was going on, and…"

Campbell sighed in exasperation. "And what?"

"I'm a little worried about Mrs. Salter being here alone. Her daughter is away and I'm not sure she's okay to be here by herself."

"She's upset?"

Zachary looked at Vera sitting there on the couch, staring at one of the pictures nearby. He got up and walked into the kitchen so that she wouldn't overhear him. Similar to the living room, it looked as if nothing had been cleaned up since the weekend.

"No," he said in a low voice. "She seems forgetful and maybe not capable of looking after herself if something was to happen."

"Call the daughter."

"The daughter already knows and is the one who left her alone like this. If I call her, she's just going to tell me that her mother is fine and to butt out of something that's not my business."

"Not bad advice."

Zachary didn't say anything. Maybe Campbell hadn't been the best person to call for advice.

"Okay, Zach," Campbell acquiesced. "I'll get a couple of officers over there for a welfare check. If they think she shouldn't be left alone, they can make the necessary calls to have her cared for until something can be arranged with the family."

"Great. Thanks. I appreciate it."

"But you know the case is closed now. So I don't expect to be getting any more calls from higher up telling me that you're still poking around and causing trouble."

"I'm not on the force," Zachary reminded him. "I'm a private citizen, so you can't tell me what to do unless I'm breaking the law. And I'm not."

It wasn't like he had planned to do any more investigating. The answers from the medical examiner's office seemed pretty conclusive. But he bristled at the order to stay off the case. He hated being told what to do, especially by someone who had no real authority over him.

"I can charge with you impeding an investigation."

"An investigation that's closed?"

"Zachary, I'm helping you out with the Salter woman. So can't we get a little bit of reciprocation here? There's nothing left to investigate."

"I'll be the one to decide that."

Before Campbell could say anything else, Zachary hung up.

<hr>

When he got back into his car, Zachary checked his phone to see if he'd missed a call back from Bridget. She was usually on her phone all of her waking hours, so it was unusual not to be able to reach her or at least get a call back pretty quickly. But she still hadn't responded. There was, however, a direct message from Rhys, continuing their conversation from earlier.

Zachary frowned as he studied the moving gif of a fat dog stuck in a toilet bowl, looking out with bulging, glistening eyes. It was captioned "help me."

Rhys had used a dog picture for his greeting the previous chat session as well. Zachary didn't know how much to read into it.

He considered the little dog for a few minutes before messaging back.

"Hi, Rhys. I was just at your house. Is everything okay?"

The reply that came eventually was a cartoon character, from Disney maybe, surrounded by walls of fire. The caption said "everything is going to be just fine."

Zachary didn't know what to make of the sarcastic meme. Did Rhys mean everything would be okay? Did he mean he was in danger? If it was just the first option that came up when Rhys typed in "everything fine," then did he really mean he was fine? Or was it intended to be sarcastic?

"Does that mean you're okay or not?"

He waited, but no answer was forthcoming. Zachary stared down at the short exchange on his phone, trying to figure it out. It seemed clear that Rhys wanted something, but Zachary didn't know what. He didn't think he could go to the authorities and get them to agree that the memes might mean Rhys was in some kind of trouble. They were pictures. Maybe they had meaning and maybe they were just random. And the words on the last one said that everything was going to be fine. The police wouldn't interpret it as meaning anything else.

There could be plenty of reasons Rhys had stopped messaging. He might have been using his phone between classes, but had to put it away when the next period started. His phone might have been taken away because he was caught using it in class. The whole thing might have been a pocket dial and randomly selected messages.

He'd just have to wait and see if he got anything else from Rhys.

20

Having returned home to work on other files, Zachary looked in his fridge, decided that he'd just have a cup of coffee, and sat down in front of his computer to work. He tried to focus, but his thoughts kept getting dragged back to Rhys and Bridget. He kept looking at his phone for any more messages from Rhys, but nothing materialized. He tried reaching Bridget by phone several times, and kept just ringing through to her voicemail.

It figured.

She had come back into his life, acting like she was ready to take him back again, and he had fallen for it. He had taken the case for her because he would do anything for her. He still cared about her and if there was any chance he could get her back, he would take it.

But she didn't feel the same way. All she wanted were his services. She had said she would pay him, and maybe that should have been the first tip-off. She wasn't looking for a favor or a relationship, just for his investigative experience. Any investigator would do, but he was the one she knew, and he came cheap.

Now that he had shown that Robin's life had, in fact, been cut short by a medical error, Bridget was satisfied. She could go on, knowing that justice had been served. She didn't have any lasting attachment to Zachary. Now that it was all sorted out, she didn't even have the time to answer a call from him. Not even to tell him to take a hike.

It was a good thing he didn't have any alcohol around, because he would have downed a whole bottle and maybe washed down a few pills while he was at it. He couldn't believe he had let himself be used by Bridget. Hadn't he figured out by now that she was the worst thing for him? How many times was he going to let himself be hurt by her?

Zachary considered throwing his phone across the room, but he couldn't be bothered to have to replace it. He placed it face-down as punishment for not being useful to him and resolved to ignore it. Even if Bridget decided to call him back, he wasn't going to answer it.

He looked back at his computer, but instead of navigating to his file system to work on reports, he clicked on the tab to see if Rhys had messaged him back again.

At ten o'clock, Zachary was crawling out of his skin. He was so anxious and agitated he couldn't stay in his apartment, even pacing, so he went out for a walk.

It maybe wasn't the best time of day to go out to burn off some steam, but his new apartment was in a reasonably nice neighborhood and it wasn't *really* late. It was still before midnight. The bars were open, so rowdies were still occupied and weren't wandering around looking for excitement. He walked in well-lit areas and kept his eyes open for signs of trouble.

All the while, his heart was pounding out an angry rhythm. Bridget didn't want him. Rhys hadn't posted again. The case was closed, but he didn't feel the sense of satisfaction and resolution he usually did when a case was resolved. Instead, it felt like an open wound. Something that needed to be properly treated and bandaged before he would feel better. It didn't make much sense. He hadn't known Robin. He had been hired—or asked as a favor —to find out why she had died so soon, and he had done that.

But Vera had been left alone and Rhys was asking for help. Gloria obviously wasn't dealing with her responsibilities to either one of them. Maybe he should go back to the house to make sure Gloria had gotten home and everybody was okay. She could have fallen back on old addictions and be out somewhere completely wasted, while her mother and son struggled to care for themselves.

Of course, it was Bridget's behavior that was really bothering Zachary. Even at their worst, darkest times, she had still called him back. Maybe she had only done it to yell at him and threaten to take out a restraining order if he didn't leave her alone, but she had still called him back.

Zachary turned back after an hour and headed back the way he had come. That way he would be back at his apartment at midnight. He could take some pills to help him sleep, and maybe in the morning, he'd be able to move on and deal with his other cases.

As Zachary approached his building, he saw a stealthy figure in the parking lot. Somebody hanging around, trying to keep to the shadows and not be seen. Zachary had done it enough times himself on surveillance to immediately recognized the movement pattern. The figure was definitely male, taller than Zachary, as most men were, broad across the shoulders. Zachary hung back and watched him, seeing what he could learn. The man put his phone to his ear and looked up at the windows of the apartment building. Watching for a figure to cross the window or a phone screen to light up the room? Or calling to report to someone on the movements of his quarry?

Zachary ducked back as the man turned around to scan the parking lot. He thought he got back behind an electrical box quickly enough that the man didn't see him. But Zachary had been able to get a full view of his face, well-lit by the phone screen.

What was Stanley Green doing hanging around in his parking lot?

———

Zachary never did get to sleep that night.

Eventually, it was late enough in the morning that he wouldn't be waking Kenzie up. If he'd timed it correctly, he figured she should be getting her coffee on her way to work. But by the way she answered the phone, he figured she hadn't had any caffeine yet.

"Case is closed, Zach. Why are you still bugging me?"

"Um…" Zachary tried to come up with a snap response and failed. He needed more time to compose an answer that would make any sense or satisfy her. "Sorry?"

"Brilliant. You're sorry. Sorry for what, should I ask?"

"I didn't… I wasn't calling to bug you about the case… not really."

"Not really. And what does that mean? Either it's about the case, or it's not."

"I was just going to tell you… about last night… nothing to do with the case, not really."

"Why should I care about it, then?"

Zachary stopped trying to explain and backed off. "What's wrong?"

"Maybe I've got my own life to deal with. My own job and my own personal problems. I don't need to deal with yours too."

"No."

"You're always wanting something from me. But what happens when Bridget shows up playing damsel in distress?"

"I fall for it," Zachary admitted. "I know I did… and now she won't even answer my calls. I gave her what she wanted and she doesn't want anything else to do with me."

"You see? I warned you. I told you not to think she was going to get back together with you. It was just a trap. That's how she gets you. She's still got you wrapped around her little finger. All she has to do is give it a little pull and you'll dance for her like a marionette on a string."

"Yeah."

"I warned you, and you didn't listen and got your hopes all built up. Now she drops out of sight, and I'm the one left to pick up the pieces."

Zachary took in a deep inhale, trying to keep his emotions under control. He sat at his desk, elbows on the table, covering his eyes. On the phone, Kenzie swore.

"You're a grown man, Zachary. Why don't you try acting like one instead of a lovestruck teenager? Your crush has moved on. Time for you to let her go."

"You're right."

There was silence from Kenzie. Zachary waited. He didn't trust his own voice. She obviously needed to blow off some steam. He hadn't registered before how irritated she'd been by Bridget's reappearance in his life.

"Okay. I'm done," Kenzie conceded. "So, what's this about last night?"

"It's not important... just... Stanley Green was hanging around my parking lot," Zachary explained, happy to move on to a less personal topic. "Robin's fiancé of ten years ago."

"Well... that's a little weird. I gather he knew you were investigating the case."

"Yes, I interviewed him Tuesday."

"Then if he wanted you, why didn't he just give you a call? That would have been easier than stalking you, surely."

"Exactly," Zachary agreed.

"What did he have to say for himself?"

"I didn't talk to him. I just called the police to say this guy was lurking around in the parking lot. I didn't say I knew who it was."

"Why not?"

"For one thing... I didn't want him to have confirmation that

I lived there. Or that I had seen him. Better if he just gets the idea that it's not a safe place for him to loiter."

"Are you safe? What if he comes back and you don't see him the next time?"

"I'll keep a close lookout. If he does show up again, I'll have to get a restraining order."

"I'd feel a lot better if I knew you were carrying a gun. All of the private eyes on TV do, why don't you?"

"Because this is real life. Real private investigators don't go around shooting everything up."

"Well, not everything, maybe, but if someone is stalking them…"

"I'll take pictures. Proof that he's following me."

Kenzie sighed. "How am I supposed to admire you for your manliness when all you do is take pictures?"

Zachary allowed himself a smile. "You'll have to take my rugged good looks instead."

Kenzie snorted.

Zachary was checking for any messages from Rhys when his phone rang. He startled so badly that he almost threw the phone in the air. He didn't recognize the number, but he answered it anyway. Maybe it would be a new client to distract him.

"Goldman Investigations."

"Zachary?"

Zachary grasped for the identity of the voice, but couldn't quite place it.

"Yes, this is Zachary."

It wasn't Stanley Green, that was the important thing. Or Joshua Campbell.

"It's Gordon Drake. Uh… Bridget's… *friend?*"

"Oh. Uh, hi Gordon. What can I do for you?" Zachary hung on to the hope that perhaps Gordon had a big corporate espionage investigation he wanted to hire Zachary for. Those could be quite profitable, from what he understood.

"I know this is going to sound a little strange, but… I was on a business trip, and when I got home today… well… Bridget isn't with you, is she?"

Goosebumps prickled up Zachary's arms. "With me? No. Why would she be with me?"

"Well, it was the only thing I could think of. I can look up her call records online, and I saw that you had phoned her a few times…"

"I've been calling her since Tuesday. I had a short conversation with her, but she had to take a call. I haven't been able to reach her since."

"That's a little odd, don't you think? She's pretty good at returning calls."

"I just figured she was avoiding me."

"She wouldn't do that," Gordon's voice was painfully frank, "not when you're conducting an investigation for her."

"That's just the thing… when I talked to her last, it was to tell her that we had figured it out. That Robin died of an iron over-dose, probably the result of medical error. Bridget had to hang up to take another call, and that was the last I heard from her. She didn't… tell you where she was going? Leave you a note?"

"No. There's nothing. I've called the appointments on her agenda yesterday… she didn't get to any of them."

Zachary felt panicked and vindicated at the same time.

Bridget wasn't just avoiding him. Bridget was missing.

In the time Zachary and Bridget had been together, it seemed like Bridget had gotten to know half the police force. She knew at least as many of them as Zachary did, maybe even more. She made friends far more quickly and naturally than Zachary, and fast became the darling of the force. By the time Zachary made it over to Gordon's and Bridget's house, at least a dozen police cars were pulled in all along the driveway and the street, both marked and unmarked cars, a testament to her many warm relationships.

Zachary pulled his car over down the block and hurried to the house. He was stopped before he even got close to the door.

"Crime scene, you can't go in there."

"I'm family," Zachary snapped at the unfamiliar police detective. "I need to get in to talk to Gordon and whoever is in charge of the investigation."

"No one is allowed past—"

"Oh, Zachary!" Jonathan Bailey spotted him and intervened. "You're here. Come on through."

The policeman who had stopped Zachary scowled in irritation, but he let Zachary past and focused on the observers that he could keep back. Zachary didn't have time to smooth over bad feelings. He allowed Bailey to escort him to the door and announce him to the crime scene investigators who were busy inside the house.

"This is Zachary Goldman. Get him in to see Lashman right away."

One of the investigators instructed Zachary to glove up and put paper booties over his shoes, and then escorted him in a circuitous route that avoided the main walking paths through the rooms, to Bridget's study. It was a bright room, lush with green plants in planters and cut flowers in a vase on the desk. That was where he found Detective Lashman and Gordon Drake. They too were wearing protective gear, and a tech was paging through her appointment calendar in front of them with gloved fingers.

"Zachary. Thanks so much for coming," Gordon welcomed him.

The investigator escorting Zachary directed him around the perimeter of the room, and Zachary joined Gordon and Lashman.

"Have you found anything?"

"So far, just eliminating possibilities," Lashman said, with a wave at the calendar. "It looks like you were the last person to talk to her. She didn't take any other calls or attend to any other responsibilities."

"She hung up on me to take another call."

"Just her maid service. Nothing there."

Zachary's hope that the call that had interrupted them would guide the direction of the investigation vanished. He felt a stab of anger that Bridget would hang up on him and his news that Robin had died because of a medical error to deal with something so routine and unimportant. He had hoped it would be a clue to what had happened to her.

"Tell me about this case you were investigating for her," Lashman said. "Mr. Drake said you had found something?"

"The medical examiner found something," Zachary corrected. "It turns out that Robin Salter didn't die of cancer, as her physician had believed. She died of an iron overdose."

Lashman's bushy black eyebrows furrowed. "Murder?"

"Medical error. Someone at the hospital gave her the wrong dosage for her anemia."

"And you had just informed Miss Downy of that fact."

"Yes. I had just told her, and she said she had to answer the other call coming in. Said she'd call me back. But then she never did. I called her back several times, but couldn't get through to her."

"You weren't concerned about her sudden unavailability?"

Zachary looked at Gordon and then looked down. He looked around the room, trying to focus on any clues it might provide as to Bridget's whereabouts instead of his own guilt and embarrassment.

"Well... no. I didn't think that anything had happened to her. She's my ex-wife, and I figured... she had the information she needed from me and didn't want to talk to me anymore."

"How would you characterize your relationship with your ex-wife?"

Zachary's stomach tied in knots. He knew his answer would make him a suspect, but lying would only make it worse.

"Well... rocky. She had been pretty angry and bitter toward me. But she still helped me out sometimes. She asked me to take this case. I thought maybe she was softening toward me." Zachary's cheeks burned at having to admit this in front of Gordon. "It wasn't a... an amicable divorce."

Lashman looked at Zachary for a long moment, then looked at Gordon for confirmation. Gordon nodded, looking as uncomfortable as Zachary felt. "Bridget's relationship with Zachary was... complicated. There were a lot of resentments. On both sides, I think."

"And you thought you would invite him to the crime scene?" Lashman challenged. "He shouldn't be in here."

"I know it sounds like the height of stupidity, but I trust Zachary. I don't believe he had anything to do with Bridget's disappearance."

"Did she ever have a protective order against him?"

Gordon cleared his throat and didn't look at Zachary. "It was discussed. But no, she never officially pursued one. And there were never any allegations of abuse."

"Then why would she want a protective order?"

"Zachary was following her. Tracking her car. Generally being obsessive about where she was and what she was doing. Bridget wanted it to stop."

Lashman looked at Zachary. "And did it?"

Zachary nodded. "I've been getting counseling. Changed my meds. I knew… if I kept it up, she was going to charge me. I was doing my best…"

"Doing your best. That sounds like maybe you weren't quite as pure and innocent as you suggest."

"I…" Zachary swallowed. He looked at Gordon. "I sometimes drove past the house. Or other places she liked to go. I didn't make contact and I didn't track her, but…"

Gordon shook his head. "Right now, I'm wishing you *had* put another tracker on her car. Then we'd know where she was."

"How did these trackers work?" Lashman asked.

Zachary explained about the app on his phone, and Lashman held his hand out.

"I want to see it. Unlocked."

Zachary complied, pulling his phone out and unlocking it. He handed it to Lashman and watched as he first reviewed the call history and texts sent and received. Lashman found the tracker app and found that access was locked. Zachary told him the password. Lashman looked at the flashing triangles on the map.

"Does it say which triangle is whom?"

Zachary nodded. "Just tap them. You can label them whatever you like. You'll want… independent confirmation that none of them are her."

Lashman looked up at Zachary briefly and agreed. "Does it keep a history?"

"In my online account. I'll give you the login. You can erase information, though. I don't know if their server keeps a backup of what's been deleted somewhere."

Lashman nodded.

"I can tell you her usual routines," Zachary said. "Where she usually went and when." He glanced at Gordon. "I haven't been tracking her lately, I just know from before."

"Empty your pockets," Lashman directed.

Zachary looked at Lashman as if he might not have heard properly. But of course he had. If he'd been a police detective, he would have asked for the same thing.

"Detective, please don't arrest Zachary," Gordon begged. "I know it looks bad, but he didn't do anything to her. He couldn't. If anyone can find her, it's Zachary. Please."

"I'm not arresting him yet. But time is of the essence here and I'm not going to be *that guy.* The stupid official who didn't see what was right in front of his own nose and didn't take all of the proper evidence. I want the contents of your pockets, Mr. Goldman. Now."

Zachary didn't like it. "Can we go to another room? Maybe the kitchen? I don't want to contaminate this scene."

Lashman scowled, looking down at Bridget's desk. Then he nodded. They moved to the kitchen, as Zachary had suggested, and laid a plastic sheet over the table so that he had somewhere clean to put the contents of his pockets without compromising any prints or evidence that might be on the table itself.

As Zachary knew he would, Lashman picked up Zachary's keys. "We have your permission to search your car?"

Gordon started to protest, but Zachary held up his hand. "No. He has to. We don't want to waste time while he gets a warrant."

Lashman gave a curt nod and took the car keys off of the ring. He handed them to another officer. "We need a search of Mr. Goldman's car. Check the interior and trunk first, then get it towed to the lab for full forensics. What is it and where is it parked, Mr. Goldman?"

Zachary told them where to find it. Lashman looked down at the rest of the items that had been in Zachary's pockets.

"What are the pills?"

"They're prescription." Zachary indicated each in turn and told Lashman what they were.

"You know better than to be carrying pills around without the prescription bottle. You could be arrested for possession of controlled substances."

"Yes, sir."

Lashman could undoubtedly see how ridiculous it would be for Zachary to carry that many bottles of pills around with him. He apparently didn't see anything else suspicious in the miscellany that had been in Zachary's pockets. He opened Zachary's wallet with his gloved hands.

"Is this your current address?" He indicated Zachary's driver's license.

"No. I've just moved."

"You know you're required to update your records with DMV."

"Yes. I will."

"You'll consent to a search of your house? What's the address?"

Zachary sighed and gave it. Gordon was red-faced with outrage.

"I called Zachary for help because he knows Bridget and is a good investigator. He is not a suspect!"

"Everybody is a suspect," Zachary told him. "But especially me. And you."

"Me?"

"The spouse or significant other is always the prime suspect. And the ex-spouse."

"But I'm the one who called the police!"

Zachary shrugged. "You had to. It would look pretty suspicious if you didn't."

Lashman nodded his agreement. "This doesn't mean that I think either one of you did it," he assured them. "But I would be negligent if I didn't treat you as suspects. We can't afford to let any evidence fall through the cracks. She's already been missing more than twenty-four hours. If we don't get a lead pretty quickly…"

The florid color drained out of Gordon's face. Zachary grasped his arm and steered him into one of the kitchen chairs.

"It will be okay," he told Gordon. "We'll find her. It's going to be okay."

Gordon's bearing, previously stoic, was breaking down. He put his hands over his eyes, trying to hold himself together.

"It doesn't make any sense, Zachary. She wouldn't just leave. Somebody must have taken her."

"I know," Zachary agreed. "We need to work through this. We need to figure out who took her and why. The police can collect all of the evidence, but you and I are the ones who know her."

Gordon nodded. He wiped moisture from his eyes. "She would think it's hilarious that I'm the one who broke down instead of you."

Zachary took a long breath in and let it out. "I'm just trying to focus on what needs to be done. Can't afford to be emotional right now."

"You're right. So. What do you need? I already showed Detective Lashman her schedule. He'll follow up with everyone she's talked to the last few days."

"Is there… anyone she's had trouble with lately? Arguments? Strange phone calls?"

Gordon shook his head. "Nothing I'm aware of. But she didn't tell me everything. As you probably gathered the other day… she hadn't even told me about Robin's death. That was a pretty big deal and she didn't even mention it."

"Did she talk to you during the day yesterday? When is the last time you heard from her?"

"Tuesday when I left. I tried her a couple of times yesterday, between meetings, but I thought I was just calling at the wrong times. While she was having her hair done or was in a meeting."

"No bedtime call?"

Gordon rubbed his forehead. "Er… no. I had clients to enter-tain until late. She goes to bed pretty early. She needs a lot of sleep." He looked at Lashman. "She had cancer. Did I tell you that? It's in remission and she is building up her strength, but she still needs a lot of rest. I wouldn't call her after eight and risk disrupting her sleep for the night. If I woke her up, she might not get back to sleep again."

Zachary nodded.

Lashman spoke up. "So, we don't know whether she disap-peared Tuesday after Mr. Goldman's call with her, or sometime Wednesday or even early today. We know she didn't show up for any appointments yesterday, so that suggests yesterday, but we can't be sure. She might simply have felt under the weather…"

"She wasn't here yesterday," Zachary told him flatly.

"How would you know that? You know she didn't answer your calls, but you said yourself she might just be avoiding your calls."

Zachary shook his head adamantly. "The flowers in her office."

"What about them?"

"The water in the vases is low and murky. Some of the flowers are starting to wilt. She didn't look after them yesterday morning and she certainly didn't change the water today."

"She might have forgotten. Been too busy."

"No. She wouldn't have neglected them."

"She might have been too sick or tired."

It was Gordon's turn to disagree. "We have a girl. She comes in and covers anything Bridget can't manage. If Bridget was too tired, all she had to do was make a phone call. Zachary's right. She wouldn't have neglected the flowers."

"It was that important to her?" Lashman was skeptical.

"They're a symbol of life and growth. Of her recovery. Neglecting them would be like…" Gordon struggled for the words.

"Like letting death into the house," Zachary suggested.

"Yes." Gordon agreed. "Like that. She would not let death into the house." He looked at Zachary. "Not knowingly."

They were both overcome for a moment.

"She's not dead," Zachary said. "I don't know what happened, but she's not dead."

"Okay." Gordon cleared his throat. As if by both of them agreeing to the fact, they could keep her alive. "She's not. She's okay. We just need to find her."

"Was your wife accustomed to taking walks? Or going off on her own to visit… I don't know… museums or craft fairs or some other interest."

"No. Bridget is very social. She isn't the type who sought out solitude. She liked to have people around her."

It had been a whole different world for Zachary. He had enjoyed it at first, having so many friends around. Being with Bridget and a coterie of admirers helped fill the empty space inside him. He'd led such a lonely existence for so many years. But it had also worn on him. Having people constantly around them. Not getting any time to just regenerate on his own. When he turned down invitations, he felt guilty and Bridget would be irritated with him. She would go on her own and he wouldn't hear the end of how she'd had to be there dateless. Bridget needed someone at her side. She needed people around her.

"How much do you know about their relationship?" Lashman asked Gordon, with a nod at Zachary. "When they were together?"

Gordon looked at Zachary uncomfortably. "Well… as much as you can know about someone else's relationship."

"Was their relationship abusive?"

Gordon's eyes avoided Zachary's and Lashman's.

"No. Not in the way you mean."

"In *any* way?"

"Zachary never did anything to harm Bridget…"

"Verbal or emotional abuse? I don't like the way you're avoiding the question, Mr. Drake."

"No, there was no verbal or emotional abuse… by Zachary."

Lashman stared at Gordon, his eyebrows drawn down, not comprehending.

"Gordon," Zachary protested.

Gordon shook his head unhappily. "If there was verbal abuse, then it was by Bridget, not Zachary."

It hadn't taken Lashman very long to decide he had reason to take Zachary in to the police station for questioning. Zachary didn't protest. He knew all of the indicators were there. He was an ex-spouse. They'd had a dysfunctional relationship when they were together and since then. Zachary was the last one to talk to her. All of those things were big red flags.

He sat alone in an interrogation room for what seemed like a long time. He was impatient to get out of there to investigate. The longer it took the police to let him go, the more time passed with Bridget gone, and the less likely it was that they'd be able to find her alive and well.

Eventually, Lashman returned to the room to continue the interview. He sat down and thumped a stack of papers down on the table in front of him.

"We've had someone looking at surveillance tapes taken in Bridget's neighborhood the past few days for any suspicious activity. Cross-checking license plates."

Zachary's stomach coiled as tightly as a spring.

"Maybe you'd like to guess at what we found."

Zachary gulped. "My license plate." His voice was strangled.

"Bingo. Your license plate. Your car. You in your car in the wee hours this morning, driving around Bridget's neighborhood. You want to explain that to me?"

He could have said it was because he had a surveillance job in the neighborhood. But there were probably enough cameras in the area that both his entrance and exit would have been well-documented, and they'd know that he hadn't been there for hours watching a certain house. He'd been there just long enough to cruise by her house a couple of times to reassure himself she was okay. Or maybe long enough to let himself in while Bridget slept and to take her away from there. Drug her, stuff her in the trunk, and take her out of there.

"I couldn't sleep. I was wound up. I was anxious. After a while, I started to worry about Bridget. If she was okay. So… yeah… I drove by her house."

"And what did you find?"

"There weren't any inside lights on. Just the usual security lights. I didn't see anybody hanging around."

"Except you."

"Only for a few minutes. I never went in. I just… checked."

"What made you think she might be in danger? It seems to me to be pretty coincidental that you would go to check on her around the time as she disappeared."

"I was worried. After seeing Stanley hanging around my apartment, it got me worrying about Bridget… if he knew who she was or where she lived—"

"Hold on." Lashman held up a hand. "Who is Stanley? What are you talking about?"

"Stanley Green. I got home at midnight, and he was loitering around the parking lot in the dark. I called the police, got them to move him on. There will be a record of it."

"Stanley Green."

"He was Robin Salter's fiancé ten years ago. Then they broke up. I talked to him about Robin and her family for some background. But then he showed up at my place…"

"Was he a suspect?"

"I... not really. He hasn't been around. He didn't visit Robin in the hospital, as far as I know, so he couldn't have given her anything."

"But then he was hanging around your apartment after that? Last night?"

Zachary nodded.

"And what did that have to do with Bridget?"

"Nothing. It just... wormed its way into my brain. I didn't know why he was there, and I started to worry about if he would go after Bridget, because she was the one who hired me." Zachary shook his head. "He didn't know Bridget. It was just... paranoia."

"You don't think he has anything to do with Bridget's disappearance."

"No. He didn't know anything about her."

"Unless he talked to someone else."

Zachary thought about that. Would Stanley have called the Salters after his interview with Zachary? To warn them about the investigation or to ask them why he was involved in it?

"I guess... but the medical examiner found cause of death, so there wasn't anything else for me to look into. I wouldn't have been investigating Stanley or anyone else any further."

Sitting in a jail cell shouldn't have been a problem for Zachary. It wasn't like he hadn't done it before. He'd been in the detention cells at Bonnie Brown, he'd been picked up by the police or put into custody while they tried to figure out what to do with him as a teenager. As a private investigator, he wasn't the type to break the law for a case. Not usually. But occasionally, he got run in anyway because of a cop who didn't like his involvement in an investigation or had some other beef with him.

But having been detained before didn't help him. Bridget was out there somewhere and he was being kept from the investigation. He should have been out there looking for her. Asking about her. Listening to the word on the street. Instead, he was stuck in a cell for just one reason: the fact that he had once been married to her. Everything else was just a nail in the coffin. His real crime was having been married to her.

Zachary paced back and forth across the small cell, which ended up being more like spinning in a circle because he couldn't take more than a couple of steps one way or the other.

"What the matter with you?" one of the other inmates demanded. As if Zachary needed to justify himself to a man whose yellow track suit made him look like a dirty banana. If wearing a getup like that wasn't a crime, it should have been. "This your first time in a cell?"

"No, it's not my first time. I'm just trying to think."

"What did you take? You're seriously amped up, dude."

"Nothing. I haven't taken anything."

"Yeah, right," the banana shared a laugh with the rest of the jailbirds. "You're that juiced but you didn't take a thing."

"Shut up and let me think."

The banana tried a few more lines, but when nothing was getting a rise out of Zachary or a laugh out of the rest of the inmates, he gave up and left him alone.

Who would want to hurt Bridget? Who would want to make her stop talking about Robin Salter? One of the medical staff? Surely they knew by now that the medical examiner had discovered Robin's iron overdose and there was no point in trying to keep Bridget quiet. Was it Stanley Green? He'd had nothing to do with Robin's death, there was no reason for him to go after Bridget. Lashman would have someone bring him in, but Zachary was confident it wouldn't amount to anything.

Maybe it was nothing to do with the investigation. Even though it was the first thing that came to Zachary's mind, there was no evidence that Bridget's disappearance had anything to do with the Salter investigation. Nothing at all.

Had a predator been watching her, observing her habits and figuring out the best time to strike?

Or was it an acquaintance or a business associate she had crossed and who wanted to get back at her? Bridget had a sharp tongue and Zachary was sure he wasn't the only one she had ever used it on. She wasn't afraid to voice her opinions. Especially after facing down cancer. *Life is too short to waste on being tactful and polite.* If people were going to be hurt by a few misplaced words, then they were going to go through life being wounded. Bridget didn't have time to be sensitive and politically correct. As numerous as the people who loved her were, she had her share of enemies or injured parties as well.

Gordon would know better than Zachary who Bridget might have had a falling out with lately. Hopefully, Gordon was telling them everything he could. Or maybe it was a business associate of Gordon's…

"Zachary."

He was so focused on his own thoughts, it took a few moments before he was able to take in Mario Bowman, standing in the corridor outside Zachary's cell, holding a folder and looking at him.

"Bowman? What are you doing here?"

"Zachary," Bowman stepped closer. His voice was low and confidential. "I had to bring these to you. I thought they might be important."

Zachary looked down at the file. Why would Bowman have any paperwork that would be important to him? His concern was with Bridget. That was where he had to stay focused. Zachary made a motion to wave him away.

"I heard about Bridget," Bowman said. His eyes were wide.

Zachary stared at Bowman hard, trying to determine whether he knew anything more than Zachary. *Was he sorry because they had found Bridget? Was she hurt? Dead?* He couldn't bear it if she were dead.

"Whoa, there." Bowman reached through the bars and held Zachary steady. "It's okay, brother."

"Have you heard something?"

"No. No one knows anything. They're looking for her. They're putting bulletins out on the TV, internet, everything. Drake has money. He'll spare no expense. They'll find her, Zachary."

Zachary nodded. He grasped the bars of the door to keep himself from shaking.

"I thought you needed these," Bowman said, proffering the file folder. "I thought they must be important."

Zachary automatically took the file folder, though he had no interest in anything except figuring out where Bridget was. He opened it and looked at the printed reports inside. Incident reports. He vaguely remembered asking Bowman for them, though all of the reasons had been driven from his mind. His hand was shaking too badly to make out the words. He sat down on the bunk and put them in his lap to hold them steady. He stared at the reports, trying to make the words stop swimming so that he could read them.

A domestic violence incident report between Robin Salter and Stanley Green. Zachary looked down the page to the description of the incident and only got a couple of lines in when he looked up at Bowman in disbelief.

"Stanley Green was the *victim?*"

Bowman nodded. "It happens more often than you might think. Sure, the majority of domestic violence reports are male on female, but there are still plenty that are women beating on men."

"Robin was the perpetrator."

"Yeah. Some of these women can be hellcats, you know." He opened his mouth to make a wisecrack, but then apparently thought better about what he was going to say and closed his mouth. "There are more in there."

Zachary flipped through the stapled reports, noting the parties on each. Robin Salter and Stanley Green. Robin Salter and Gloria Salter. Robin Salter and Vera Salter and Gloria Salter.

Zachary sat there on the bunk, his vision going white. Everything around him dissolved.

Robin Salter wasn't the victim of domestic violence. She was the abuser. The things Stanley had told Zachary came into sharp focus. *There were things happening in that family… it was very unhealthy. People… are not always what they seem. Relationships that look healthy from the outside… sometimes they aren't.* Zachary had thought that Stanley meant Grandpa Clarence was abusive. But he hadn't. He'd meant Robin.

She knew how to persuade other people around her to do things the 'right' way

She got more extreme. More… angry.

How had Zachary missed what Stanley was really trying to tell him? Zachary had taken one look at the big, broad man and assumed he was the abuser. It never occurred to him that the small, sick woman whose death Zachary was investigating had once terrorized him.

Zachary's head whirled. He pressed his fist to his forehead, trying to keep it all in logical order.

Where had Robin been when Clarence had died? Clarence and Rhys were at home, and Vera and Gloria were out, but where was Robin? Her name had been left out of the story completely. Had she been at Stanley's house? Out partying? Were the two of them out to dinner or running errands?

Someone had gone into the house and shot Clarence as he sat at the kitchen table. There hadn't been a fight. A burglary gone wrong, the police had suggested. But what would it take to make it look like a burglary? Move the electronics into a pile. Leave a few drawers open. A broken window would help to set the scene, but wasn't necessary. A high percentage of burglars simply entered through unlocked doors.

"Bowman."

The jail cell reformed around him. Bowman was still standing there, wide-eyed at Zachary's reaction to the reports.

"Yeah, I'm here, Zachary."

"I need Lashman. I need him right now."

"I don't think he's here. He's running the investigation into Bridget's disappearance…"

"I know. But this changes everything. I was wrong."

"About what?"

"About everything. Nothing is what it looked like. I need to tell him what's going on. Right now."

Bowman seemed to finally be getting the urgency of the situation. "This is something to do with Bridget?" he asked, pointing at the file folder.

"Yes. We need to get to her before it's too late." Zachary clutched the file. "If it's not too late already."

"Okay. I'll get ahold of him. I know who to call."

If anyone would know who to call, it was Bowman. He was the only person in the world who understood all of the politics and inner workings and motivations of the police department. It didn't matter if Lashman had said he wasn't to be disturbed, Bowman would find a way to get to him.

23

When Lashman got there and gave Zachary the stink-eye before unlocking the door to the cell, he wasn't prepared for the earful he was about to get.

"It wasn't Stanley," Zachary said urgently. "It wasn't Stanley and it wasn't a medical mistake. It was retribution. She had to make Robin suffer. She couldn't just let her die of natural causes. That wouldn't have served justice."

"What the hell are you talking about?"

Zachary waved the file folder at him. "I thought Stanley was abusive of Robin, but the domestic violence incident reports show that *she* was the aggressor, not him."

Lashman's eyes followed the folder. "Quit waving it in my face and let me see it," he growled, opening the cell door and taking the file folder from Zachary. "Slow down and start at the beginning."

Zachary let him have the folder. He blathered away to Lashman as they walked down the hallway, and it wasn't until they reached the end of the corridor that he realized the detective hadn't heard a word he had said. Zachary closed his mouth and waited. Lashman skimmed through the incident reports and then looked at Zachary, nodding.

"Okay, Robin Salter was the abuser, not the abused. Why does that matter?" Lashman led the way to an interview room. He motioned for Zachary to take a seat, but Zachary couldn't sit down, not with everything bubbling up inside him.

"She was physically violent. It wasn't just verbal abuse, there was physical violence." Zachary tried to find the place in one of the incident reports. "She broke bones. She used weapons. If she didn't like the way you were doing something, she would show you the light. She wasn't a nice person."

"And you think that means what? I don't follow what it has to do with Bridget's disappearance."

"Her father was murdered."

Lashman blinked at him. "Mr. Goldman... those pills that you had with you earlier today...?"

"What?" Zachary didn't understand the segue.

"You missed taking something, didn't you?"

"No. I don't want to take anything. I need to stay clear."

"You're not making sense. I know you think you are, but you're not. I think you're... getting yourself confused."

"No." Zachary scowled. "You need to listen to the rest. This is bigger than anything we ever thought."

"Okay... tell me the rest. But realize that while you are explaining, you're keeping me from finding Bridget."

Zachary blew out his breath in exasperation. "You're not going to find her without me. I'm the only one who has put it together."

"Go." Lashman made an impatient motion. "Let's hear it."

"Robin's father was murdered. Clarence. At the time, the police thought it was a burglar, but it wasn't. Robin wanted every-thing done her way, and if it wasn't, she got mad. She got violent. I don't know what her father did that day, but she killed him. It wasn't a burglar. It was *Robin*."

"What's your evidence?"

"Her family knew. Maybe they were the ones who made up the burglary story in the first place. They covered for Robin. But they didn't know how it was going to affect the family. How it was going to *keep* affecting their lives for the next decade."

Lashman shook his head, but he was following Zachary so far.

"Gloria's son, Rhys, was home that night. He must have seen or known what happened. He had a nervous breakdown. He was just a little kid. They probably told him he dreamed it. They thought he would just forget it and that everyone could just go on as they had before."

Lashman swore. Zachary knew exactly how he felt.

"Yeah. They all stayed together. Rhys had to keep living in the same house as his grandfather's murderer. By now, maybe he's completely forgotten what happened, but the feelings aren't gone. He's still mute. He hasn't been able to deal with the fear and betrayal."

Zachary started to pace. He knew Lashman wanted him to sit down and take some kind of tranquilizer to settle him down, but it was suddenly all clear, and he couldn't waste one extra second explaining it.

"They were all still living together. Gloria started standing up for herself and her son and got her life together. But it was too late for Rhys, he was already damaged. Vera was starting to get forgetful. Maybe to the point where she couldn't remember what had really happened anymore."

"You don't know that, though. You're only speculating."

"I *know*. I can see it. I need my phone. Can someone get me my phone?"

"It's in evidence."

"I need it. I'll show you. You'll see."

Lashman shook his head in irritation, but he popped out the door to flag down another officer and explain what he needed. He returned to his conversation with Zachary.

"And how does this explain everything? It seems to me that you're just muddying the waters further. This doesn't bring us any kind of clarity."

"Robin was diagnosed with cancer. Whatever Gloria had been

dreaming of doing to make things right, it was too late. She couldn't turn Robin in and expose her to the world. Robin would be dead before she could get to trial. There wouldn't be any justice. Robin would never have to pay the piper. Gloria had to think of something else to do instead."

"And you think she poisoned Robin," Lashman sighed, connecting it up at last.

"I know she did!" Zachary insisted.

The officer eventually returned with Zachary's phone. Zachary powered it on.

"Look. Look at this." Zachary went through his photographs. He found the ones he had taken of the Salters' medicine cabinet. "I took this picture before we knew what it was that had killed Robin. I was looking for insulin—which I now know would actually have been in the fridge. There were other prescriptions, so I took a picture of them… just in case. I thought maybe one of them had tried to stop Robin's suffering. A mercy killing. Euthanasia. Maybe even assisted suicide, without a physician's involvement. But it wasn't. Her death was meant to be painful. The hospital had to keep increasing her painkillers because of the damage the poison was doing to her system."

Lashman looked at the small screen. "I'm sorry, I'm supposed to be looking for…"

Zachary zoomed the image in. A pink and blue bottle from the hospital pharmacy. The silhouette of a woman on the front. 'Fe' in big block letters

"Iron."

Seconds ticked by while Lashman processed this.

"I'm sure a lot of women have iron supplements."

"It's clear liquid," Zachary pointed out. "Not pills. It could be injected directly into Robin's IV. No one would be the wiser."

"That's not proof."

"You need to get someone over to the house. Find out whose fingerprints are on the bottle. See if there are any syringes around. Find out if either Vera or Gloria was anemic. Find out if there was enough iron in that bottle to kill Robin, when added to the amount the hospital was giving her."

Lashman picked up his own phone and talked quietly to some assistant at a desk somewhere about getting a warrant for the Salter house to search for evidence that Vera or Gloria had given Robin a fatal dose of iron. He hung up.

"Now then; what does that have to do with Bridget?"

Zachary looked up from his phone. "Bridget stuck her nose into it. She wouldn't believe that Robin's death was natural. She asked me to investigate. The Salters all knew I was there because of Bridget. Gloria needed me to stop asking questions and knew I was only asking questions because Bridget was pushing me."

"But if Bridget disappeared, you wouldn't have any reason to keep investigating."

"Right."

"Wouldn't Gloria know that you would look into Bridget's disappearance? You would still be investigating, just from the other end of the problem."

"She must not have thought I would see the connection between Robin's death and Bridget's disappearance."

Lashman gave a grim smile. "Well, she was wrong there, wasn't she?"

Lashman returned and put a cup of coffee down on the table for Zachary.

"There's no one home at the Salters' house. Search team says it looks like they packed up and left in a hurry."

Zachary had been holding out hope that they would still be at the house, that maybe they would be holding Bridget there tied up in the basement. All they would have to do was search the house, Bridget would be found, and that would be all the proof they needed that Gloria had been involved in Robin's death and Bridget's kidnapping.

"What happened the last time you were there?" Lashman asked.

"At the house?" Zachary frowned. "I went over there after I heard what the medical examiner had found. Yesterday."

"To ask them about the iron in the medicine cabinet?"

"No. To tell them it had been a medical error. I didn't realize then that it had been intentional. I didn't know it was Gloria."

"If they knew the medical examiner thought it was accidental, why would they run?"

"Gloria wasn't there. She was at work. Rhys was at school. It was just Vera home alone. I don't know if she really understood what I was trying to explain to her. She was a little… distant."

"Do you think Gloria had already run?"

"No, they hadn't run yet, Vera was still home."

"There was a notice left at the house that Social Services was taking Vera into care. Dated yesterday."

Zachary swallowed and nodded. "I asked for a welfare check. The officers who came by said they would talk to Social Services and get ahold of Gloria. They told me to hit the road. I just assumed they would call Gloria home from work to deal with it…"

"Apparently they weren't able to contact Gloria. She hasn't been home or answered any calls."

"Then Gloria *had* already run when I went there. Monday or Tuesday. That would make sense… she knew an autopsy had been ordered, but didn't know the results yet. She was still ahead of the game." Zachary closed his eyes, concentrating on a mental image of the house that day. He reviewed the memory as if it were a photograph he had taken. "Rhys's book bag was on the floor. I thought he was at school, but he couldn't have been at school without his books. The house was a mess… like Vera might have been left alone to fend for herself for a couple of days…"

Lashman nodded. "Long enough to track Bridget down and to make a plan to take her. I'll get an APB out on Gloria's car."

24

The door opened, and instead of Lashman, it was Kenzie. Zachary blinked at her.

"Kenzie…? What are you doing here?"

"A mutual friend asked me to check in on you."

For just an instant, Zachary's mind went to Bridget. It made perfect sense, in that split-second leap, that it had been Bridget who had called Kenzie. But of course, it hadn't been. Bridget was gone and she had no way of even knowing where Zachary was, let alone that he could use a visitor.

"Bowman," he guessed.

"Yeah. He didn't want to make a second appearance in case there was trouble, so he asked if I would stop in." Kenzie looked around the bare interview room, as if looking for something to talk about. But of course, there wasn't anything. "Are you okay?"

Zachary gave a wide shrug. He didn't know how much she already knew about what was going on and he didn't know where to start

"Bridget is missing?" Kenzie said softly.

"You heard… yeah. I think she was kidnapped. I *hope*," Zachary's voice hitched on the word, "she was kidnapped."

Because the alternative was just too awful. If Gloria had

murdered her sister, would she hesitate to kill again to cover it up? Zachary shut this thought away, pushing it out of his mind and refusing to consider it.

"Do you know who? Where she is?"

"It was Gloria Salter."

"Robin's sister?"

"Yes. Because she's the one who killed Robin." Zachary raised his eyes to Kenzie's. "It wasn't a medical error. It was intentional."

Kenzie's mouth hung open. She didn't argue and say that it wasn't possible, as Zachary had expected. Finally, Kenzie shook her head and spoke. "Are you sure?"

"It's the only thing that makes sense. And she's missing. Gloria. Looks like she ran a few days ago. Then took Bridget… Tuesday night, Wednesday morning… It's Thursday afternoon now." He swallowed, but it didn't get rid of the lump in his throat. "Bridget will think I don't care. She'll think I'm not coming."

"She knows you care," Kenzie assured him. "There can't be any doubt of that. She knows you'll be looking for her and you won't give up until you find her."

"How am I going to find her? I can't even get out of here. I can't do anything." Zachary smacked his palm down on the table, frustrated.

"If they know it's Gloria Salter who took Bridget, then they've got to release you."

"Tell Lashman that. I wasn't arrested as a suspect. He's holding me as a material witness."

"We both know that's just semantics. I'll go talk to him."

Zachary hadn't expected that Kenzie would actually talk to Lashman, but Kenzie ducked back out of the room and went to find him. Zachary watched the clock on his phone, getting more and more wound up, until he again couldn't sit still and got up to pace.

Lashman returned with Kenzie. He scowled at Zachary. "I don't want you getting in the way of this investigation."

"I'm not going to get in your way."

"What are you going to do? Because I don't believe for a minute that you're just going to drop it and leave finding Bridget Downy all up to us."

Zachary chewed on his lip. "Vera, I guess. She's the only one who might be able to tell us where Gloria would go."

"I've already had officers talking to her. She's too confused to be of any help."

"With all due respect," Kenzie said aggressively, "the odds that your officers will be able to drag information out of a senile old lady and the chances that Zachary can sit down with her and tease something useful out are not even in the same league."

Lashman bristled at this. "We can't have him contaminating a witness."

"If she's too confused for your officers to get the story out of her, then what's the problem with me talking to her?" Zachary asked. "You can't exactly get *less* than nothing out of her."

Kenzie snorted and covered her mouth.

Lashman glared, but Zachary thought he saw a hint of a smile on Lashman's lips as well. "I doubt she has any idea where Gloria went. Gloria wouldn't have told her and then left her behind."

"I'm not going to ask her where Gloria went."

The police detective gave Zachary a look like he was crazy. A look Zachary had seen plenty of times before. "Then what are you going to ask her?"

"I'm just going to have a chat with her. I might not ask her anything at all."

Kenzie laughed at Lashman's perplexed expression. "You've got to trust the process, detective. Come on. What's it going to hurt to let Zachary out of here? If he can find Gloria or Bridget, then that's good for everyone, isn't it?"

"What are people going to say if you don't let me?" Zachary played on the weakness Lashman had already shown, his worry about being the stupid cop. The one who let something important just slip through his fingers. "They'll say that you just let a resource go to waste. Someone who knew Bridget and was a skilled investigator. Someone who was more invested than anyone else in finding her. And instead of using me, you just kept me locked up."

"I don't know…" Lashman was softening. "If I screw this up by letting you go…"

"What if I stay with him?" Kenzie suggested. "I can keep an eye on him, make sure he's not going to run or screw up your investigation…"

Zachary glanced over at Kenzie, surprised. Did she want to be with him? Or did she just want to give Bridget the best chance at survival? Did she care about her rival? She'd been pretty chilly toward Zachary since he had taken Bridget's case on.

"Fine." Lashman growled. "If you think you can crack this case before the police department, you're welcome to it. But if I get word from my officers that you're getting in the way, or you mess with any of my witnesses and end up screwing up the case, don't think there won't be consequences."

Zachary was on his feet, nodding his agreement. "Yes, sir. I'm not going to screw anything up. Thank you!"

He didn't wait for Lashman to tell him they had to fill out a bunch of paperwork to get released. He didn't ask for the possessions he had turned over to the detective to be returned to him. He had his phone and nothing else was worth worrying about.

"Uh… I guess I need to know the facility they put Vera into, if you're willing to give it to me. And I wonder if I could go by her house and get a few things…"

"I can't have you touching things and contaminating evidence."

"Someone can go in with me. I won't touch anything important. I just want to get a few things that might help her to feel more at home. The more comfortable she is, the better the chances are that she'll be able to tell me something helpful."

"You're a pain, you know that? This is why we don't like private detectives."

Kenzie opened her mouth to protest.

"Yes, sir," Zachary agreed, motioning Kenzie to silence.

The detective looked sourly at the two of them. "Fine, then. She's at the East Side Care Center and I'll have someone meet you at the house. Are you going straight over there now?"

"Yes."

"Someone will be waiting for you."

Zachary took his leave before Lashman could think of anything else to delay them. "You can drive?" he asked Kenzie.

"You don't want to take your car?"

He shook his head quickly. "It's… unavailable right now."

"Oh." She paused, considering whether to get more details, then decided not. "Well, you know I love to drive, so that's fine. And it's been in the police parking garage, so I know it hasn't been tampered with."

Zachary was thinking about his spark plugs being pulled as he folded himself into Kenzie's little red sports car.

"So, what are you picking up at the house?" Kenzie asked, after getting the address.

"Just some things to make her comfortable," Zachary repeated.

Kenzie kept looking at him expectantly when the police officer let them into the Salters' house. Like she was expecting him to suddenly find Bridget or an important clue, or maybe to do a back flip. She didn't believe that he was just there to pick up items to make Vera more comfortable and at home.

Zachary didn't want to take too long, but he didn't want to rush it, either. It was probably his only opportunity to look through the house, so he didn't want to miss anything important.

"Take pictures of each room," he suggested to Kenzie, motioning to her phone. "Just in case we miss something."

"What do you want me to take pictures of?"

"Everything you can."

"Hey," the policeman objected, when Kenzie started to do so. "You can't do that."

"We're not tampering with anything," Zachary said. "And we're not sending them to anyone. They're just for reference in the investigation."

"You don't have permission to do that."

"I have permission to be here. No one said we couldn't take pictures."

The house was just as Zachary had left it on Wednesday when he talked to Vera and had the police check on her welfare. They had taken her out of the home, and no one had been there until the police arrived to execute their search warrant.

It was obvious that Gloria had left in a hurry. There was a lot of stuff thrown around the rooms in the whirlwind of packing in both Gloria's and Rhys's rooms. Vera's and Robin's did not appear to have been touched.

The police had processed the house. The iron supplement was gone from the bathroom and the mirror and other surfaces had been dusted for prints. They didn't appear to have touched much else.

Kenzie studied each of the items Zachary picked up and showed to the police officer to get permission for their removal. A quilt. A sweater. A photo album.

"I don't really understand this. Why are these things important?"

Zachary glanced at the policeman. "They're not. They're completely unimportant." He looked through the living room and kitchen to find Vera's favorite mug. She'd had it on the table beside her both times he had visited her. He found it in the kitchen and showed it to the officer.

"Can I take that? It's dirty, I'll need to wash it."

The policeman inspected the mug, then shrugged. "Go ahead."

"Why don't you find the tea while I'm washing this?" Zachary suggested to Kenzie. "It smelled like peppermint."

Kenzie didn't move. Zachary cleared enough space in the sink to wash the mug, and while he scrubbed it, she finally did as he asked and looked through the drawers and the canisters on the counters until she came up with a tin of tea bags. The peppermint smell wafted over Zachary when she popped the lid to have a look inside.

"That's it," he confirmed.

"Okay. We've got her mug and her tea. And her blanket, sweater, and photo album."

"That should do it."

The police officer had one more look through everything before allowing Kenzie and Zachary to take them out of the house. Zachary packed everything but the photo album carefully into the small trunk of the sportster. He put the photo album in his lap and paged through it as Kenzie drove them to the care facility.

Vera sat in a bed in a hospital-like room at the care facility, looking anxious and confused. She didn't remember who Zachary was and snapped at him about when she was going to be able to go home.

When Zachary brought out the quilt and spread it over the bed, she patted at it, making soothing sounds. She pulled it close and snuggled into it.

"You probably don't need this," Zachary displayed the sweater. "Not with the quilt on. But if you decide to get up and walk around, you might want something to put on."

"No, I want it now," Vera disagreed. "Help me put it on."

She leaned forward away from the pillows and Zachary helped her to thread her arms into the sleeves and straightened it out. She lay back again, and he did the zipper up.

"There. That's very pretty. It's a nice color on you."

Vera smiled and patted at her hair, making sure it was all neatly in place. Zachary reached back to take the mug of hot tea from Kenzie. One of the nurses had been kind enough to let him use the electric teakettle in the staff kitchen to prepare it.

"Here, it's very hot, so you'll have to be careful and let it cool down for a few minutes."

Vera held the mug under her face and inhaled the peppermint scented steam. "Oh, this is my favorite," she said happily. "How did you know that?"

Zachary sat down on the visitor chair, which put him closer to her eye level. "There, that's better, isn't it?"

Vera nodded. She reached out for Zachary, and when he extended his hand, she patted it. "You're such a nice boy. How did you know just what to do?"

Zachary shrugged. He'd been moved around enough times to understand how much a few precious possessions could mean. "How are you feeling? Are you okay?"

"Oh, yes. I feel fine. I don't know why they brought me here. I'm not sick."

"I think they were just worried about you being alone, with Gloria being away."

Vera thought about that for a minute. "But where did she go? This is all so sudden!"

"I know. She and Rhys had to go, didn't they? It must have felt strange, being all alone in the house."

"I'm used to being alone. During the day, anyway. The girls work, and Rhys goes to school. Clarence is long gone, so it's just me there during the day. At night..." She frowned and shook her head. "I'm not used to that. It's a little bit *scary*."

"You must be glad that you were here last night, where you didn't have to be alone."

Vera brightened at that. "Yes. It was much better."

Zachary didn't look at Kenzie. They had both heard the staff talking about how Vera had whined and complained all night that she just wanted to go back home. It was better if Vera remembered being happy to be there at night, even if it wasn't true.

"I brought some pictures." Zachary pulled out the photo album and rested it across Vera's lap. "I thought you could tell me about your family. About Clarence, and the girls when they were younger. And Rhys."

Vera squealed in delight. She ran her hands over the ornate

cover as if she hadn't seen it in years, instead of having looked at it with Zachary only a few days earlier. "You brought my pictures! You are in for a real treat. Let me show you…" She opened the photo album reverently. Zachary scooted closer to look at it. It was the same album as he'd looked at with Vera before, but he knew more about the family this time. He wasn't going into it blind like he had at the beginning. If he was right, Clarence had been murdered by his own daughter, not killed in a burglary. And the others had covered it up. Gloria, at least, knew what had happened. Maybe she knew at the time, and maybe she had learned since, but she hadn't gone to the police and told them what she knew. Her son had suffered for years and the resentment between Robin and Gloria had grown.

"Here is me and Clarence." Vera started at the beginning, with what might have been an engagement photo of her and her husband. As much as Zachary wanted to race on ahead, he looked at their faces and their body language and tried to put together the story that they told without words. Vera took him through the births of the two girls.

Zachary looked at them together, looked at them with their father. He was still suspicious of Clarence abusing the girls. That was the story he was accustomed to hearing. Robin must have had a good reason for killing him. Women didn't just go around killing their fathers out of the blue. Had Clarence abused them as little girls? Had he been too strict? Molested them? Zachary wouldn't have guessed it from the pictures. The girls were usually smiling or laughing. They didn't seem awkward or afraid when Clarence was in the same picture.

"What was Clarence like as a father?"

"He was a good daddy." Vera sighed. "I know he wished that he could have been home more to spend more time with them. He worked a lot when they were little. Long hours. They barely saw him during the week. Just on the weekend, when he got a break. And he'd be so tired he'd just fall asleep in front of the game on the TV."

"Did he get mad when they bothered him? Yell at them?"

"Everybody yells sometimes. He was a good daddy."

Vera reached for her mug. Zachary handed it to her and watched like a hawk to make sure she was steady enough to take it and that it wasn't too hot. He didn't need her dumping scalding tea all over herself. When she'd had a sip, he took it from her and put it down on the side table.

"And then when they were older, he didn't have to work so much?"

Vera was looking at pictures of the girls as they got older. Graduation pictures. Boyfriend pictures. The pictures of Gloria with Rhys, looking awkward and posed.

"How did Clarence feel about Gloria getting pregnant? I'll bet that was a shock."

"Well, neither of us was happy about it, I'll tell you that. But shocked? No. Gloria was wild. She wouldn't listen. Sneaked out at night. Who knows how much drinking and drugging she was doing. She wasn't a nice girl. Not like Robin."

"Robin didn't run wild like that?"

"No. She was more careful. The older one is always the perfectionist. Tries to show Mom and Dad that they can do everything right. Gloria was never like that. She was always looking for her own way to do everything."

"But you took her and the baby back."

"How could we not? She couldn't take care of a baby by herself. That child would have been abandoned in a garbage can or on the street. We had to look after him. And we hoped that she would learn to take some responsibility, get back on track. Turn her life around."

"I guess it worked," Zachary offered. "She seems much better now."

Vera frowned for a moment, then her brow smoothed again. "Yes, she's a very nice girl now. Very responsible. A good mom to Rhys. It took her a long time to get there, but she got herself turned around."

Zachary looked down at the page. Gloria with Rhys. Grandpa Clarence holding Rhys, laughing. A couple of random shots of Robin or Gloria by themselves. Robin and Vera making Christmas cookies.

Zachary's stomach tightened, thinking of Christmas preparations. He still couldn't think about getting ready for Christmas without a feeling of panic.

"How did Gloria and Robin get along, after Rhys was born? Robin was older, it must have been strange for her to have a little sister with a baby."

"Yes, they didn't get along too well together." Vera's lips twitched. She was looking at the pictures, her eyes far away. "Robin was going through a difficult time."

"Oh?" Zachary glanced over at Kenzie. She sat quietly, listening to the stories, staying out of Zachary's way and not attracting Vera's attention. Vera might not have even been aware that Kenzie was in the room. "What was she having a difficult time with? I'll bet it was boys."

Vera chuckled. "Robin never had problems with boys. She always had a boyfriend, and others waiting in the wings for her to break up and give them a chance. She was my social butterfly. Always getting ready for this party or that dance. She knew everybody in her school. She even ran for school president."

"She seems like a very capable woman. So what was bothering her? You said she was going through a difficult time."

"You know how it is." Vera sighed. "When they go through puberty, things can get a little crazy. Teenage girls are so emotional. They can get quite unbalanced."

"What did she do?"

Vera turned over the next page slowly. "It wasn't one thing… it was a build-up over time. We just didn't know what to do with her. She would get angry over the littlest thing. Hysterical tears. All kinds of drama. Everybody was out to get her. Nobody understood her. Everybody was talking about her behind her back."

"Was she just hormonal? Or mentally ill?"

"There wasn't anything wrong with her," Vera assured him. "She's a very nice girl and everything is good now. She just went through that little stretch as a teenager. It was hard for her after Rhys was born. Here was her sister getting all kinds of attention and Robin, the perfectionist, wasn't getting any. We were too busy trying to raise Rhys and get Gloria onto a better track. We didn't have any time to give to Robin." Vera raised her eyes from the photographs and looked at Zachary. "It was a matter of life and death," she said. "Robin didn't understand that, but it was true. She couldn't see that we were trying to keep Gloria from doing something that would harm Rhys, or harm herself. She thought Gloria was just being a bratty little sister."

"Did she… get any treatment? Counseling?"

Vera turned the page. Rhys older in these pictures. Sitting in his mother's lap. Sitting in Robin's. A round-faced, smiley little toddler, beaming at the camera.

"She needed some help," Vera admitted. "She needed someone to talk to. It was hard for her. She didn't understand that what she was going through was normal. Everybody has a hard time. Growing up isn't easy."

"No. Is that what the doctor said? That she was just acting out?"

"Oh, what do doctors know?" Vera asked irritably. "They put us off for years. There's nothing wrong, it's just hormones. Try these antidepressants. Try tough love. Make her do things for her sister. She tried. We all tried."

Zachary looked down at the pictures. Robin's smiling face, carefully posed for the camera, gave nothing away. She had put up walls. She had tried, like Zachary had tried, to deal with the meds and their side effects and the doctors with conflicting opinions, and with parents who couldn't understand what she was going through. And she'd put on a brave front and tried to pretend to be normal for everyone else. While under the surface, the anger bubbled away.

Was it the first time she had been violent? All of the incident reports Zachary had were after Clarence's murder. Had they been afraid to do anything before that? Afraid that if they reported Robin, it would ruin her life? So they kept ignoring it and sweeping it under the carpet, until everything exploded and it was too late to put Humpty Dumpty together again.

"Robin fought with Clarence, didn't she?" he suggested.

"All kids fight with their parents. It's part of growing up. They need to learn to be independent."

"She wasn't a teenager anymore," Zachary pointed to a picture of Robin. "She must have been out of school at this point. She should have been past all of the rampaging hormones and been settling down."

"She was trying. I know she was trying. She struggled so hard to be what everyone wanted her to be. The perfect student. The perfect daughter. The perfect worker. I told her she didn't have to be perfect for me. It was okay for her to make mistakes and to let us know when she was feeling down. She didn't have to be happy and gracious all the time for everyone."

"Wearing a mask."

"That's what she said. She always had to wear a mask. She could never show anybody what she was really like underneath. Because it was too awful. I didn't believe that. I knew she was mixed up. Things were messy inside. But she was my daughter. I knew she was a good girl. No matter how hard it was for her to do the right things, she was really a good girl inside."

Vera turned a couple more pictures. Zachary knew they would soon reach the end of the pictures of Clarence. Clarence most often was with Rhys. Fishing with him, doing woodwork or other kinds of handyman work. The boy obviously idolized his grandpa and spent as much time as he could with him.

"Grandpa's little shadow."

Vera nodded, a sweet, sad smile on her face. "Oh, yes. Grandpa's little shadow. They were inseparable. I always said to Clarence, 'what are you going to do when he has to go to school? How is he going to be able to go by himself when you spoil him all the time?'

He always just shook his head and said it would all work out in good time. Who knew how long he had to spend with his grandson?"

Tears started to leak out the corners of her eyes. Because Clarence had been right. He had been right to spend as much time as he could with his grandson, because in the end, he was going to be taken away long before his time.

"And then you came home one day, and you saw what Robin had done."

Vera didn't disagree. She continued to dab at the tears, mourning her departed husband.

"Did you know before then that she might hurt someone? Had she ever hurt anyone before that?"

Vera sniffled. "Not… like that. She would get out of control. I knew it wasn't her fault. She couldn't help it."

"And what would happen? She hit you?"

Kenzie shifted in her seat, distracting Zachary's attention. He darted a look over at her, and saw her wide, worried eyes. He pushed them out of his mind and focused on Vera.

"She'd hit you," he suggested. "Probably more than once. She'd left you with bruises."

"It wasn't her fault. The doctor kept saying that if he could just get her medications right, she would be fine."

"She'd broken bones. You didn't tell anyone?"

"We said… they were accidents. And they were, because they were out of her control. She never meant to hurt anybody."

"And Rhys?"

Vera shook her head slowly. "You have no idea what it was like trying to raise that boy. His mother running around all over town, acting like a little hussy. Coming home drunk or as high as a kite. So irresponsible. And Robin… she was trying so hard. She wanted so badly to be a good girl. She really did. But no matter what they gave her…"

"It never worked."

"She didn't deserve to be punished." Vera blinked her big,

dark eyes at Zachary. "Gloria said she should be punished for what she did. Put in prison. Gloria was the irresponsible one. Robin shouldn't have to be put in prison when she was trying so hard."

"You all knew she was the one who had killed Clarence. You knew there was no burglary."

"We didn't know what had happened," Vera insisted. "We didn't see it. We could only piece it together, we could only guess."

"What about Rhys? Was he a witness? Grandpa's little shadow?"

"He was in his bed, curled up tight in a little ball. *Just stop it. Just stop it.*"

"Stop what?"

"It was Robin's voice. What Robin would say when someone was 'driving her crazy.' Chewing too loudly or fidgeting or doing something else she couldn't stand. Rhys kept repeating it over and over. *Just stop it.*"

Vera reached to turn the page. Zachary put his hand out to stop her from turning it. He wanted to hear more about that day. To understand why Clarence had died and why everyone had covered it up.

Vera glared at him and with a force he hadn't expected, pulled the photo album away from him and turned to the next page.

"Poor little Rhys," she said in a faraway voice. "He was so sad after Clarence died."

"He had to go to an institution."

"You don't put a little boy in a place like that… but we didn't know what else to do. He was falling apart."

"And Robin? Did you send her away?"

She wasn't in any of the pictures on that page, nor on the next.

"I couldn't," Vera said. "People would know what had happened. We had to make things look normal. She was different after that." Vera's brows furrowed, and she shook her head. "She had changed."

"How had she changed?"

"She wasn't my sweet girl anymore. She wasn't... innocent anymore."

Or maybe Vera had stopped seeing her as the little girl trying to be good and saw what she had become; a jealous woman who had to have everything her way. Who had taken her own father's life over some petty bother.

"You started calling the police when she got out of control."

"She was very angry about that. Stanley left her, said he couldn't deal with it anymore. Up until then... I had thought she would settle down with him. She would get married and she'd have someone giving her all of the attention she needed. She would be out of the house and we could live in peace."

"You must have found something that worked eventually. The calls to the police stopped. Rhys came home and you were all living together again."

"It was a hard time." Zachary was sure that was an understatement. "Making sure that Rhys was safe... Robin knew if she ever did anything to hurt him, she would go to jail. We didn't talk about it, but we never left him alone with her. Never left her to watch him."

Zachary couldn't imagine what it had been like for the boy. To have had to live in the same house as a woman he knew to be a murderer. Unable to tell anyone what had happened. He looked at the boy's sad face in all of the pictures after Clarence's death. Gloria had finally grown up and taken responsibility, but she couldn't fix the damage that had been done. She lived every day with the knowledge that Robin had never been punished for what she had done. Then she was faced with the fact that Robin was going to die without ever being punished. Poisoning her must have seemed like such a small satisfaction. A few days of suffering, after all that they had suffered over the years. One tiny retribution; depriving Robin of her last few months of her life.

Zachary wondered whether Vera knew what Gloria had done. Had Gloria told her? Had she watched Gloria inject the iron into the IV? Approved of it? As much as he wanted to know and to get a clear picture, that wasn't the most important thing. It was more important to keep Vera talking. If she clammed up, there was no chance of finding out where Gloria might have gone with Bridget. Zachary studied the pictures as Vera turned the pages. Rhys's growing-up years. Moving from boyhood to a gangly teenager. His face always worried or sad.

There was a candid shot of him looking down, intent on something in his hands. Playing an electronic game or texting with a friend.

Zachary's sudden movement startled Vera. She looked at him, eyes wide as he dug the phone out of his pocket. "Did you get a call? I didn't hear it ring."

Zachary shook his head. "Does Rhys ever send you messages on your phone? Maybe pictures or a text message?"

Vera's eyes were wide.

"Rhys sent me a few messages," Zachary said. He was working out the timeline in his head. The friend request from Rhys had come Monday after Zachary had been at the house. Rhys had come out to see his grandma while Zachary was there and had been hustled back away to his room. After Zachary had left, Rhys had tracked down Zachary's social media account to connect with him. Vera must have told him who Zachary was and why he was there.

Zachary looked at those first messages. Sad faces. First the basset hound and then the emoticon. Zachary had thought that Rhys was sad about Robin's death. But Rhys had been sad a lot longer than that. He was sad about losing his grandpa. About the horrible situation he found himself in, living with someone who might cause him harm if given the opportunity. Unable to make his voice heard and to be safe.

When Zachary had said he was sorry about Robin's death, Rhys had responded with a picture of his family. The three women together, with him posed in front of them. What had he been trying to tell Zachary? Not that he missed Robin and was sad she had died, but that this was how he had lived, trapped in a home built of secrets, lies, and abuse? How had he felt looking at that picture, with the women's plastic smiles trying to hide what had happened all those years ago? Did Rhys remember what had happened? Or had they managed to erase that night from Rhys's conscious memories, leaving him with just a feeling of dread and danger and deep unhappiness day after day.

"You must miss her a lot," Zachary had written back, not understanding, and Rhys had not responded.

Were they already on the run? Was Zachary the one lifeline that Rhys had reached out to, hoping a private investigator would understand and be able to help? But Zachary had not understood.

"What did he send you?" Vera asked, her head turned to try to see the messages Zachary was looking at.

Zachary thumbed to the next message. Wednesday. The day Gloria had taken Bridget. Zachary held the phone where Vera could see the picture of the moving gif of a fat dog stuck in a toilet bowl. *Help me.*

"Oh, look at that," Vera said, with a catch in her throat. "Isn't that funny."

But she didn't say it like it was funny. Did she know that Rhys really had been begging for help? She had known the boy since he was born. She had communicated with him throughout all of his mute years and had probably seen similar pictures or messages. She had the insight into Rhys's mind that Zachary lacked. She probably knew that, far from simply sharing a funny picture with Zachary, Rhys had been reaching out, begging for help.

And then the last picture Rhys had sent to him. He didn't show that one to Vera. A cartoon character surrounded by walls of flame. *Everything is going to be just fine.*

Knowing what he did now, Zachary had a chill at the ominous picture. Where was Rhys? What hell was he going through? Did he know that Gloria had killed Robin? Did he understand why Gloria had taken Bridget? Did he know what was going to happen next?

Zachary had waited patiently for responses from Rhys. He had not wanted to push Rhys away by being too nosy. He had just accepted that Rhys would message him back again when he was comfortable doing so, sending him another amusing picture or cryptic message.

But he couldn't wait any longer. Zachary tapped the field to enter his own message to Rhys.

Where are you?

He looked over at Kenzie. She inched her chair a little closer to him. "Rhys has been messaging with you?"

"Just twice," Zachary said, looking down at his phone and willing Rhys to message him back again. "On Monday and on Wednesday."

"And Wednesday…" Kenzie trailed off.

Zachary nodded.

Vera was watching them, looking troubled. Zachary drew her attention back to the photo album. "Did you ever go somewhere on vacation?" he prompted. "Somewhere you went with the whole family? Or maybe somewhere you and the girls and Clarence went, when they were young? Before Gloria started getting into trouble."

Vera looked back down at the album. She turned a couple of pages slowly. "We didn't have a lot of money. There was no Disneyland or anything like that."

"No," Zachary agreed. "Maybe a road trip? A cabin in the woods or somewhere Gloria really loved?"

Vera's expression was vague. Her eyes went over the pictures of Rhys and her daughters. "A cabin?" she echoed. Zachary watched her eyes, trying to read whether she was remembering something or just repeating his words.

Zachary's phone vibrated in his hand and he looked down at it. There was an answer from Rhys, but again, it was in the form of a picture. Zachary stifled a groan. Rhys was capable of writing a short answer, that's what Gloria had told him. So why couldn't he give Zachary a word or two pinpointing his location instead of making him interpret a picture?

"What is it?" Kenzie asked.

"A fish." Zachary showed it to Vera. "Where would Gloria and Rhys go that there were fish?"

Vera smiled. "Rhys used to love to fish."

"He used to go with Clarence, didn't he?" Zachary encouraged. "Where did they like to go?"

"They went lots of different places. There are many good fishing spots around here."

"Yes, there are," Zachary agreed. He had never been fishing in his life and had no idea where the popular fishing spots would be. "Did Gloria ever go with them?"

Vera shook her head. "Gloria didn't like fishing. Neither of the girls did. They were city girls, both of them."

"They never went somewhere there was also fishing?"

Vera looked blank.

Frustrated, Zachary tapped a message back to Rhys.

Need more. Want to help but don't know where u r.

Zachary pictured Rhys, hunched over his phone in some McDonalds or somewhere else with public wifi, pretending he was playing a game while Gloria ordered their dinner. Or closeted in a bathroom out of her sight, with only a few minutes to get his message to Zachary.

The phone vibrated. Zachary stared at the picture of Snoopy from the Peanuts comic strip. Smiling and dancing with his feathered friends.

"Come on, Rhys," he murmured. "I'm not getting it. Kenzie, can you think of anything? Vera?"

He showed the picture to each of them. Vera smiled and said "Snoopy!"

"Does Snoopy mean anything? Did Rhys go somewhere with Snoopy as a kid? Did he have a Snoopy toy? A dog? A beagle?"

"No. We never had a dog, though Rhys has always liked them. We couldn't have one; Robin was allergic."

Vera's forehead wrinkled and she looked to the side, giving off clear signals she was lying. She reached for her tea and Zachary again guided her hands to make sure she was steady with it. Though it was cooling now and would only be uncomfortable if she spilled it.

"Robin wasn't allergic to dogs," he said.

Vera's lip stuck out in an exaggerated pout. Kenzie looked at Zachary. "How do you know that?"

"Because she wasn't, was she?" Zachary directed it back at Vera again, who shook her head and didn't fill in the rest of the details. "But maybe it was Robin that prevented you from having a dog even though Rhys loved them." He searched her eyes. "Did Robin not like dogs, so Rhys couldn't have one? Or maybe you were afraid she would hurt a dog. You couldn't get one in case it got underfoot and Robin hurt it. It was hard enough keeping track of Rhys and keeping him out of her way."

Vera looked at Zachary in dismay. Zachary pursued it, not because he wanted to hurt her, but because he had to figure out where Gloria had gone with Rhys.

"Was there a place they would go to get a dog? If Gloria decided it was okay to have a dog now that Robin wasn't around anymore, was there a farm or supplier that they might have gone to?"

"No."

"Rhys never had a dog? Even for a few days? A stray he had to get rid of?"

"No," Vera insisted. "We never had any animals. It just wouldn't have been good. Things upset Robin. Things irritated her. Animals... you can train a dog, but you can't make sure it never does anything to irritate her"

"What do you think of when you look at this picture?" Zachary showed it to them each again. "Snoopy... happy... dancing..."

"Peanuts, Charlie Brown," Kenzie contributed. "Charles Schultz. Chuck."

"Flying, birds," Vera said, getting into the spirit of things. "Yellow. Flapping. Woodstock."

"Woodstock!" Zachary said. "That's it. That's gotta be it. Did Rhys or Gloria ever go to Woodstock?"

"The music festival?" Kenzie asked, puzzled.

"No. Woodstock, New Hampshire." Zachary looked at Vera. "Did any of you ever go to Woodstock, New Hampshire?"

"Rhys went fishing there with Clarence," Vera said slowly, seeming uncertain. "Is that… is that what you meant?"

"Yes. Tell me about that. Where did they go in Woodstock? Where did they stay? In a hotel? Did they camp?"

"I don't know…" Vera touched the photo album uncertainly.

Zachary reached over and turned the pages, running the clock back until he saw a picture of Clarence again. "Is there a picture in here? Of Woodstock?"

"Maybe…" Vera's voice wavered.

Zachary scoured the pages. He pointed to a picture of Rhys standing with his grandfather, green leaves behind them.

"What about that? Is that in Woodstock?"

"It might be…" Vera leaned over it to study it more carefully. "Yes… I think it might be…"

Kenzie got up from her chair and leaned over the picture as well.

"Where did they stay?" Zachary prompted again. "This looks very rustic." He could see just the corner of a building, gray weathered wood. "Did they have a cabin here? Was there a fishing lodge?"

Vera nodded. "I don't remember the name of it. Clarence rented it from an Indian fellow. He wanted a real fishing experience with Rhys. Getting up before the dawn. Frying their own fish over the fire for breakfast. It was supposed to be a *guys'* vacation."

Zachary cocked his head at her wording. "It was *supposed to be*. But then what happened?"

"Gloria decided that Rhys was too young. He couldn't go with Clarence without Gloria or me there to supervise. Clarence was wonderful with Rhys, but he wasn't a mother. A mother knows when her child is sick and what to do about it. And doesn't let him get caught on a fishhook. Or fall in the lake and drown. She didn't think that Clarence would be responsible enough. And she thought that Rhys might miss her and get homesick. Then they would have to come back and not have their special weekend."

"She wanted to go along," Zachary summarized.

"Well, what woman would want to go along on a fishing trip like that? She didn't want to, but she didn't think Rhys was old enough to go on his own. So she insisted she had to come along too."

Zachary exchanged looks with Kenzie. "So she went. She knows where this cabin is."

"Cabin!" Vera made a noise. "It wasn't anything more than a shack. Gloria said it had running water, but no electricity, no shops within walking distance. It was in the middle of nowhere."

"Do you know exactly where it was? Do you have a map? The name of the fellow Clarence rented it from?"

"No… I don't know. I wasn't there, so I don't know, exactly. But it was Woodstock," Vera nodded definitely. "I know that for sure."

"We'll find it," Zachary said. "Woodstock is no bigger than a postage stamp. There could only be a handful of people renting out cabins there. I might be able to get more details from Rhys once we're there and he can tell us what's close by."

"You did it," Kenzie breathed. "I can't believe you figured it out. We should call Detective Lashman and let him know."

Zachary swore.

Kenzie looked at him, frowning. "What? What's wrong?"

"They crossed state lines."

"Is that a problem?"

"Not only is it out of Lashman's jurisdiction, that makes it an FBI case."

"That's good. FBI has great resources."

Zachary looked at the time on his phone. If he told Lashman and Lashman told the FBI, they would start looking Saturday morning. Bridget would have been missing for four days. Being past the first forty-eight hours, the FBI would assign it a lower priority. There was less likelihood of retrieval. If Gloria had not been taking care of Bridget's needs, death was a real possibility.

He wished he'd been able to ask Rhys more questions and that Rhys had been able to answer him more clearly.

"We have to go. We'll call Lashman on the way and give him a heads-up. He can call the feds, and if they get there before we do, more power to them. But I can't sit and wait on them."

"I don't know…"

"If you're afraid of getting in trouble, I can take your keys and go without you. Just give me a head start before you call and report it." Zachary stood up.

"Oh, you're not driving my baby without me!" Kenzie shot back.

"Then let's go. If you really don't want to come, then drop me at a car rental. But if you're just afraid of what the cops or Dr. Wiltshire will say, I'll happily agree that I coerced you. Or that you were worried about my stability." He gave her a hard, forced smile. "You *are* worried about my stability, aren't you?"

"I'm always worried about your stability," Kenzie agreed. "Especially wherever Bridget is concerned."

"Then let's hit the road."

Vera was looking at them, a puzzled crease in her forehead. Zachary bent over and kissed her cheek.

"Thank you, Vera. You were a big help. We're going to go now, to go help Rhys."

"Okay," Vera agreed, giving him an uncertain smile. "Thank you."

They hit the road. It was probably a good thing that Kenzie was the one who was driving, because once Zachary sat down in the car, he found himself shaking all over. Kenzie didn't say anything at first as they headed east on the highway. But after a while, she looked over at him.

"Are you okay?"

"How could I be? Bridget could be hurt or sick. She could be dying. She's going through who-knows-what hell, and I'm sitting around having tea and looking at pictures with an old woman. Do you know how that feels?"

"But it worked. You never would have been able to figure it out without getting Vera to talk to you. You did the right thing."

"I should have figured it out sooner. I should have figured out that Bridget was missing on Tuesday! How could she be missing for three days before I knew it?" Zachary's voice rose. He knew it wasn't Kenzie's fault. He shouldn't be yelling at her. But he was feeling bad. Overwhelmed and inadequate and too late.

"Because you thought she was just avoiding you. You thought she had what she needed and just didn't want to talk to you."

"How could I think that about her?"

"Because it's probably true," Kenzie said calmly. "That's exactly what she would do. Why feel guilty for that? You're doing every-thing you can to help her. You've been able to get further than Detective Lashman with all of his personnel and resources. That's why Gordon called you."

"He called me to find out if Bridget was with me."

Kenzie turned her gaze away from the highway to look at him. "Do you seriously think he thought Bridget was with you? When he realized that she hadn't been home in a day or two, he thought maybe she had shacked up at your place? Or maybe the two of you were out having brunch? Gordon Drake didn't get to where he is today by being stupid. He called you because he knew you were the best man for the job. He called the police to cover all his bases, but he called you first."

It was hard for Zachary to believe. He shook his head and looked out the window, wishing that they could get to Woodstock faster. Should they have gone to the airport instead? Would that have gotten them there any sooner? Probably not. They would have to make arrangements, wait for flights, deal with security and delays. Maybe the FBI would block him from flying in an effort to keep him out of the case. Driving was better. Short of setting up road blocks, there was no way the FBI could stop him from driving there.

Rhys lay as still as he could, listening to his mother breathing. Gloria was restless, and stayed up late muttering to herself, watching reruns of American Idol on her phone, and frequently going to the windows to peer outside and make sure no one was going to sneak up on them.

A few times, Rhys had dozed, the restless kind of sleep he experienced when he had to sleep somewhere other than his own bed. He would stay awake late into the night, and not until he became convinced that he was not going to sleep at all would he finally drift off into restless dreams about coyotes and

Grandpa Clarence and things that had happened when he was little.

But it had been several days, and his body wanted to sleep, even though he was trying to stay awake.

It was a long time before Gloria's breathing finally settled into a long, slow rhythm and Rhys was sure she was asleep. He counted to one hundred slowly in his head. If she made any noise or movement, he would start over again, so that he could be sure she was soundly asleep.

Then he left his blanket on the floor and crept over to where the other woman, Bridget, moved around restlessly. She wasn't trying to sleep and she had no blanket or warm jacket or anything else to make her comfortable. He had seen her fall asleep sitting up several times during the day, her chin gradually lowering to her chest until she startled and sat up again.

She saw him moving toward her but didn't make any sound. Not a single whisper or movement that might rouse Gloria out of her restless sleep. Rhys drew up close to her until they were nearly touching. Bridget's white skin seemed to glow in the moonlight.

Rhys worked the paper-wrapped half hamburger out of his pocket. It was squashed flat, but Bridget didn't seem to take any notice. She eagerly took it from him and took a bite. In a few moments, it was gone. She licked at the wrapper. Rhys dug into his other pocket and pulled out the remains of a cookie. His stomach was grumbling, but he knew Bridget was in worse shape than he was. He could only save so much for her without Gloria noticing. The bit of cookie was polished off just as quickly as the hamburger. Bridget looked at him to see if there were anything else. Rhys shook his head regretfully.

She drew a finger down her throat. *A drink?*

Rhys looked over at Gloria. She hadn't moved. He stood up and tiptoed over to the bathroom. He didn't turn on the light, but he knew where everything was in the tiny bathroom. He felt for the cup he'd left there earlier in the day. He positioned it under the faucet and trickled water into it. If Gloria woke up, he would just drink it himself. She couldn't prove he was getting it for Bridget unless she caught him giving it to her.

Since his stomach was growling, he downed a glass himself first, and then refilled it for Bridget. He stopped in the bathroom doorway and listened for Gloria's breathing to reassure himself she was still asleep, then went over to Bridget with the water. She gulped it down. Rhys could tell by the way she pressed her hand over her stomach that she had eaten and drunk too fast. She pressed the cup back into Rhys's hand, smiling her thanks. Her lips were rough and cracked.

Rhys pulled out his iPod and navigated to the games folder where he'd hidden his messaging app. He tapped on the message thread, positioned the messages, and turned it around so Bridget could see. Her eyes darted over the contents, then went back to Rhys, questioning, hopeful. He nodded. Then he deleted each one so that if Gloria ever looked at it, there would be no evidence of his communication. He met Bridget's eyes one more time, imploring her to be careful and not do anything to upset Gloria.

Then he went back over to his blanket and lay down.

2 8

Pinpointing the cabin where Gloria was likely to have taken Rhys and Bridget was not as easy as Zachary had hoped. He had imagined that with the small population of Woodstock, he'd be able to find out who had cabins that might have been used as fishing lodges in the past ten years, who was still renting them out, and quickly narrow down which one Gloria was using.

But he wasn't a native of Woodstock and hadn't been prepared for the suspicion that he would face as an outsider.

"I just want to find out who owns the cabin that my father rented a few years ago," he told yet another resident. "He said he got it from a native fellow. He kept talking about how remote it was. Not even any electricity, just running water pumped by a generator. Very rustic."

But the woman selling ice cream cones was having none of it. "I don't know," she said stubbornly. "Everybody in these parts has somewhere they go. The woods are littered with 'rustic' shacks and shanties. Anyone who rents one of those deserves what they get!"

"No, he liked it," Zachary protested. "I wanted to find the place he stayed… take some pictures…"

The woman just shook her head and continued to scoop ice cream. Zachary and Kenzie cycled through various different

250

stories, trying to find something that would gain the trust of the Woodstock residents.

"They think they're going to get into some kind of trouble," Kenzie said. "They're getting cash and not declaring it as income or they're afraid you want to sue them. Asking questions is just making people more and more suspicious, no matter what kind of story you have about a relative who came here once and stayed there."

"Then what are we going to do? If I had the time, we could just surveil the area, watch the main services and wait for Gloria to show up. But we don't have the time. In the amount of time it would take to find her, Bridget could…"

"Well, then… we're not looking for a specific cabin. We're just looking for one we can rent. Somewhere no one will bother us. If someone has something promising, we go take a look. If they say it's already rented…"

"Then we see who rented it," Zachary finished, "and if they match Gloria's and Rhys's descriptions."

"And if we happen to find a Native renting out his old shack, one that was old and falling down ten years ago, we take a look at that one for sure. Whether he remembers an old black man coming out here with his grandson ten years ago or not."

Zachary nodded his agreement. "Do we stay together or split up?"

"Let's split up… we've both got phones and can reach each other if we get a promising lead. Cover twice as much ground."

"Okay. But if you get a bad vibe from anyone… we get back together. I don't want you running into any danger alone."

"Or you," Kenzie declared. "You're the one who keeps landing in hospital."

"Uh… or me," he agreed.

"And you promise me you won't go off on your own or do anything stupid. As soon as you get a lead, you let me know."

Zachary nodded.

"What about calling the authorities?" Kenzie suggested. "Do you think it's time?"

"When we find out where they are. Right now... if you fill this town full of FBI agents... word is going to get back to Gloria in two seconds. I don't want to put Rhys or Bridget in danger."

"Have you messaged Rhys? To see if you can get any details from him? It would be a lot easier if we had some better clues as to where they are."

"I've messaged him, but I haven't gotten anything back. I'm thinking that if they don't have any electricity, he might not be able to keep his phone charged. Or they might be out of cell range some of the time. It seems like he can only message me once a day, so I'm thinking that might be when they go into town for something else."

"Well, we'll keep our eyes open. I take it you don't want me to ask the restaurant owners whether they have seen a black boy and his mother...? You have that picture on your phone you could show around."

"Too dangerous. I can't risk tipping them off. We have to find out where they are staying. If they come into town and someone says there's been people asking questions about them... they may take off without going back to get Bridget, and if we don't know where they're staying and she's being kept, then..."

Kenzie nodded, conceding the point. "Then I'm off to see if someone has a cabin I could rent for a couple of days."

"We need to leave today," Gloria told Rhys.

Rhys was sitting on his blankets on the floor. He stared at her and shook his head, not understanding.

"We've been here long enough," she told him. "People are going to start to ask questions. It's a small town. They're used to tourists coming through for a few days and then leaving again. We can't stay here forever."

Rhys looked over at Bridget.

"We'll leave her here," Gloria said. "That should make you happy. We'll leave her here and she'll be fine. We'll find another house and start a new life, just you and me."

Rhys closed his eyes and tried to picture it. How many times over his life had he dreamed of just that? Being able to leave Aunt Robin and his old life behind. He would be like a new person, undamaged, able to talk like anyone else and not plagued by nightmares.

But Gloria had brought him new nightmares. He would never be able to forget the pretty, blond Bridget and how her eyes had become more dull and sunken with each passing day. Her features would be burned into his brain for the rest of his life, just like Grandpa's face. He'd always seen Aunt Robin as the monster, and his mother as his protector, but that had changed. When Aunt Robin died, Gloria had changed and had taken her place, angry and snapping at Rhys and taking this woman who she saw as a threat. He would never have predicted that his mother would have done those things.

"I think maybe we'll go south," Gloria suggested, "settle down somewhere it doesn't snow. How would you like that? No heavy coats and gloves and traipsing to school through all of that ice and snow."

Rhys looked away from her. He took out his iPod and tapped through the screens to find a game to play.

"Rhys!" Gloria's voice was sharp. "Look at me. Don't ignore me!"

He didn't look up. Gloria strode across the room toward him. Rhys tensed, bracing himself against her anger, but still didn't look up at her. Gloria snatched the iPod out of his hand and flung it to the side, making it clatter across the floor. She grabbed his upper arm and shook him.

"I said look at me!"

Rhys did as he was told, his heart beating hard and fast, a lump in his throat.

"I'm doing this for you!" Gloria shouted. "All of this is for you! You think I'm doing it for my own good? I'm doing it to give you a life. You deserve to have a real life!"

Rhys shook his head and blinked out tears. That wasn't what he wanted. Not if it meant hurting other people and losing his mother. He wanted her to be the woman she'd always been for him.

Gloria shoved Rhys, pushing him over. She turned her back on him, isolating him to emphasize her anger.

Rhys didn't move for a long time, just lying on the floor where she'd discarded him. She picked up her coil notebook and started to write notes furiously. After her attention had been distracted from him for a while, Rhys reached out for his iPod. It was a few feet out of his reach, so he crawled over to it, then pulled it to him and held it protectively against his body. He stayed there motionless for a long time, just curled up on the floor, watching Gloria. Out the corner of his eye, he saw Bridget shift her position, silently and very slowly. So she was awake, even though she'd pretended to be asleep or unconscious when Gloria had checked on her earlier.

Rhys sat up and moved so that his back was against the wall. He looked down at his iPod. The screen was cracked, two long lines that angled toward each other and joined in a V at the edge. Rhys woke it up with the press of a button and was relieved to see that it still powered on and was readable in spite of the damage.

He wished that Gloria would take him back into town so he could get a wifi connection and see if Zachary had sent him any more messages. He wanted to send Zachary a few words or a picture to make sure he knew where to find them. Zachary had to find them before Gloria decided to leave Woodstock. Rhys didn't know if his mother planned to do something to Bridget to make sure she couldn't follow them or give them away, or if she just planned to leave Bridget chained up there to starve to death before someone found her. If Rhys hadn't been surreptitiously giving

Bridget food and water, he was pretty sure she would already be dead.

He had one other option, and that was to try to tether his iPod to Gloria's new phone. She had given it to him to set it up for her, but he hadn't had the nerve to piggyback it. If he could connect to it and it had a strong enough signal, he might be able to contact Zachary without going back to town. But he ran the risk of Gloria realizing what he was doing and taking measures to make sure he couldn't do it again.

He watched her writing in her notebook and tried to decide whether to attempt it.

It was almost lunchtime when Zachary and Kenzie got back together at a rustic-themed diner to compare notes. Zachary ordered a coffee for himself and a sandwich for Kenzie, knowing she would be hungry after their busy morning.

"I've got a couple of possibilities," Kenzie said. "Nothing that immediately felt like 'this is the one,' but they fit the profile closely enough."

Zachary nodded. "Me too."

"But the trouble is, they either aren't rented or the person who rented them doesn't match Gloria's description. You don't think she's working with someone else, do you? A boyfriend…?"

"I don't think so. Other than Rhys, and he couldn't pass as an adult. The thing is, she might *not* be renting it. She might have just found it empty and used it."

Kenzie nodded. She took a big bite of the sandwich and didn't say anything else while she chewed.

"I found a couple." Zachary pulled up the notes he had made on his phone. "They might be the same ones as you found…"

He put the phone on the table and slid it across to Kenzie. Kenzie leaned over it to read the details, nodding.

The phone gave a short vibration. Kenzie looked up at Zachary. "It's him."

"Rhys?"

Zachary grabbed the phone and turned it back around to look. The banner announcing Rhys's message disappeared, and Zachary switched apps to find it. He could see the last message he had sent to Rhys.

We are coming to Woodstock. Where r u staying?

And then Rhys's reply, a picture that appeared to be a photo he had taken himself rather than a meme or gif available within the app. It was a low angle, showing a wood plank floor and a steel bed frame, with just a piece of Robin sitting on the thin mattress covered with a gray wool blanket.

"Okay, we're right, it is a cabin," Zachary said, showing it to Kenzie. "Do you think there is enough for anyone to recognize?"

"Maybe for whoever owns it. But they're going to be suspicious about why we're asking."

Zachary concentrated on the problem, then texted back.

Did Gloria rent it?

The reply came back quickly.

No.

"No," Kenzie repeated aloud. "Then it could be Old Bear's cabin. It's supposed to be empty right now."

Before they could send anything back to Rhys, another message came in. Another photo Rhys had taken himself. There was a heap of clothes in a corner, difficult to see in the dim lighting. Zachary studied it, trying to make out the details to see what else Rhys was trying to tell him. Obviously, Rhys had to be careful and could not use his flash and attract Gloria' attention.

Zachary realized it wasn't a pile of clothes. It was the shape of a woman.

Bridget.

R hys deliberately moved slowly. *Where was Zachary?* Rhys thought Zachary had understood where they were, but maybe he'd gone to the wrong cabin. There had to be dozens of them in the wilderness surrounding Woodstock.

If Zachary had gone to the wrong one, all hope was lost. Rhys was convinced Gloria intended to do something to Bridget before they hit the road. Gloria hadn't told Rhys so, but Rhys was afraid of what was in the first aid kit Gloria brought with her and kept eyeing as she waited for Rhys to get ready to go.

Gloria had become more and more obsessed with medical matters since Aunt Robin had been diagnosed. She got thick texts out of the library and spent hours researching different therapies and medications that might help Aunt Robin. But as it had turned out, all of her research was for naught, since Aunt Robin had ended up dying even sooner than the doctors had predicted.

"Come on, I told you it's time to go," Gloria urged.

Rhys hesitated. He could squeeze a few more minutes out with a trip to the bathroom, but that would also mean leaving Gloria alone with Bridget, and Rhys was worried about what Gloria might do.

He walked to the cabin door with his bag. He opened the

door and scanned the clearing for any sign of Zachary or someone who could help him. All was quiet. Rhys offered his bag to his mother with a head-jerk toward the car, then hooked his thumb back toward the bathroom indicating that he wanted to use it before leaving.

Gloria sighed in exasperation and took the bag from him. "Honestly, Rhys. I wanted to be on the road an hour ago!"

He waited until he was sure she was on her way to the car to put their bags inside before heading to the bathroom. Bridget lay in the corner of the cabin, unmoving. Rhys pulled out his iPod as soon as he was through the bathroom door, looking for an update from Zachary. But there was nothing, and with Gloria out at the car, she was too far away for Rhys to piggyback on her signal again.

He filled the cup he had left on the edge of the sink, thinking that he might have enough time to give Bridget one more drink before Gloria returned. But when he opened the door to check her position, his heart jumped. Gloria was bending over Bridget.

"Ma—no!"

Gloria whirled around at the sound of his voice, dropping what was in her hand with a clatter. Her eyes were wild. "Go out to the car, Rhys!"

Rhys shook his head. His mouth moved as he tried to form words again, but his exclamation had drained his speech reserves.

"Go on. Go sit down and get yourself settled. You've done everything you need to do to get ready at least twice."

Rhys couldn't find any more excuses. But he couldn't let her do anything to Bridget. He shook his head again, refusing.

Gloria marched across the room to him. Rhys stubbornly stood his ground. She slapped him across the face, the blow so hard it made him see stars. His mother had never before hit him. He could see the shock and horror in her own face at what she had done, but she didn't apologize.

"Look what you made me do!" Her voice cracked. "You do what I tell you, Rhys. This is important. I know you don't understand what's going on, but you need to listen to me. Now go out to the car."

Rhys shook his head. He held his hand up in front of his face to block her from slapping him again. Gloria grabbed his wrist and wrenched his arm to the side.

"The car!" she insisted.

Rhys's face throbbed. Hot tears leaked out the corners of his eyes and a lump formed in his throat so big that he could barely breathe. He tried to get words out, but between his brain and the lump in his throat, he knew he couldn't speak. He grasped her hands. Not violent, like she'd been toward him, but soft and gentle. He lifted each up and kissed it, begging her with his eyes. Gloria was his mother and she knew him almost as well as Grandma, all of his facial expressions and body language. He silently begged her for all he was worth not to hurt Bridget. She wavered.

"Rhys…" she murmured. "I just want to protect you."

He continued to hold her hands, warm and smooth in his, praying for her to listen.

Finally, Gloria turned toward the outside door. Rhys let her pull her hands out of his and followed her out of the shack. She had nearly reached the car when an authoritative voice shouted over the stillness of the clearing.

"Freeze! Federal agents! Stay where you are!"

Gloria's head snapped around to look at Rhys to make sure he was okay. Rhys lifted his hands in surrender. How many times had she lectured him on how to behave if he were ever stopped by the police? How many times had she warned him about the hazards of being a young black man, especially one who couldn't say 'yes, sir' to a policeman? Gloria stared at Rhys for a minute, then mirrored his movement, raising her hands.

The peace of the forest clearing was broken by a swarm of black-uniformed men with big guns, overwhelming the unarmed woman and youth. Rhys kept his body soft, letting them pat him down and move him without resistance. They handcuffed Gloria, but not Rhys. When the all-clear had been called, Zachary entered the clearing.

Rhys let his breath out with a soft puff. Zachary approached him, both hands extended to either hug Rhys or give him a two-handed handshake. But Rhys moved away, taking hold of one of Zachary's hands and leading him into the cabin. There were already a couple of FBI agents there, bending over Bridget. Zachary rushed over; calling her name, swearing, and apologizing to her all in a jumble. The agents moved out of the way to allow Zachary to see her. One of them had picked up the syringe Gloria had dropped. Rhys retrieved the cup from the bathroom and inserted himself beside Bridget as well. Her eyes were open and she was attempting to smile at Zachary and reassure him. Her lips were cracked and swollen and her eyes deeply sunken. Rhys put the cup into her grasp and Zachary helped steady her shaking hands and raise it to her mouth. He kept the angle low, forcing her to sip it slowly instead of gulping it down.

Bridget licked her lips and cleared her throat. "He's my hero," she whispered. "She was going to kill me. Rhys wouldn't let her kill me."

Zachary put an arm around Rhys and pulled him close. Tears were streaming down his face.

"Thank you, Rhys. Thank you so much."

Rhys didn't try to squirm out of Zachary's hold. He just let Zachary hold him tight, both of their faces wet with tears.

3 0

O ne of the police officers held a cup of coffee in front of
Zachary's face. He looked up from the chair in the hospital
waiting room and saw that it was Joshua Campbell. He nodded
his thanks and took the coffee, taking a sip of the hot, rich blend
to steady his nerves.

"Another feather in your cap," Campbell observed, sitting
down in one of the other chairs. "You're getting quite a reputation
for being the guy to solve murders that weren't supposed to be
murders."

Zachary gave a self-deprecating shrug. "Sometimes the family
—or friends—know instinctively what the police or medical
examiner could never have known. I'm just following the direction
they point me."

"Well, I've known you were a good investigator for a long
time. Nice that you're getting some recognition."

Zachary's ears got warm. He was tongue-tied for a moment.
He never had gotten the knack for graciously accepting a
compliment.

"These murder cases," Campbell said, "that woman principal a
few months back, the abuses at Summit…"

Zachary nodded and took another sip of coffee. "Yeah, I guess.

Sometimes it feels like it's all skip tracing and cheating spouses, but there have been a few more interesting cases lately."

"And Lucas at the hospital," Campbell added to his list of Zachary's cases.

Lucas. Zachary had to think for a minute before he remembered the hospital worker who had upset Ruth Wicker during the Salter investigation.

"Lucas. I forgot about him. You looked into him? Did you find something?"

"Nothing we can charge him with, but enough to drop a word to the hospital on the QT that they might want to find a reason to let him go."

Zachary thought back to the way the hospital worker had behaved. Ignoring Ruth's protests, trying to bully his way through when confronted by Zachary, insisting he had the right to do whatever needed to be done for Ruth and that she owed him her gratitude for it. Then the way he had reported that Zachary had threatened him and kidnapped Ruth, which could very well have landed Zachary in jail if Ruth hadn't been able to verify his story and Campbell hadn't shown up when he did.

"That weasel," Zachary said. "What did you find out?"

"He's had various assault charges against him in the past. Not by hospital patients… but his work history is very checkered. He doesn't stay anywhere for long, and his previous employers say things like 'we cannot comment on that matter.'"

"They're gagged. They told him he could leave quietly and they would keep whatever had happened confidential."

"That's my impression," Campbell agreed. "In a case like this, if you fire the guy and refuse to give him references, then he sues you for termination without cause. That blows up into some big media circus and a legal case that costs thousands of dollars, if not hundreds of thousands. Cheaper to pay him out, give him a reference, and keep quiet."

"Especially when you can't prove he's done anything illegal or harmful to a patient."

"Exactly."

"Is the hospital going to send him on his way?"

"They're talking to their legal department."

So Lucas would be gone and no longer be a danger to vulnerable patients like Ruth.

Until he got another job.

Zachary wasn't able to see Bridget that first day, but when she asked him to visit her at the hospital the next, it sent his heart soaring. He knew she wasn't calling him about Robin's death, because she already knew Gloria had been the one to give Robin the iron that had caused her death.

That meant that Bridget wanted him for something else.

Maybe she had realized, when her own life was in jeopardy, that she really did love Zachary and wanted to get back together with him. Her relationship with Gordon could be no more than a sham when compared to the love Bridget and Zachary had shared together, the love that had driven Zachary to find Bridget and bring the forces of the FBI to bear just in time to save Bridget and apprehend Gloria before she could run again.

Zachary thought everything through before he went to see her. He showered, carefully shaved, and put on clean, neat clothes, a good notch or two higher than his usual jeans-and-tee combination. He went to a flower store. Not the hospital flower store with its sad little arrangements, but a real flower store. He didn't buy her red roses. Instead, he picked from the varieties of flowers that he had seen at the house, having the florist design a bright and cheerful arrangement in an elegant vase. He didn't buy her chocolates. That would be going too far, and he knew that since the chemo, she eschewed sugar and would not want to compromise her health. She needed to heal from her ordeal and overloading her system with sugar would just lower her immunity.

Then he headed to the hospital. He had her unit and room

number, and followed the hospital color and letter codes to get to the right place.

When he walked into the room, his heart sank. Gordon sat beside the bed, talking with Bridget in a low voice, holding hands with her. They both looked up when Zachary arrived. Bridget pulled her fingers out of Gordon's grip.

"Gordon, dear, would you mind…?"

Gordon nodded briskly and stood up. "I'll give the two of you some time alone."

Zachary strove to keep his expression blank as Gordon left the hospital room. He didn't want to sneer at Gordon or to give him a gloating look over Bridget's dismissing him. Zachary could be gracious whether he were the loser or the winner. For once, he was actually going to be the winner.

With Gordon out of the way, Zachary walked the rest of the way into the room. He showed Bridget the flowers and let her smell them, then put them down where she directed. Bridget stared at the arrangement for a few long seconds, giving no sign of what she was thinking. She motioned for Zachary to sit in the chair that Gordon had just vacated so he could sit at eye level with her. He could still feel the warmth from Gordon's body there.

"How are you feeling?" Zachary asked.

"I'm doing much better. So good to get properly hydrated and to be able to eat at regular intervals. It really is amazing how we take food for granted! We've always had what we need, so we don't understand what it is like to want."

Zachary nodded his understanding. He had experienced plenty of lean times as a child. Times when they simply didn't have food to put on the table and the children went to bed with empty stomachs. But Bridget wasn't thinking about that. She wasn't asking him whether he had ever experienced it. She was just sharing her experience with him.

"You're looking a lot better." It was amazing how much of a difference one day could make. Her color was better. The hollows in her skin had filled in. Her eyes were bright and alive with interest. He'd been afraid when he'd seen her at the cabin. She had looked so close to death. She had not been able to sit up or to raise the cup of water to her mouth on her own.

"I hope so!" Bridget patted at her hair. "I must have looked a fright…"

"No. Just… sick. I was worried about you."

"I wanted to thank you for everything you've done. For investigating Robin's death and figuring out what had happened. And then for searching for me and tracking me down. You really are… an amazing investigator."

Zachary smiled sheepishly, his face getting warm. "I had to find you. When I knew how long it had been, and that you would be waiting for me, wondering why I hadn't come…"

"It was the only thing I had any hope for. The police and the FBI…" She shrugged expressively. "I trusted your investigative skills and your… passion."

Zachary hadn't thought it was possible for him to blush even more, but he did, his ears and cheeks on fire. He reached for Bridget's hand.

"I care about you, Bridge… I couldn't live without you. If I had let something happen to you…" he trailed off. He wanted to tell her that he loved her. But the last few times he had said it, she had brushed his feelings off, even mocked him for making such a ridiculous statement in the midst of the dissolution of their marriage. *You don't even know what love is. You don't want a wife, you want a mother.*

"Zachary… no. Don't say anything else."

He was quiet, waiting.

"I care about what happens to you too. But… let's not go too far here. You and I… we're never going to be a couple again."

He felt like she had just stabbed him in the gut. She lay there and smiled sweetly as she twisted the knife.

"Gordon and I are not breaking up. I don't want to be with you again. We weren't good for each other."

"But—"

She shook her head. "You come here all cleaned up, with your flowers and your company manners... it's obvious what you're thinking. But we're over, Zachary. I can't ever be with you like that again."

Zachary took a long, shuddering breath. He nodded stoically. "Okay. Got it."

He stood up. He didn't know whether to shake her hand or kiss her on the cheek. He ended up doing neither.

"I'll, uh, see you around, then."

She reached toward him, eyes soft and concerned. "Are you okay, Zachary? Will you be okay?"

"Sure. Of course. Don't you worry about me."

EPILOGUE

Zachary had been holed up in his apartment for some time. Long enough that he'd lost count of the days and frequently had to look at the date on his phone or computer to orient himself. He had plenty of computer work and other desk work that he could do without going out or having to talk to anyone, so that was what he worked on.

Some friends or clients had called him and left messages. Zachary replied to them by email so he wouldn't actually have to speak to anyone. He'd finally ordered a couch for his living room that fit through the apartment door, and that was where he was spending his nights, watching TV until he fell asleep, the nights he actually managed to fall asleep.

There was a persistent knocking on the apartment door. Zachary ignored it for a good ten minutes, but whoever was there was not taking no for an answer, so they probably knew he was home and had not left the apartment in days. Zachary went to the door and looked through the peephole. He sighed and opened the door, stepping back to let Kenzie in.

"Hey," Kenzie said brightly. "I wondered where you'd gotten to. Glad to see you're still around."

Since he'd texted her answers to her voicemails, she really

couldn't complain that he hadn't responded or that she thought something had happened to him.

"Hi. Yeah. I've been busy with work."

"Any interesting cases?" She followed him into the living room and sat down on the new couch, testing it out. "Oh, this is nice! Comfy?"

"Sure."

Kenzie glanced over at the TV, which had pretty much been playing 24/7 for however long it had been since Zachary had gotten home from visiting Bridget at the hospital. He didn't like it when it was too quiet. "Are you watching something, or could we shut that off?"

Zachary wasn't even sure what time of day it was, let alone what program was on. He slipped out his phone and covertly checked the time and date on his way over to shut off the TV.

"Are you out of work early, or didn't you have a shift today?" he asked.

"I've been working overtime, so I took off early today."

"That's good," Zachary said without enthusiasm. "It's important to take care of yourself."

Kenzie snorted. He sat back down and glanced over at her.

"It's time to pick yourself up and dust yourself off, Zach."

"I'm fine."

"No, I don't think you are. I think you're spending your life holed up over here, moping over Bridget again. I told you from the start she wasn't interested in getting back together with you. She wanted your investigative services. She should have just hired someone out of the phonebook. That would have been a lot kinder."

"Someone else would not have dug down deep enough to find the truth. They probably wouldn't even have taken the case."

"And what would that matter? I'm sure homicides like this usually go undetected. Robin was dying anyway. All Gloria did was hurry things along. If you hadn't been digging into it, Gloria would never have gone after Bridget. She would have just stayed home with Rhys and gone on with her life."

"But that wouldn't have been *right*," Zachary pointed out. "That wouldn't have been justice."

"By whose definition? Robin was a killer, don't forget. She had ruined their lives. Especially Rhys's. Would her just living out her normal lifespan without ever having to confront what she had done be justice?"

"Turning her in ten years ago would have been justice. What Gloria did wasn't justice. It was revenge."

Kenzie shrugged. "Whatever. You still need to get past this and go on with your life." She raised a finger when Zachary opened his mouth to respond. "And that is not what you are doing."

"Maybe I'm not ready."

"Then it's time to see your psychiatrist. Get some help."

Zachary drew in a deep breath. It wasn't the first time he'd fallen into such a depression. Kenzie was probably right.

"Fine. I'll make an appointment."

"And start taking your meds."

He looked for an argument, then shrugged, conceding.

"Let Bridget go. She's with Gordon Drake now. So you're not getting her back, no matter what she led you to believe. You need to let that whole notion go."

"That's not as easy as you think. I made vows. I promised…"

"She's released you from them. So go on."

Zachary shook his head and didn't try to explain how impossible that was for him.

"You're taking me out for dinner tonight," Kenzie informed him. "You choose the place."

"I'm not hungry."

"Then just order an appetizer. We'll head over there after. Maybe you'll be hungry in a couple of hours."

"After? After what?"

She shook her head, her hair bouncing around her face, bright red lips curved in a smile. "After we go see Rhys."

Once again showered, changed, and dressed in fresh clothes, Zachary headed out with Kenzie. She wouldn't give him any details about where Rhys was or how he was doing. She told him to just go with her and see for himself, and he couldn't argue with her logic. It was the first thing that had interested him since seeing Bridget at the hospital. Bridget would be back home and completely recovered. Since Zachary hadn't left the apartment, he hadn't even driven by her house since she'd been released and could only assume that everything was back to normal for her.

"Good to feel the sun on your face and the wind in your hair?" Kenzie asked, winding through the streets with the top down. Zachary brushed his hand over his hair with one hand, but it was short enough that the wind couldn't mess it up.

"Yeah, it's nice," he agreed.

She turned up the radio to eliminate the need for more conversation. Zachary watched the streets pass by, his arm resting on the window ledge.

He was surprised when they pulled up to the Salter house. He had assumed that Rhys would be in foster care, maybe even institutionalized, given his mutism and the trauma of the kidnapping and his mother's behavior. He'd had to go to a facility once before, after Clarence's death and, in Zachary's experience, one institutionalization led to another.

"But who's…?" Zachary shook his head, not even finishing the sentence, because he knew Kenzie wouldn't answer it. There must have been some other relative willing to move into the house to look after Rhys. Some cousin.

Kenzie just smiled and walked up the sidewalk, using her fingers to comb her hair back into shape after the ride in the convertible. She rang the bell.

Zachary nearly fell over when Vera answered the door. He hadn't expected to ever see her outside of a care facility again.

How could they have released her? She couldn't possibly be taking care of Rhys, and Rhys couldn't be taking care of her.

"Mr. Goldman, I'm so glad you could come. Come in, come in."

Kenzie and Zachary entered.

The house was spotless, everything put away in its proper place. Even the shoes at the door and Rhys's skateboard were neat and tidy. Zachary sat down on the couch with Vera. She put her arm around his shoulders and gave him a hug.

"I wanted to thank you for everything you did. I don't know what would have happened if you hadn't stepped in."

Zachary looked at her and shook his head. "I don't understand. The last time we talked to you, you were..." he trailed off, not sure of a tactful way to say that she'd appeared to have dementia. When now, she obviously didn't.

"Gloria again," Kenzie said. "It looks like she was intentionally giving Vera drugs that would make her muddled. So she wouldn't understand what was going on or be able to tell anything to the police."

Zachary blinked. "That's... I don't know. That's *devious*."

Kenzie laughed. Vera sighed and shrugged. "I guess so. I really don't know what to think of this all. I started to feel better after a few days off of those pills. Like myself again. I'm still not sure of everything that happened while she was giving them to me, or how long she was doing it for. She was always in charge of dividing up my pills into daily doses for me. I just... took what she gave me."

"So, you're better now... and you can take care of Rhys."

Vera nodded. "That's right." She raised her voice. "Rhys? Where are you? Are you going to come in to see Mr. Goldman or not?"

Zachary looked up at a heavy approaching footfall. But it wasn't Rhys he saw, it was Stanley Green. Tall and broad and looking like he owned the place.

Zachary's jaw dropped open. He looked at Vera and Kenzie,

but neither of them seemed to be surprised or alarmed, so obviously they had already known that Stanley was there or was going to be. Both women looked at him expectantly.

"What... what are you doing here?" Zachary asked, fumbling his words. "I thought... what?"

Stanley scratched his ear, a slightly sheepish grin on his face. "After you told me about Robin's death... I couldn't get it out of my mind. I wanted to reconnect with Rhys, see if I could help him out. I was very close to the family, once. If Robin hadn't been so..." Stanley looked over at Vera. "...uh, so volatile..."

Vera nodded. She looked down at her hands. "It wasn't Stanley's fault," she reassured Zachary. "He was never the one who started things."

Zachary nodded. "I know. I read the police incident reports. That's when it all came together."

They were all silent, not sure where to go next.

"I'm sorry about scaring you that night," Stanley said, looking down in embarrassment. "I never meant to freak you out. You weren't even supposed to see me."

"Why would you even come by?" Zachary asked. "Why didn't you just call me? Set up a meeting? Or email me?"

"I didn't really know what else to say to you. I didn't want to leave things where they were... I realized that you thought I was abusive toward Robin, when that wasn't the way things were. I wanted to straighten things out. But what could I say?" Stanley gave a shrug. "Here I am this big guy... who's going to believe that Robin was the aggressor? Or that I couldn't make her stop?"

Zachary thought about Mrs. Phipps at Ptarmigan House, one of the group homes he had been in. She was a little, wizened old woman with a bad leg, but she could whale the hell out of a boy with her cane if she caught him disobeying the rules. At fourteen, even with his stunted growth, Zachary had been bigger than she was, and logic dictated she was the one who should fear him. But the *thunk* of her cane on the floor and the drag of her bad leg was all it took to send his heart racing wildly, even if he couldn't think of anything he'd done wrong. Especially if he didn't know what he'd done wrong.

"It's okay," he told Stanley. "I get it."

"I was trying to think things through. Sometimes… I have to physically go somewhere to make sense of a thing. I thought if I was there, where you lived… I could figure it out. Decide what to do next."

Like Zachary's compulsions to drive by Bridget's house. Even though he couldn't see her car in the garage and couldn't see if she were sleeping soundly in the house, it comforted him to be there. He had to go by there to settle his brain down and reassure himself she was okay. Nothing else would work. He had gone to Bridget's the same night as Stanley had come to his apartment, both of them driven to put themselves in a specific place to work through their thoughts.

"I get it. Sometimes… you just have to do something."

Zachary looked up when he heard another set of approaching feet, and this time it was Rhys's familiar lanky figure. Rhys gave a little wave and a nod to Zachary. He stood there looking at Zachary, then looked at his grandmother.

"Rhys wanted to see you," Vera said. "He wanted to thank you for helping him. For finding him and saving him and Bridget."

Zachary met Rhys's eyes and nodded. Rhys still looked sad, but there was something looser and more comfortable about him. Like a great weight had been lifted off his shoulders.

"Thank you for helping me to find you," Zachary told Rhys. "And for helping Bridget. She would have died if you hadn't helped look after her." Zachary swallowed. He wasn't sure he could express to Rhys how much Bridget meant to him and how much he appreciated what the boy had done. Faced with being loyal to his mother or with helping a woman he'd never even met before, Rhys had done what was right, even though it meant his mother had to go to jail.

Rhys nodded. He held out a hand to Zachary and they shook.

"I tried to do the right thing for our family," Vera said quietly.

"When Clarence died… it felt like the most important thing to do was to shelter Robin from the consequences. I couldn't bear to think that she could go to prison for what she had done. She really wasn't well." Vera looked over at Rhys. "I guess… that's what I told myself. It was something she couldn't control. But…" She grimaced. "She could have, couldn't she? She made her choices. And we chose to protect her."

Rhys gave a shrug. Not an 'it doesn't matter' shrug, but one that said that what was done was done. They couldn't undo the past.

"How are you, Rhys?" Zachary asked, searching Rhys's face for the answer. "Are you okay?"

Rhys cleared his throat. He looked at his grandma for reassurance before answering. "It's gonna be okay."

It was a long utterance for him. Zachary took in a deep breath and let the words wash over him.

Was it?

Was it going to be okay for Zachary, too? Was he going to be able to get out of the funk he was stuck in and move on?

There were other cases to be solved, other questions left unanswered. And supper with Kenzie. Rhys was safe with Vera, with Stanley Green around to lend a hand and be there when he needed a man's guiding hand. Thanks to Rhys, Bridget had survived her ordeal. Zachary couldn't imagine the darkness he would be in if she hadn't.

But Bridget was alive and happy. So Zachary would go on, just as he had before.

It was gonna be okay.

Did you enjoy this book? Reviews and recommendations are vital to making a book successful.

Please leave a review at your favorite book store or review site and share it with your friends.

Don't miss the following bonus material:
Sign up for mailing list to get a free ebook
Read a sneak preview chapter
Other books by P.D. Workman
Learn more about the author

Sign up for my mailing list at pdworkman.com and get Gluten-Free Murder for free!

PREVIEW OF HER WORK WAS EVERYTHING

1

Zachary had heard about the death of Lauren Barclay in the news before he was contacted by Barbara Lee. It seemed like such a tragic waste. A promising young investment banker, she had been tragically killed in a slip-and-fall accident in her home. It wasn't particularly newsworthy, except for the fact that she had been an attractive, brilliant young woman, and that played well in the press on a slow news day. There were a lot of quotes from family and friends about how awful it was and what a wonderful person she had been. There would be a lot of mourners at her funeral.

But he hadn't really given it anything more than a passing thought. He had that little twinge of regret that he got when he read about a tragic death, but since he hadn't known her and there didn't seem to be anything unusual about her death, he had just given himself a second to feel bad for her and her family, and then moved on with his day.

Barbara Lee had told him that she wanted to meet about the death of a friend, but it wasn't until they sat down together for coffee that Zachary found out the friend was Lauren Barclay.

"I just can't believe it." Barbara sniffled and wiped at the corner of her eye. "She was so brilliant, so full of life, I can't believe she's gone. It just isn't fair. She was so young!"

Zachary nodded. "I read a little bit about it… there wasn't any hint in the news that there was foul play, though. They said it was an accident. She slipped in the tub?"

"I can't believe that. You don't think that's really what happened, do you?"

He looked into her bloodshot eyes. She was probably an attractive woman when she wasn't a complete mess. Her eyes were red, her face was blotchy; it looked like her hair had been put up into a partial bun at some point, but she had wisps of hair going in every direction and she might have slept on it once or twice since she had put it up. She smelled of sweat.

"I don't know anything about it, so I wouldn't venture a guess," he said. "Why don't you tell me what you know about it? Why don't you think she slipped?"

Barbara rummaged in her handbag for a tissue and wiped her red nose. "I didn't even know she was home. She worked all hours, she was always at the office. I hadn't seen her for days. Then I got home… it was the middle of the day, and I could tell that she'd been there. I called out to her, but she didn't answer. I figured she probably came home to change and then had left again. Or maybe she'd fallen into bed and was catching a few winks before she had to go back. But she wasn't usually home during the day, so I didn't expect… to find her…"

Zachary thought he should touch her arm or make some other comforting gesture, but he wouldn't want it to be taken the wrong way. She might not think he was professional and decide not to hire him.

"I'm so sorry… you were the one who found her?"

Barbara nodded, giving another sob. A bubble of snot blew out her nose and she wiped it away. If she had been the one to find her friend's body, it was no wonder she was such a mess. He couldn't imagine what that would have been like for her.

"Take your time," he told her. "You don't need to rush into this."

"I just want… to get it all out. Everybody wants to know, but nobody wants to hear about it. They all think that they want to hear the details, but… it isn't like watching a murder mystery on TV. It's something that… it's so unreal. I didn't know what to do. It was such a shock finding her, I felt like she was a mannequin or it was a prank, I just didn't want to believe it. I couldn't touch her. I called 9-1-1. And then… the police came, and the paramedics, and they all wanted me to tell them about finding her. I had to keep repeating it over and over again."

She stopped talking to wipe and blow again. Her nose was red and raw.

"But they didn't think there was any foul play?" Zachary prompted.

"No. But they didn't ask if there was anyone who wanted her dead or if she had a boyfriend that was violent or she had just broken up with, or anything like that. Not like on a cop show or in a mystery book. They just asked about… when I'd been home last, what time I had found her, when she would have gotten home. The paramedics asked if she had a history of epilepsy or fainting spells. Just… like it was an accident."

Zachary nodded. He sipped his coffee, which was still a bit too hot, but he wanted to give her time to think and to calm down a little. He would get more out of her if she were relaxed and composed than if she got all wound up and couldn't think straight.

"So what was the timing? You said she wasn't usually home during the day?"

"No. She worked really long hours. They were supposed to be at the office before their boss got in, so like six-thirty or seven at the latest. And she would work past dark. She would come home late, sleep for a few hours, and then be back at the office before I even had breakfast. Her hours were crazy."

"How long could she keep up like that? She must have had to

take breaks on the weekend at least. Did she get a day off? Sunday?"

"She worked every day. It wasn't a rule that they had to work on weekends, but everybody did. It was so competitive. If the other interns were there on the weekend, then Lauren *had* to be there on the weekend. Otherwise, people would think that she wasn't as dedicated, and when her internship was up, they would just say goodbye and she'd have to find something else. No other investment banking firm was going to take her if she failed her internship there. She'd be... damaged goods. She'd have to find a job in something else, and she really wanted to be in finance. She really did."

"Why was it so cutthroat? Is that normal?"

"For investment banking, I guess it is. They're all like that. And Chase Gold is just a small firm, so if she couldn't make it there, there's no way that some Wall Street or Japanese company would look at her. She had to get a permanent position with Chase and work there for three years before she could go on to look for something else. No one would look at her otherwise."

Zachary shook his head. "Why would anyone want to work like that?"

Barbara pushed tendrils of hair away from her face, making a half-hearted attempt to push them back into the bun. "Lots of professions are like that, not just finance. Look at doctors and nurses. They're the same way. Long-distance trucking. Cab drivers."

"They all have rules now about not being able to work more than a certain number of hours in a row to prevent people from falling asleep at the wheel or cutting off the wrong leg."

"I guess. But this isn't that kind of place. I don't think there are any rules about not being able to work that long. She always worked for hours and hours. She slept at the office on the floor sometimes. Or didn't sleep at all for two or three days. You can't even imagine how bad it was."

Zachary thought about that. He pulled out his notepad and

jotted down a few notes to himself. Avenues to pursue. Things not to forget. Barbara's eyes tracked his pencil as he scratched out the lines.

"You look like you've never held a pen before," she commented.

Zachary's cheeks heated. He looked down at his awkward grip on his pencil. Many teachers had tried to correct it during school. He'd moved among a lot of different schools, classrooms, and institutions, and the first thing they always tried to do was correct his grip.

"I have dysgraphia," he said. "That's the only way I can write. I know it looks bad to you, but it's the only thing that feels right to me. It's the only way I can see what I'm doing and form the letters."

She shook her head and didn't make any comment on his chicken scratch. He *could* write neatly. He did when he was filling out forms or writing something down for someone else. But it took two or three times as long if he wanted to make it tidy. When he was writing for himself, he could scrawl it however he wanted to. He could still read it. Usually. Sometimes. He could normally figure out what he had meant, even if he couldn't read every word.

"Lauren had beautiful handwriting," Barbara said, tears starting to make their way down her cheeks. "She should have been a schoolteacher, it looked like something out of a handwriting textbook. But..." she sniffled, "of course, teachers don't make anything, and Lauren wanted to make a lot of money. A lot of money."

"I don't really know what an investment banker does," Zachary said, "but I know it *is* something that I associate with making a lot of money. She was pretty wealthy, then?" He was thinking about motives. If there were anything to Barbara's fears—and he had to assume for the purposes of his investigation that there was —then whoever had killed her needed a motive. And money was always a good motive.

"No, not yet," Barbara said. "She was just starting out, so she wasn't making a whole lot. We rented an apartment together, and it's a nice one, not some little rat's nest, but neither of us could have afforded it on our own. Maybe we could, but only if we didn't need to eat or pay for heating or internet."

Zachary nodded. "And if she was just starting, then she probably still had school loans to worry about too."

"Yeah. All of that stuff. She wanted to get rich, but she wasn't there yet. We are—were—both making good money for our age, but nothing like it would be if she got to be a permanent employee with a few years under her belt."

"That makes sense. What's the name of the place that she worked?"

"I have to look it up…" She pulled out her phone and fiddled with it. "We always just called it 'Chase Gold,' because it was close to that, and that's really what they were trying to do. Chase after the gold and get as much as they could. For themselves and their clients."

Zachary waited while she tapped through a few screens on her phone, searching for it in her contacts or on an internet browser. He made a couple of other short notes while he waited. Things to look into. Questions to ask. Who would want to kill a young woman who spent all of her time working and was still in debt?

"Yeah, here it is," Barbara offered. "Drake, Chase, Gould." She spelled Gould for him to make sure he got it right. "She was really devoted to her job. And I don't just mean that she liked it or put a lot of hours in. She did, but there was more to it than that. She thought they were the best company to work for, and that they were going to get her everything she wanted. She was always saying how good the management was, how well they took care of their employees, how good the other people she worked with were. She thought they were going right to the top. That they would compete with the Goldman Sachs and Wells Fargos of the world. They just started up a few years ago, and their portfolios were amazing, especially considering how short they had been in business. Or so she told me." Barbara sniffed and rolled her eyes. "Multiple times."

Zachary smiled at that. Nice to hear about someone who liked her job. "That's great."

He leaned back in his seat. The coffee shop didn't have particularly comfortable chairs. He supposed it was to encourage people to have their coffees and to move on, not to just camp there drinking lattes and using the free Wi-Fi all day long. He looked at Barbara.

"So what makes you think it wasn't an accident? Tell me about the things that made you concerned."

"You think I'm just crazy, don't you? Everybody just looks at me like I've got two heads. How could a slip in the bathtub *not* be an accident? It's like being hit by a bus, the classic accident that everyone uses as an example."

Zachary waited. He wasn't the one who was doubting her opinion or sanity. He waited for her to stop defending herself and to fill the silence with her concerns. She would, if he just waited.

"It just doesn't fit that Lauren was even home," Barbara said. "Like I said, she was never home during the day. Between ten in the evening and six in the morning, if she was lucky. That's it. No weekends. No days off. No afternoons going home to have a nap. She just shouldn't have been home."

"What was the time of death?"

Barbara looked at him. She shook her head. "I don't know."

"What time had she gotten home? You were out of the apartment from when until when?"

"I was out with a friend overnight. So I didn't get back until… ten or eleven o'clock. That's when I found her. But she was never home at that time of day."

"But if she had been running a bath at six, and hit her head then, that would make sense."

Barbara sighed. "I know. Everybody says it makes perfect sense. But it doesn't. She was young and healthy. She wouldn't just fall down and die. She wasn't drunk or doing drugs. She didn't have any diseases that would have made her pass out. To just step into the tub and fall down and die…? That doesn't make sense either."

"Sure. I understand that. No one expects something like this to happen. But she could have had the flu, or just wasn't paying attention and slipped."

"She wasn't an old lady. Maybe old ladies slip and fall like that, but Lauren never did. If she slipped, she would have caught herself. If she got hurt, she would have called someone to help her."

Zachary made a couple of notes of questions to pursue. He'd

have to talk to the medical examiner's office, and he really didn't want to. He would have to psych himself up for it.

"What was the mechanism of death?"

Barbara frowned. "She… fell…?"

"Yeah. Did she drown? Or did she die from the blow to the head? Brain swelling or bleeding?"

"Drowning, I guess. She did hit her head, but then she went into the water. That's where I found her. I guess… she knocked herself out, and then she didn't know that she was drowning, couldn't do anything about it."

"The medical examiner hasn't made a finding yet?"

"I don't know. I guess that's what they're working on right now."

"Okay. We'll need a copy of their report once there is a finding. I'll put in a requisition for it."

Which meant that he would take the elevator down to the basement level at the police station. He would walk up to the desk and fill out one of the forms in his neatest printing, trying his best to avoid an intensely awkward situation with Kenzie.

He wasn't sure how she was going to react. Things had been pretty quiet since they had broken up. He felt horrible about the way everything had ended, but he hadn't called her and begged for her to come back. He hadn't given her excuses for his behavior or followed her around in his car. He had done his best to just back out of her life and forget about what they had shared together.

But going back there, onto her turf, he didn't know how she was going to treat him. Would she yell at him and call him out the way that Bridget did? Would she go all quiet or ignore him? Or just stare at him with her dark, intense eyes boring into him, hating him for the time she had wasted on him?

"Uh… Mr. Goldman?"

Zachary blinked and refocused on Barbara. It was Barbara he had to talk to and interact with. He needed to stay focused on her. "Sorry, just thinking about something. What was that?"

"If the medical examiner says that it was just an accident, that will be the end of it, won't it? The police won't investigate it as a homicide. They won't hold anyone responsible."

"No. But if I find something, we can get them to open an investigation. I've done it before. I'm assuming you already know that. That's probably why you picked me out, isn't it?"

She gave an embarrassed little shrug and nodded.

"I can't guarantee anything," Zachary said. "I don't know whether it was an accident or something else… but it sounds like it's going to be pretty hard to find evidence that it was anything else. I'll look. I'm just warning you… Don't expect miracles. Just because I've been able to prove that other deaths were homicides, that doesn't mean that I can prove any death was. Some of them are going to be just what they look like."

"I know. But… no matter what anyone else says… I want to do everything I can for Lauren. I can't just close my eyes and say 'oh, what a bizarre accident.' I need to know. I need to do everything I can to bring the responsible party to justice. If there is a responsible party."

"You said before that the police hadn't asked you anything about an ex-boyfriend or anyone who might have wanted to harm her."

"Yes. I mean no. They didn't. They didn't want to know anything like that."

"Does that mean that she *did* have an ex-boyfriend who might have wanted to harm her?"

Barbara's eyes widened. "Oh, no. I didn't mean to imply anything like that… She did have ex-boyfriends, of course, but no one who was bitter or anything. No one who ever threatened her or stalked her."

"Was there anyone who was abusive while they were together? She might not have told you that he hit her, but was there ever anyone that you suspected… that you thought might have hurt her? Even someone who was verbally or emotionally abusive. Someone you didn't feel comfortable around or were glad that she broke up with him."

"No… I don't think so… everyone that she was with was pretty casual… it isn't like she had any time for a relationship. She would take someone to a firm event, or sometimes she brought someone home from work… but she didn't really have a life outside of the office."

"She dated people from the office?"

"Yes… she went out for a meal with them, maybe brought one or two back to the apartment to…" she shrugged uncomfortably, "…to sleep it off. Just to crash somewhere before they had to go back to the office again in a few hours. There just was so little time, and she was under so much pressure… it didn't leave time for a real relationship."

"Even if it isn't what you would call a relationship… men can still decide that they want what they can't have. They might think that she should have spent more time with them, given them more attention, maybe not gone on to see someone else so soon… if they went out to eat, or he went home with her, then he might have expected more. He might have thought that it was turning into a committed relationship when it wasn't."

"I guess so. I don't know. I never saw anything like that. The guys that I met from Chase Gold always seemed pretty casual. Not like they were pining after her or acting possessive."

"Do you have the names of some of the men that she dated? Maybe an address list?"

"All of her numbers would be on her phone… I guess it's at the apartment. The police didn't take it, I don't think. They just took a quick look at her electronics, but there wasn't anything that didn't look right to them, so they said they didn't need to take anything with them."

"Who is the detective on the case?"

"I don't think there was a detective. Just… whoever comes out to have a look when someone dies suddenly. They're not really investigating it. Just filling out the forms."

"Someone would have been assigned to it. I'll look into it. See if they have any thoughts."

"They aren't going to. They are just going to think that it was an accident, like a million other accidents that happen every day."

Her Work Was Everything, Book #3 of the *Zachary Goldman Mysteries series* by P.D. Workman can be purchased at pdwork-man.com

ABOUT THE AUTHOR

Award-winning and USA Today bestselling author P.D. (Pamela) Workman writes riveting mystery/suspense and young adult books dealing with mental illness, addiction, abuse, and other real-life issues. For as long as she can remember, the blank page has held an incredible allure and from a very young age she was trying to write her own books.

Workman wrote her first complete novel at the age of twelve and continued to write as a hobby for many years. She started publishing in 2013. She has won several literary awards from Library Services for Youth in Custody for her young adult fiction. She currently has over 50 published titles and can be found at pdworkman.com.

Born and raised in Alberta, Workman has been married for over 25 years and has one son.

Please visit P.D. Workman at pdworkman.com to see what else she is working on, to join her mailing list, and to link to her social networks.

If you enjoyed this book, please take the time to recommend it to other purchasers with a review or star rating and share it with your friends!

facebook.com/pdworkmanauthor

twitter.com/pdworkmanauthor

instagram.com/pdworkmanauthor

amazon.com/author/pdworkman

bookbub.com/authors/p-d-workman

goodreads.com/pdworkman

linkedin.com/in/pdworkman

pinterest.com/pdworkmanauthor

youtube.com/pdworkman